D1760967

E.R. PUNSHON
EVERYBODY ALWAYS TELLS

ERNEST ROBERTSON PUNSHON was born in London in 1872.

At the age of fourteen he started life in an office. His employers soon informed him that he would never make a really satisfactory clerk, and he, agreeing, spent the next few years wandering about Canada and the United States, endeavouring without great success to earn a living in any occupation that offered. Returning home by way of working a passage on a cattle boat, he began to write. He contributed to many magazines and periodicals, wrote plays, and published nearly fifty novels, among which his detective stories proved the most popular and enduring.

He died in 1956.

The Bobby Owen Mysteries

E.R. PUNSHON

EVERYBODY ALWAYS TELLS

With an introduction
by Curtis Evans

DEAN STREET PRESS

Detective Stories, the Detection Club and Death: The Final Years of E. R. Punshon

> ... but, they dead,
> Death has so many doors to let out life,
> I will not long survive them.
>
> *The Custom of the Country* (c. 1619-23; 1647)
> JOHN FLETCHER AND PHILLIP MASSINGER

WHEN IN 1949 E.R. Punshon published *So Many Doors*, his twenty-sixth Bobby Owen detective novel, the Englishman was seventy-seven years old, with nearly a half-century of published novels behind him and a comparatively scant seven years of life and letters remaining before him. 1901, the year of the appearance of Punshon's first novel, *Earth's Great Lord*, saw the death of Queen Victoria, the long reigning granddaughter of King George III for whom a regal age of European global dominion has been named; while 1949, a year during which a convalescent Europe was still bleakly recovering from a world war that had reduced much of its civilization to ashes and rubble, saw the testing by the USSR of its first atomic bomb and the proclamation of the formation of the People's Republic of China. The world was changing with a fearsome fleetness that not merely old men who had first glimpsed light in the Victorian era were finding hard to follow.

Rapidly changing too was the craft of crime and mystery fiction that E.R. Punshon had long practiced (this admittedly a minor thing compared to unsettling phenomena like armed revolution and atom splitting). Like the once seemingly imperishable British Empire, the hegemony of the between-the-wars "Golden Age" clue-puzzle detective novel was breaking asunder, under pressure from increasingly popular rival forms of mystery fiction, such as hard-boiled, noir, psychological suspense and espionage. Already stalked by Raymond Chandler's famous gumshoe, Philip Marlowe, as well as ill-humored and hard-drinking would-be Marlowe doppelgangers like Mickey Spillane's brutish Mike Hammer, Punshon's well-born English policeman Bobby Owen, along with other of his surviving gentlemanly detective colleagues from the era of classic crime fiction, soon found himself in the sights of no less deadly a professional killer than James Bond. Agent 007's creator, Ian Fleming, who cited as his literary influences Raymond Chandler, Dashiell Hammett, Eric Ambler and Graham Greene, published his first Bond spy novel, *Casino Royale*, in the United Kingdom in 1953, where it enjoyed immediate popular and critical success. In the United States, where the novel appeared in 1954, the same year as Raymond Chandler's much-lauded *The Long Goodbye*, *Time* magazine wryly declared that "Bond . . . might well be [Philip] Marlowe's younger brother, except that he never takes coffee for a bracer, just one large martini laced with vodka."

Upon the publication of *So Many Doors* in the UK and the US (in the latter country it would prove the last Punshon mystery published during the author's lifetime), crime fiction reviewers deemed the novel and its author representatives of a vanished era. "The twenties were the plotter's heyday (consider Freeman Wills Crofts, J.J. Connington, Dorothy Sayers)," observed the Democratic-Socialist *London Tribune* in its review of the "well-plotted" and "studiously told" *So Many Doors*, "and to the twenties, in spirit at least, belongs Mr. Punshon." In the United States, Anthony Boucher, dean of American mystery critics, allowed in the *New York Times Book Review* that the narration of *So Many Doors* was "leisurely"; yet, after noting the seventeenth-century English stage derivation of the novel's title, he approvingly added that there "is something Elizabethan, even Jacobean, about the obscure destinies that drive [Punshon's] obsessed and tormented characters, and about the frightful violence that concludes the story." Punshon, it seemed, still had something to say in the harried and hectic atomic age, when crime fiction reviewers and readers alike seemed increasingly to believe that brevity was the soul of death.

* * * * *

To his death in 1956 E.R. Punshon maintained a loyal following in the United Kingdom among readers who staunchly adhered to the strict standard of fair play puzzle plotting associated with Golden Age detective fiction. During the Fifties the aging but seemingly indefatigable author, who still lived quietly with his wife Sarah at their house at 23 Nimrod Road, Streatham, produced, through the medium of his prestigious longtime publisher Victor Gollancz, nine new mystery titles--*Everybody Always Tells* (1950), *The Secret Search* (1951), The Golden Dagger (1951), *The Attending Truth* (1952), *Strange Ending* (1953), *Brought to Light* (1954), *Dark Is the Clue* (1955), *Triple Quest* (1955) and *Six Were Present* (1956)—that detailed the final criminal investigations of his longtime series police detective, Bobby Owen, now risen to the august rank of Commander (unattached), Metropolitan Police. Additionally Punshon continued to remain active in his cherished Detection Club, a London-based social organization of distinguished detective novelists, in which the author had been inducted, along with Anthony Gilbert and Gladys Mitchell, in 1933, three years after the Club's founding, joining such luminaries from the crime writing world as G.K. Chesterton, Dorothy L. Sayers, Agatha Christie, E.C. Bentley, Anthony Berkeley, R. Austin Freeman and Freeman Wills Crofts.

Like other British institutions the Detection Club from 1939 to 1945 bore the bitter burdens of war, including the devastating Nazi air raids known collectively as "the Blitz." When the Club revived its meetings and annual dinners in 1946, it became immediately apparent that time had wrought cruel changes with its membership. On seeing his brother and sister detective novelists again at the Club premises after the long interval of war years, John Dickson Carr, a comparative stripling at the age of forty, recalled that he had been "shocked" by their appearance, which he had found decidedly "greyer and more worn."

By 1946 eight of the original twenty-eight Detection Club members, including G.K. Chesterton, R. Austin Freeman and Helen Simpson, had passed away and many other members were now elderly and inactive. Several more members would expire over the next few years. Even the formerly quite engaged Freeman Wills Crofts and John Rhode (Cecil John Charles Street), now in their sixties and living in the country, became markedly less involved with Club affairs, as did an increasingly infirm Henry Wade (the landed baronet Henry Lancelot Aubrey-Fletcher). For his part, John Dickson Carr, deeming British life under postwar conditions and the governance of the Labour party intolerable, would in 1948 depart for his native United States. Besides Punshon, only Christie, John Rhode and Henry Wade, among original members, and Anthony Gilbert, Gladys Mitchell, Margery Allingham, John Dickson Carr, Nicholas Blake, Christopher Bush and E.C.R. Lorac, among the smaller number of Thirties inductees, remained substantially active as crime writers into the 1950s. Of these Lorac and Wade, like Punshon, would not survive the decade, and another, John Rhode, would barely outlast it.

Clearly some new blood was badly needed. During Punshon's remaining span of life the aged and ailing Detection Club received transfusions, so to speak, from seventeen new members. Although with the deaths of Baroness Emma Orczy and A.E.W. Mason (in 1947 and 1948 respectively), Punshon became the oldest surviving member of the Detection Club, the author, who served as Club treasurer between 1946 and 1949, during the postwar years remained extensively involved in Club affairs, actively participating in hearty debates concerning prospective new members, like Christianna Brand, Michael Innes, Michael Gilbert, Elizabeth Ferrars and Julian Symons, as to whether or not they practiced fair play and sufficiently respected the King's (later Queen's) English, the Club's chief requirements for induction. (These debates are chronicled in detail in my CADS booklet *Was Corinne's Murder Clued? The Detection Club and Fair Play, 1930-1953*.)

In 1949 Punshon found himself at odds over the matter of new enrollments with the man who unquestionably was the Club's crankiest and most cantankerous member: Anthony Berkeley, famed author of *The Poisoned Chocolates Case* (1928) and, under the pseudonym Francis Iles, of *Malice Aforethought* (1931) and *Before the Fact* (1932), three of the best regarded British crime novels from the Golden Age. In April Berkeley wrote a provocative letter to Punshon in which he claimed that as the Club's "First Freeman" he possessed blanket veto power over prospective members, despite the fact that he no longer served on the membership committee. During the early days of the Detection Club, Berkeley had observed at a meeting that the Club had two "Freemans" as members (R. Austin Freeman and Freeman Wills Crofts), and he pronounced that as the person who had originally suggested forming the Club he would be its "First Freeman." To this suggestion everyone else had laughingly assented, taking the office as a joke; yet now, nearly two decades later, it seemed that Berkeley had not been joking.

Incensed by Berkeley's gambit and the rude language in which he had couched it, Punshon wrote Sayers, enclosing his antagonist's "offensive" letter (which evidently has not survived) and warning that "[Berkeley] intends to make some sort of fuss." Punshon speculated that "possibly it is better to take no notice [of the letter], except perhaps as regards the absurd claim of his to hold some special position as what he calls 'First Freeman.' I have a vague idea that once before he put forward a claim to be a permanent member of the [membership] committee on the same ground." He noted dryly that while he had forborne responding to the specifics of Berkeley's letter, he had sent the notoriously tightfisted "First Freeman" a reminder that his annual membership fee was due, to which he had received no reply.

"Bother AB!" responded Sayers in a letter to Punshon that she composed the day after receiving his missive. "I do wish he was not so rude and silly." She entirely concurred with Punshon's recollection of the once comical but now rather annoying office of First Freeman and added resignedly: "If he tries to make a fuss at the meeting, the committee will have to cope; but I hope he will have more sense. I am sorry he should have written to you so impertinently."

By the summer of 1949 the First Freeman's irksome machinations had been checked--but only, Punshon feared, for the moment. With considerable skepticism Punshon wrote Sayers, "I gather the reconciliation with Anthony Berkeley is now complete and the hatchet well and truly buried. Until dug up again." Sayers, who soon would succeed E.C. Bentley as President of the Detection Club, advised members to tread carefully around Berkeley's tender sensibilities. "Let a (more or less) sleeping Berkeley lie," she urged. Nevertheless Sayers agreed with Punshon that the Club members would have to keep Berkeley off the membership committee, because were he to be on it the Club would "never get any new member . . . he turns them all down on sight." She lamented that "Berkeley is a difficult man to work with."

Sayers found working with Punshon, whose detective fiction she had enthusiastically promoted as a book reviewer for the *Sunday Times* between 1933 and 1935, to be an altogether more pleasant experience. Surviving correspondence between the two authors suggests that Punshon was, along with Anthony Gilbert (Lucy Beatrice Malleson), the Detection Club member with whom Sayers got along most amicably at this time. The two communicated fairly frequently during the postwar years, chatting not only about Detection Club matters, but more personal affairs as well.

As treasurer of the Detection Club, Punshon gave his attention to matters large--such as any taxes the Club might have to pay to a revenue-hungry British government ("we have to remember that we may be dropped on by the Income tax people")—and matters small. As an example of the latter, Punshon advised Sayers in December 1948 that the Club should give a "small Christmas present" to Mrs. Buchanan, caretaker of the Club premises at 12 Kingly Street, Soho. ("A room and loo in a clergy house," Christianna Brand bluntly recalled of the locale.) Although payment for services was included with the rent, Punshon pointed out that "services included are very often badly neglected and so far as I have noticed in this case they have been quite well carried out and the room always seemed neat and tidy." "[E]ven in this sordid age," he reflected with characteristic gentle irony, "a few thanks and expressions of satisfaction . . . often please as much as gifts—at any rate if accompanied by a gift." A few days later Sayers gave Mrs. Buchanan a £1 Christmas tip (about £32 today).

Sadly, Punshon suffered a serious setback to his health in August 1949, not long after a busy summer that saw the English publication of *So Many Doors*, his nettlesome skirmish with Anthony Berkeley and the annual Detection Club dinner at the Hotel Café Royal, Piccadilly. (Recorded treasurer Punshon of the latter event: "L87/9/9—Miss Gilbert paid L6/9/4 for after dinner drinks. I gave the head waiter L1. Total 95/9/1. Great success.") After writing Freeman Wills Crofts and John Rhode to inform them about the Berkeley brouhaha, Punshon went into hospital for an operation. In September Sayers wrote Punshon that she was pleased to hear from his wife that he was "making a really good convalescence," adding: "We will miss you greatly at the October meeting, but of course you must have a good long holiday and get quite fit."

By early November Punshon, recuperating at Christopher Bush's house, Little Horsepen, near Rye in East Sussex, was able to report that he was "very much better," though the same month he resigned as Detection Club treasurer. (Christopher Bush succeeded him to the office.) Later that month Punshon wrote Sayers from Bournemouth, where he was taking a "long rest." He wished her good fortune with the recently published Penguin paperback edition of her translation of Dante's *Inferno*, remarking, "I don't know any translation of Dante except the old one [1805] by [Henry Francis] Cary, and that was a fairly pedestrian performance." He also heaped praise on Penguin's ambitious paperback publishing scheme, deeming it a "very praiseworthy attempt to turn us into a nation of book buyers instead of borrowers. A Real Revolution—if they can bring it off." Punshon had particular reason to applaud Penguin's effort, as the previous year the company had issued a pair of 1930s Bobby Owen mystery titles as paperbacks. (Three more titles would follow in the next half-dozen years.)

Punshon remained active in Detection Club affairs in 1950, though he urged that Michael Gilbert be tapped to replace him on the membership committee. "Would [Anthony Berkeley] take the suggestion as an insult," he sarcastically queried Sayers, obviously still smarting over the events of the previous year. Punshon also participated in evaluations of the work of proposed new member Julian Symons (1912-1994), one of Britain's new wave of consciously self-styled "crime writers." Of Symons's recent *Bland Beginning* (1949), a novel based, as was Punshon's own *Comes a Stranger* (1938), on the Thomas J. Wise literary forgery scandal, Punshon wrote Sayers, "On the whole I should be inclined to say 'yes,' even though I think the character drawing deplorable and the construction and final explanation a bit shaky. But he does manage to produce a readable story and it is certainly an intelligent and clever book."

By 1952, however, Punshon's health had declined to the point where he felt unable to attend the Detection Club's annual dinner. "[A]s they used to say in the war, the situation on the (health) front has deteriorated," he mordantly wrote Sayers, adding ominously that he had scheduled an "appointment with a specialist." The next year, however, both he and his wife, now octogenarians, managed to make it to the dinner, much to the pleasure of Sayers, who promised, "you shan't be bothered with the [initiation] ceremony at all—there will be plenty of people to carry candles." Sayers promised the Punshons good seats at the High Table to hear philosopher Bertrand Russell speak, and in contemporary letter Christianna Brand somewhat cattily reported observing

Mrs. Punshon sitting "terribly close to the speakers so as not to miss a word, and sound asleep."

Sometime in the 1950s an increasingly fragile Punshon took a dreadful tumble down the landing steps at the Detection Club premises at Kingly Street, an event Christianna Brand vividly recollected many years later in 1979, with what seems rather callous amusement on her part:

> My last memory, or the most abiding one, of the club room in the clergy house, was of an evening when two members were initiated there instead of at the annual dinner [possibly Glyn Carr and Roy Vickers, 1955 initiates]. As they left, they stepped over the body of an elderly gentleman lying with his head in a pool of blood, just outside the door. . . . dear old Mr. Punshon, E.R. Punshon, tottering up the stone stair steps upon his private business, had fallen all the way down again and severely lacerated his scalp. My [physician] husband, groaning, dealt with all but the gore, which remained in a slowly congealing pool upon the clergy house floor. . . . However, Miss Sayers had, predictably, just the right guest for such an event, a small, brisk lady, delighted to cope. She came out on the landing and stood for a moment peering down at the unlovely mess. Not myself one to delight in hospital matters, I hovered ineffectively as much as possible in the rear. She made up her mind. "Well, I think we can manage *that* all right. Can you find me a tablespoon?"
>
> The club room was unaccountably lacking in tablespoons. I went out and diffidently offered a large fork. "A fork? Oh, well . . ." She bent again and studied the pool of gore. "I think we can manage," she said again, cheerfully. "It's splendidly clotted."
>
> I returned once more to the club room and closed the door; and I can only report that when it opened again, not a sign remained of any blood, anywhere. "I thought," said my husband as we took our departure before even worse

might befall, "that in your oath you foreswore vampires."
"She was only a *guest*," I said apologetically.

"Dear old Mr. Punshon," no vampire he, passed through a door to death in his 84th year on 23 October 1956, four years after his elder brother, Robert Halket Punshon. On 25 January 1957 the widowed Sarah Punshon presented Dorothy L. Sayers with a copy of her husband's thirty-fifth and final Bobby Owen mystery, the charmingly retrospective *Six Were Present*. "He would like to think that you had one," wrote Sarah, warmly thanking Sayers "for your appreciation of my husband's work during his writing life" and wistfully adding that she would miss her "occasional visits to the club evenings." Sayers obligingly invited Sarah to the next Detection Club dinner as her guest, but Sarah died in May, having survived her longtime spouse by merely seven months. Sayers herself would not outlast the year. As Christianna Brand rather flippantly reports, Sayers was discovered, just eight days before Christmas, collapsed dead "at the foot of the stairs in her house surrounded by bereaved cats." Having ascended and descended the stairs after a busy day of shopping, Sayers had discovered her own door to death.

* * * * *

Dorothy L. Sayers's literary reputation has risen ever higher in the years since her demise, with modern authorities like the esteemed late crime writer P.D. James particularly lauding Sayers's ambitious penultimate Peter Wimsey mystery, *Gaudy Night*--a novel E.R. Punshon himself had lavishly praised in his review column in the *Manchester Guardian*--as not only a great detective novel but a great novel, with no delimiting qualification. Although he was one of Sayers's favorite crime writers, Punshon was not so fortunate with his own reputation, with his work falling into unmerited neglect for more than a half-century after his death. With the reprinting by Dean Street Press of Punshon's complete set of Bobby Owen mystery investigations—chronicled in 35 novels, five short stories and a radio play—this long period of neglect now happily has ended, however, allowing a major writer from the Golden Age of detective fiction a golden opportunity to receive, six decades after his death, his full and lasting due.

Crime Fiction Reviews by E.R. Punshon

E.R. PUNSHON reviewed crime fiction for the *Manchester Guardian*, a newspaper congenial to his own Liberal Party sympathies, in 70 insightful and witty columns published between 13 November 1935 and 27 May 1942. A total of 369 books were included in Punshon's near-monthly column, making his reviews one of the larger bodies of crime fiction criticism by a Golden Age detective novelist. (In Punshon's company we also find, among others, Dashiell Hammett, Anthony Boucher and Punshon's Detection Club colleagues Dorothy L. Sayers, John Dickson Carr, Anthony Berkeley, Milward Kennedy, Julian Symons and Edmund Crispin.)

Punshon's crime fiction reviews, selections from which are included in Dean Street Press's new editions of the novels *So Many Doors*, *Everybody Always Tells*, *The Secret Search* and *The Golden Dagger*, indicate a partiality on the author and critic's part toward classical detective fiction, especially works by present and future Detection Club members, including, for example, both richly literary whodunits by Dorothy L. Sayers, E.C. Bentley and Michael Innes and ingenious yet austere efforts by John Rhode, J.J. Connington and Freeman Wills Crofts. Yet though Punshon figuratively threw bouquets at the feet of Dorothy L. Sayers, whose own rave review of Punshon's first Bobby Owen detective novel, *Information Received* (1933), was a great boon to Punshon's career as a mystery writer, in his columns he forbore neither from occasionally criticizing works by other Detection Club members nor from tendering advice on improvement. He also demonstrated interest in American crime fiction, reviewing not just detective novels by classicists like S.S.

Van Dine and Ellery Queen, but suspense novels by Mignon Eberhart and tougher fare like Raymond Chandler's *Farewell, My Lovely*. Altogether Punshon's crime fiction reviews offer both the mystery scholar a valuable research tool and the mystery fan wise pointers for further reading.

Curtis Evans

CHAPTER I
"I SAW IT MYSELF"

THIS FAMOUS London store was not holding a sale. Its large full-page advertisements had merely stated modestly that it was offering to its customers an unparalleled opportunity for securing unrepeatable bargains. Bobby Owen, quite an important person nowadays at Scotland Yard, and at the moment enjoying a day's leave, was following, faint but pursuing, in the wake of Olive, his wife. His arms were full of parcels, his legs were weary, his mind was all one great wistful thought of lunch, his eyes had all they could do to keep themselves fixed on Olive, as sometimes she pressed fiercely forward to her distant objective of that special unheard-of bargain which had chiefly excited her desire, and sometimes swerved through the press to discover why the fray seemed thickest round this or that counter. Who could tell but that there might be precisely what one needed above all else?

On a sudden Bobby was aware of a little grey lady standing by his side. There was a large paper parcel under her arm. Evidently she had secured her bargain early, and now was looking round for another. She was so completely one with all the rest of that busy crowd that nobody could possibly have thought of giving her a second glance. Unless of envy that she had secured her purchase already. She looked up at Bobby imploringly, as if wondering if she dared ask him the time or something like that. Bobby looked back at her reproachfully. Then, with a guilty start, he looked away. Alas! in this one brief moment in which he had removed his eyes from Olive's distant figure she had vanished as for ever in that vast eddy of eager, hurrying femininity.

Fortunately he had taken the precaution of warning Olive that if they became separated they would meet in the lounge of the store restaurant. So, giving up all hope of finding her again till then, he shifted the burden of his parcels, in an effort to relieve the arm that seemed to ache most, and wandered abstractedly away in the wake of the little grey lady, who for her part had wandered, equally abstractedly, to a spot, deserted and lonely, because there were offered no such absolutely unique opportunities as blossomed in their hundreds and their thousands elsewhere. To her Bobby said, still reproachfully:

"I was sorry to hear, Miss Rice, that you had resigned. It's difficult for us at the Yard to carry on if all our best people keep on leaving."

"I was offered twice what I was getting," Miss Rice answered simply.

Bobby, recognizing the force of this argument, did not attempt to reply, and took the opportunity of relieving himself of his parcels by depositing them in a heap on an adjacent counter. Miss Rice said:

"You ought to have a shopping-bag to put them in."

"You mean a portmanteau, don't you?" Bobby corrected her. "I see you've got your bargain all right," he added.

"Stuffed with tissue paper," Miss Rice informed him, balancing that large parcel on an outstretched forefinger. "Store detectives, especially head store detectives, are not allowed. We get a chance only at what's left over. Ever heard of Lord Newdagonby?"

"Not that I remember," Bobby answered. "Why? Has he a record?"

"Well, he's a peer of the realm," Miss Rice explained, slightly shocked.

"His misfortune or his fault?" Bobby asked.

"Enormously wealthy, or at least as enormously wealthy as anyone can be nowadays," continued Miss Rice. "He is one of our directors, and in 'Who's Who' he gives his recreations as mathematics and philosophy."

"What a rollicking time he must have!" murmured Bobby, doing his best to sound envious.

"And I've just seen him pick up something from the jewellery—I couldn't see exactly what—and slip it into Mrs Owen's handbag when she wasn't looking."

Bobby had seen and known too much that was strange to be easily surprised, but this time he fairly gasped.

"Are you sure?" he asked, rather feebly, for Miss Rice, as he very well knew, was not the sort of person to make such a statement without very good reason.

"I saw it myself," Miss Rice answered. "One of my girls had noticed him. She didn't know who he was, and she thought he was acting suspiciously. She said he seemed to be following Mrs Owen. Of course, she didn't know Mrs Owen either, and she thought perhaps they were working it together. Couples do sometimes, you know. One to take, and one to keep. She told me, and I said I would watch. I'm sure Lord Newdagonby saw me. And I saw him pass his hand over Mrs Owen's handbag and drop something in. I believe he meant me to see."

"Do you think possibly he had really taken it?" Bobby asked, "and then he saw you and decided he had better get rid of it, and so just pushed it into the first handbag he saw half-open—as," Bobby added, "most of 'em are half of the time, and I daresay my wife's like the rest."

"Don't I know it?" retorted Miss Rice. "Or else a shopping-basket in provisions with a purse on top shouting 'Won't someone please go off with me?' But Mrs Owen's was only open just that minute while she was paying for what she had been buying."

"Another parcel coming?" Bobby sighed, glancing at the pile on the nearby counter.

"A silk head-scarf," Miss Rice told him, "and will go in your pocket easily, so don't grumble at nothing, and one of the really, real bargains. Most people never notice, but Mrs Owen spotted it. The Buyer tipped me off, and I'm hoping one or two will be left so I can get one after closing."

A voice from behind said:

"If I'm interrupting a hot flirtation, don't mind me."

"Hullo, Olive," Bobby exclaimed, turning round. "How on earth have you managed to find me in this hullabaloo?"

"What hullabaloo?" asked Olive. "They are a bit busy," she admitted, looking round.

"Talking of hot flirtations," Bobby said, "have you been having one yourself with Lord Newdagonby?"

"Who is Lord Newdagonby?" Olive asked.

"He seems to have been making subtle advances to you," Bobby told her.

"Oh, how nice!" cried Olive, enchanted.

"Look in your handbag," said Bobby.

"What for?" asked Olive.

"Do as you are told," said Bobby with firm, husbandly authority.

"Oh, my lord and master, to hear is to obey," said Olive with true wifely meekness, and did so. Then she said, "Oh".

For there, lying on the top of a varied contents, ranging from a small paper-bag of chocolates to scraps of material preserved for matching, was a string of artificial pearls of the kind sold before the second world war for a guinea or two, and today for ten times as much.

"From the jewellery counter," said Miss Rice. "Price not reduced. He must have had it all ready to pop in."

"Who had?" said Olive, very bewildered and a little alarmed as well.

"Lord Newdagonby," said Bobby. "Miss Rice was just telling me. She saw him slip it into your bag when you weren't looking."

"Who is Lord Newdagonby?" Olive repeated.

"The point is," Bobby said, "what was he up to? Of course, if it was the beginning or continuation of a courtship, of which I as a stern husband . . ."

"Don't be silly," snapped Olive, really cross. "Miss Rice, if Mr Owen can't be a little bit sensible, who is Lord Newdagonby?"

"One of our directors," Miss Rice explained. "Very rich and important and all that. His daughter is the Miss Dagon, that's the family name, who was in the news a year or two ago when she left a sisterhood she had joined because she said she had found there was nothing to religion. She's married now. I saw him put that necklace in your bag."

"What for?" asked Olive.

"And I'm perfectly sure he wanted me to see him do it," Miss Rice added.

"Well, what for?" Olive persisted.

"That," said Bobby, "is what I would like to know. An attack of kleptomania? But that's chiefly a feminine disease, and Miss Rice says she feels sure Lord Newdagonby wanted her to see what he was doing. Temporary insanity? But that only applies in cases of suicide."

"Temporary insanity indeed," sniffed Miss Rice. "He's all there all right, trust me."

"Because he wanted the thing but couldn't afford to buy it?" Bobby went on. "But Miss Rice says he is a rich man. Where does he get his money from? Do you know, Miss Rice?"

"Stock Exchange," Miss Rice explained. "He is always buying and selling, and always at a profit."

"Oh, come, not always," Bobby protested incredulously.

"Well, that's what they say," Miss Rice persisted. "He has a flair."

This silenced Bobby, because, though he had no idea what the word meant, he knew that he himself had been credited with having it—much to his surprise.

"What's a flair?" asked Olive, also curious to know what this strange thing was that her man was said to possess.

"I think it means being always right," Miss Rice explained.

"Then I certainly haven't got it," declared Bobby, much relieved.

"They say," Miss Rice went on, "that a college at Oxford or somewhere was very hard up, so they asked him, because he had been there, and he said: 'How much do you want?' and they said: 'All we can get,' and he said, 'Would fifty thousand do?' and they said: 'Very nicely,' so he said he would send them a cheque after next settling day, and he did."

"Just like that?" asked Bobby.

"Just like that," repeated Miss Rice firmly. "All out of Stock Exchange dealings."

"Very nice, too," said Bobby, much impressed. "Talk about giving to airy nothings a local habitation and a cheque book."

Both the ladies looked as if they wondered what he was talking about. He went on, rather hurriedly: "How about drifting along to the jewellery department and seeing if they've missed any odd pearl necklaces recently?"

Thither accordingly the three of them drifted, if that can be called drifting which was in fact one long, stern fight against a whirling tide of opposing currents. However, finally they reached their destination, a little breathless but otherwise not much the worse for wear. There they found a very perturbed young lady. Yes, Lord Newdagonby had been there. He had wanted to see some of their good-class imitation pearl necklaces. He had asked that three of them should be kept out of the showcase while he went to find his friend for her to make her choice. He would be back in less than a minute, he said, but in fact had not been seen since. She, the young lady in charge of the counter, was most emphatic that she had never taken her eyes off the three necklaces for one single second. All the same, one had disappeared, and what had happened to it she couldn't think. But if the firm wanted her to pay for it she couldn't and wouldn't, so there.

Bobby relieved her fears by producing the one found in Olive's handbag. This she at once identified, since the price ticket was still attached. Bobby told her he would have to keep it for the present, but gave her a receipt for it, and then allowed his thoughts to wander in the direction of lunch. Olive protested against wasting time in eating that could be devoted to bargain hunting. Bobby said simply that he was at the point of death from sheer exhaustion. A little alarmed lest this might be true, Olive yielded. Bobby said gloomily that he supposed by now there would be a queue all round the restaurant lounge and back again. Miss Rice at once offered to fix that for them. Olive said, "Oh, thank you so much," before Bobby had time to voice a high-minded refusal to take advantage of such gross, back-stairs influence. So instead he followed, silently protestant but also very hungry, to a table specially provided for them.

"Yes, but, Bobby, what does it mean?" Olive asked, as they settled themselves in their places and smugly surveyed that interminable queue, hungry, patient, well trained, at the tail end of which they should now, by all the canons of justice, be taking their stand. "It all," said Olive, musing over a very satisfactory menu, "it all seems so silly. I do hope they know how to make decent coffee here."

"It does seem silly and meaningless," Bobby agreed. "But is it? Or is there behind it something very far from silly?"

CHAPTER II
"DISCUSSING MY MURDER?"

LATER ON that day there were two telephone messages. One was from Miss Rice to Bobby, telling him that a cheque had been received from Lord Newdagonby in payment for an artificial pearl necklace purchased that day. The matter was therefore closed so far as her firm was concerned. The second was from Bobby to his lordship, asking if he, Bobby, might call next day.

"Must you?" Olive asked doubtfully when Bobby told her he meant to do this. "What for? Miss Rice says it's all finished."

"I don't like people who push necklaces into other people's handbags," Bobby remarked. "Prejudice on my part perhaps, but there it is. And I want rather badly to know what's up. At present I'm in possession of a necklace priced at thirteen guineas according to the price ticket."

"One guinea before the war," Olive interposed, indignation in her voice.

"Apparently," Bobby went on, "it's the one Lord Newdagonby bought, and certainly the one he wished on you. Anyhow I've got to return it to him."

"What you mean," Olive told him, the touch of indignation in her voice giving place to reproach, "is that you're never happy till you're trying to get to the bottom of some silly thing or another. Oh, why," she appealed to the Fates, "why haven't I a nice quiet husband in a nice quiet office just writing nice quiet letters all day long about yours to hand and same duly noted?"

"Well, they do other things as well in offices," Bobby protested mildly, "or so I'm told."

Olive, resigned, said no more, and Bobby went to the 'phone. He got a reply that Lord Newdagonby would be delighted to see him next morning at any time he liked before lunch. Lord Newdagonby expected, he said, to be in all morning.

So at a gloomy old town house, a white elephant of a house, an unwanted whale of a house, most of it on a kind of care-and- maintenance basis for lack of the dozen or so servants it needed, Bobby duly presented himself next day soon after eleven. He was admitted by a charwoman, pail and mop complete, and one almost saw the sad, lamenting ghosts of former stately butlers hovering aghast in the background. Then came a small, thin, elderly woman, appearing so silently and unexpectedly at his side that Bobby was not quite sure whence she had produced herself. He thought most likely from the entrance to a corridor that, though it was broad daylight, seemed shrouded in perpetual shade. A cast in one eye, not pronounced enough to be called a squint, made it a little difficult to be sure at what she was looking. He got the impression, however, that she was aware of his identity, aware, too, of his errand, and the cause of it, and that this knowledge filled her with a secret excitement. Nor did he much like the thin, tight-lipped mouth, drawn down at the corners, where now and then appeared a slight quivering movement. A somewhat disturbing personality, Bobby thought. She asked him to wait for a moment or two while she informed Lord Newdagonby of his presence and with that glided, rather than walked, away down that gloomy and hidden corridor from which he thought she had emerged. She returned presently to say that Lord Newdagonby was not in his room, and she didn't know what had become of him. He was, however, certainly somewhere in the house, if the gentleman wouldn't mind waiting a few minutes.

Then she vanished again in that peculiar silent way of hers, but before very long was back to say that Lord Newdagonby had merely been in the library, where she had failed to notice him at first, hidden as he had been behind one of the great protruding bookshelves, but that he was now back in his study. Would the gentleman please come this way?

Bobby followed her accordingly down that dark and airless and seemingly endless corridor into a huge, cavern-like apartment, once the last of a whole series of reception rooms, and now used by Lord Newdagonby as his study. The walls were lined with low bookshelves, filled with books that had the air, not always noticeable with books on shelves, of being in frequent use. Above these shelves were a number of paintings of the most modern school, one or two probably even just a trifle too advanced even for that most modern of institutions, the Tate Gallery. The furniture was mostly early Victorian, mahogany of a massive type, built for permanence in days when permanence seemed—well, permanent. Bobby noticed also the great fireplace in white marble, big enough to consume in a week a year's supply of fuel as we know supplies to-day, and supported by two finely carved figures, nearly life size, half-fish and half-human.

A large electric radiator had been installed to provide warmth for a room that seemed to Bobby as he entered to be deathly cold. But this radiator was now out of action, as a power unit cut was in progress. Near it, as near as he could get, as if hoping that some warmth still lingered in its neighbourhood, a man was sitting, holding on his knee a pad on which he had been writing. As Bobby entered he laid this aside and rose from his chair, giving in doing so an impression of being nearer seven feet in height than his actual six. It almost seemed indeed as if there would be no end to it as he slowly unwound himself from his former huddled position to stand at last upright at the full stretch of his abnormally thin body, a body so thin, so immaterial almost, one had the idea that it might very well vanish soon, like the fabled genii of the east, into a column of smoke. Crowning this strange body was an enormous head (size eight in hats) almost entirely bald, with two very bright bead-like eyes on each side of an enormous nose so like a beak that Bobby was irresistibly reminded of a vulture watching and waiting for its prey. Beneath this fantastic nose was a small, red mouth above a chin that tapered away nearly to a point. But it was in a low, pleasant voice, almost a caressing voice, that Bobby was greeted by this odd personality in whom he had no difficulty in recognizing Lord Newdagonby. Bobby offered his apologies for disturbing his lordship, and his lordship apologized in return for the cold room, but hoped the electricity supply would soon come into action again.

The polite preliminaries over, Lord Newdagonby went on to express his pleasure at meeting Bobby, of whom he had often heard, both through the press and from a relative in the Home Office. But he had not fully understood the message received. Certainly he had purchased a string of pearl beads ("a ridiculous price, I thought of keeping it to show at our next board meeting and of asking how long the public was going to stand for that sort of thing"). But instead he had given it to the young lady he had bought it for, and very likely it was at that moment around her very charming neck.

"That detail is, of course, strictly confidential," explained Lord Newdagonby, and twisted his features into a sort of grimace that instantly changed his resemblance to a watchful vulture into that of a grinning gnome. "Can't afford," he explained, "to let my daughter know. Henpecking by a wife is nothing to henpecking by a daughter. You can't divorce a daughter. And if Kitty got to know, I don't suppose she would ever speak to me again. She has ideals—so delightful of her. But somehow it makes me mistrust her. Ideals are so unpredictable."

Bobby produced the necklace found so mysteriously in Olive's handbag.

"It has been identified by the price ticket," Bobby explained, "as one of the three or four shown to you. You bought one, I understand. The others are safe back in the show-case. This was later picked up in the shop."

Lord Newdagonby took the necklace from Bobby and examined it closely.

"Very like the one I bought," he agreed, "Probably the same factory or wherever these things come from. But certainly not the same thing. As I told you, that is in the possession of a most charming young lady. Identified, you say? It must surely be very difficult to tell these things apart?"

"The assistant seemed sure enough," Bobby answered. "There's always the price ticket, I suppose."

"I shouldn't wonder," Lord Newdagonby murmured, "if these shop-lifter people don't keep a supply of price tickets in their pockets. If they are challenged in shop 'A', then they produce the thing with the price ticket of shop 'B' on it. Clear proof of innocence."

"Well, I've certainly never heard of that piece of technique," observed Bobby, rising to his feet in preparation for departure. "Very ingenious idea, but not, I think, very practical. Still, what you tell me closes the matter as far as we are concerned. Of course, there may be developments later. One never knows. The necklace will have to go to Lost Property, I suppose. And all I can do is to offer you my apologies once again for having troubled you so unnecessarily."

"Not at all, not at all," protested Lord Newdagonby, as once more he began that long, seemingly interminable process of unfolding himself to his full height. "A privilege to meet you, Mr Owen."

"Too good of you to say so," declared Bobby; and for a moment his own clear and steady gaze met full that of those little bright bead-like eyes on each side of that enormous nose, so that once again he was reminded of a great watchful bird of prey, and in his mind was the certainty that this was not the end but the beginning.

Oddly enough, too, he had a feeling that Lord Newdagonby had suddenly lost his former self-possession and calm certainty that he controlled the situation. It was exactly as if all at once, for some reason Bobby could not even guess at, he had felt his grip abruptly slacken. With a certain hurried suggestion of a wish to change the subject, he now waved a hand towards those rather astonishing pictures on the room walls.

"I saw you looking at my little collection, Mr Owen," he said. "The new French school mostly, but a few striking examples of some of our own more advanced workers. I wonder what you think of them?"

"Oh, well, I'm a traditionalist, I suppose," Bobby explained. "I follow Mr Churchill's example and thoroughly enjoy playing about with paints and brushes when I've time. Teaches you to look, too. Look. Stare. Not just give a stray glance. But always traditional."

"Oh, yes, traditional," Lord Newdagonby repeated, much as if for some obscure reason this word reassured him, relieved as it were the momentary doubt or unease or whatever it was that for a moment had appeared to trouble his supreme self-confidence. He emitted a sudden harsh sound that Bobby was to come to know as the Newdagonby version of a chuckle. He went on: "Very suitable, too. A police force should be traditional—like the Chantry Bequest and all that. Admirable work in its time, no doubt." In saying this, his tone was exactly like that a scientist of to-day might use in commenting on a prehistoric stone axe. With a motion this time of his hand towards the fireplace, he added: "What do you think of those two supporters? They are traditional if you like. Body and head of a fish. Arms and legs of a man."

"Well, I did rather wonder," Bobby admitted, "if there was any connection with the old man-fish god of the Philistines, wasn't it? Dagon, I think, and I thought your name might mean the new farm or bye dedicated to Dagon."

Again Lord Newdagonby looked slightly taken aback, as if he had never supposed that a policeman was at all likely to have heard of any of the gods of the ancient east or to know what the termination 'by' might mean.

"There is an old family legend like that," he remarked. "We are supposed to descend from a Roman legionary, possibly of Arab origin, and a worshipper of Dagon. Thank God."

Bobby, a little puzzled at first by this pious exclamation, saw then that it was due to the fact that the power cut was over and the electric radiator once more in action. At the same moment the door opened and a deep, harsh, husky voice said:

"Discussing my murder, are you?"

CHAPTER III
"BEELZEBUB"

STARTLED BY this remark, which seemed to chime so well with his uneasy feeling that in all this there was much more than appeared on the surface, Bobby turned quickly to see a woman standing in the doorway. Behind her was a little, round man, half-hidden by her and giving a curious impression of peeping shyly round the flowing, fur-trimmed cape she wore. She was a tall, palely handsome woman with a high, pale forehead; and small, restless, uneasy eyes that somehow gave an odd impression of seeking a road it was both impossible and imperative to find. Yet the lower part of the face, with its rather too large mouth set in firm, hard lines above a chin, square and protuberant, seemed to contradict this first impression Bobby had received as of one who had lost her way and was seeking almost desperately to find it again. Then, too, there was about her a kind of aggressive air, a suggestion of a hungry ruthlessness, as if to match that likeness to a seeking bird of prey Bobby had found in Lord Newdagonby. For though no single feature in this new-comer bore any resemblance to any one of Lord Newdagonby's, yet the total effect was of a general family likeness suggesting close relationship. Bobby guessed at once that she must be the daughter of whom he had heard, as having spent eighteen months or so in an Anglican sisterhood and then leaving it on the ground that she had found there was 'nothing to religion'.

"Murder is an ugly word," Bobby said to her.

"Murder is an ugly thing," she retorted, and her small, restless eyes grew suddenly intent upon him. "Isn't it, Charley?"

From behind her flowing cape, as in speaking she came farther into the room, now emerged the little, smiling man Bobby had only seen before in partial eclipse. He was comparatively young, that is somewhere about forty, and he beamed approvingly upon the world in general, and those present in particular, through a pair of those large, gold-rimmed spectacles, once associated with elderly benevolence but now grown rare, now that gold has been dethroned as the universal touchstone of value and thereby become three times as valuable as before.

He said rebukingly, in answer to his companion's question:

"Now, now, Sibby, murder's not a thing to talk about like that."

"Oh, shut up," she retorted.

But this was spoken without heat, even without much interest, almost indifferently indeed.

"My daughter, Mrs Findlay," Lord Newdagonby said to Bobby. "Oh, a friend of hers—Mr Acton."

"The Mr Acton," explained Mrs Findlay. "Charley Acton—every one ought to know his name. Every one will some day if only for what he's done already that they haven't heard about yet."

She had been walking slowly across the floor of that enormous room while she was speaking till she was quite close to Bobby, at whom she looked with a kind of detached curiosity, as one might look at something in a glass case in a museum, something one knew to be of interest but had no idea why nor greatly cared. Behind her trotted 'the' Charley Acton. 'Trotted', however, must be understood in a purely impressionist sense, for in fact he progressed in a completely normal manner, but none the less managed to convey a reminder of a pet dog trotting after its mistress—on a leash. To Bobby, when she was quite close to him, she said in her cool, uninterested tone:

"Policeman, aren't you?"

Bobby was only just in time to grab hold of his temper before he lost it. Few things annoyed him more than when perfect strangers pretended to recognize his profession at first sight. Besides, he was always sure it was a pretence and that those making the claim had been 'tipped off' in advance. Now he made a slight bow which he hoped was reserved, dignified, and aloof. She rewarded him with one of her faint, almost illusory, yet rather charming smiles. He said:

"Because of that fact, I was interested in what I heard you say about having been murdered recently. If I may say so, you seem to have survived the experience very successfully."

She had been turning away but now looked back at him, frowning slightly, and this time those small, worried eyes of hers showed a quick, new interest or perhaps surprise.

"Prospective, purely prospective," she said. "But not to be so for long, I understand." To her father, she said: "What have you been telling him, Loo?"

"The modern young woman," commented Lord Newdagonby, shaking disapprovingly that enormous head of his which had the air of being perched so insecurely on so thin a body, on such narrow shoulders. He was regarding his daughter with obvious pride and affection. Strange indeed to see how the rather bizarre, slightly inhuman impression he had conveyed at first, changed now into warm, natural human love. Not that Mrs Findlay seemed to notice. Perhaps she had grown so used to it that she had really become unaware of, or indifferent to, this strong affection her father had for her. Not to her but to Bobby, Lord Newdagonby went on: "My first name is Louis, and so my daughter calls me 'Loo' after some ridiculous, old, forgotten card game. Probably she thinks I'm ridiculous, old, and forgotten."

"Oh, I do," Mrs Findlay remarked carelessly.

"Now, now, Sibby," said 'the' Charley Acton.

"Shut up," said Mrs Findlay—or 'Sibby'.

"In the golden days of good Queen Vicky," said Lord Newdagonby, "I should have been cut off with a shilling if I had dared talk to my father like that—or sent to my room on bread and water for a week."

"These aren't the golden days of good Queen Anyone," retorted Mrs Findlay. "They are the very drab, leaden, totalitarianly dull days of good King George—fifth or sixth, I never can remember which."

"Do you really find these days dull?" Bobby asked. "Does a woman find childbirth dull? Critical, painful, dangerous. Yes. But dull?"

Mrs Findlay stared at him for quite a long time before she spoke. Bobby felt that Charley Acton wanted very much to say "Now, now, Sibby," but knew that if he did she would hardly hear, though certainly she would tell him to shut up. So he turned his attention to one of the more repellent of the pictures on the walls. Mrs Findlay said:

"How the devil do you manage it?"

"Manage what?" Bobby asked.

"To look so ordinary, so damnably commonplace, when you're nothing of the sort."

"Oh, that," Bobby answered brightly, "that's just part of our police training. They lay great stress on it. Shall we talk about your prospective murder you mentioned just now? I'm interested professionally, you see."

"I say," Mr Acton interrupted, still examining the painting that had attracted him, "this is jolly fine. Superb. Quite new, isn't it? Not signed. It isn't a Picasso, is it?"

"No, a young English artist," Lord Newdagonby told him. "Unknown at present, but in my opinion, a coming man. Unfortunate name and why it's not signed. He must change it. It's Bill Brown."

"Most unfortunate," agreed Mr Acton in a very shocked tone.

"More unfortunate still," Lord Newdagonby continued, "he was christened or registered, or whatever they do to babies, as 'Bill'. His father said if they called him William he would be 'Bill' anyhow, so he might as well be 'Bill' from the start."

"I suggest," observed Mrs Findlay thoughtfully, "Bertie Brenda Browskyvitch. Bertie as he's a man. Brenda because a combination of masculine and feminine is always so fascinating, Browskyvitch because you've got to be foreign if you want the critics to take you seriously. Also he could sign as 'B.B.B.', and initials are all the go. You must be in the go. Essential."

"I say you know," declared Mr Acton in a low, hushed, reverent voice, "there's a touch of genius in this thing."

"Shut up," said Mrs Findlay, quite automatically, for she had not caught the remark, uttered as it had been almost in a whisper.

"I mean this painting," explained Mr Acton, looking hurt.

"You don't care to talk about your apparently contemplated murder?" Bobby asked Mrs Findlay.

"Ask Loo," said Mrs Findlay, and strolled away to join Acton before the painting he admired so much. Over her shoulder, she said: "Charley Acton is a born art critic. He ought to have been one instead of a scientist, inventing things better left uninvented. His response is instinctive. He—knows, and that's all there's to it."

This mention of Mr Charley Acton as an inventor woke memories in Bobby's mind. He recollected the excitement in some of the sillier papers when Mr Acton had announced a new method of manufacturing artificial diamonds of a reasonable size. Unfortunately the process proved to cost more than the diamonds produced were worth. Then again there had been his project for storing sun heat in the tropics by means of enormous mirrors. A by-product of this idea had been a plan for storing electricity in great cisterns, like enormous water-tanks. But it was understood that the working out of these plans, though far advanced, was in abeyance, as Mr Acton was now concentrating on the use of atomic energy, which he considered might well, and comparatively soon, supersede electricity altogether. In an article in a prominent scientific journal he had pointed out that the sun is merely a great factory for splitting the atom and releasing atomic energy. He had gone on to suggest that it might be possible to manufacture a smaller artificial sun to accompany the planet Mars in its orbit, and so make Mars available for human habitation. The idea had aroused much interest—and controversy.

Fortunately he had inherited a good deal of money, and so was able to some extent to finance his own research. But for this he might have encountered considerable difficulty in getting his ideas listened to, as some people of standing denounced him as a charlatan. But this opposition came chiefly from the older universities, and all know how conservative and unprogressive they are apt to be—homes of ancient, lost, forgotten causes as Mr Acton himself remarked occasionally. At any rate, some of his minor inventions had had considerable success. A dripless teapot, for example, that, however, didn't drip only because it wouldn't pour. And an admirable device for threading needles, though few women seemed interested in it. They appeared to think they could thread their own needles for themselves without buying a gadget to do it for them. Now it was understood he had produced an everlasting razor blade. It was already in production though only on a very small scale and samples of it had been tested continuously for months at a time with complete success. Negotiations were in progress for the flotation of a company with a very large capital.

At the moment, however, this scientist of so many revolutionary ideas was completely lost in the art lover. Busily, even excitedly, he was pointing out the insight, the power, the significance of the painting he was admiring. Bobby could not resist going to get a closer view of what was rousing so much enthusiasm in a man 'born to be an art critic' as Mrs Findlay said.

He contemplated it with some awe. There was a border of what seemed to be meant for kettles, frying-pans, and so on, but like no kettles or frying-pans or anything else that human kitchen had ever seen. "Their inner essence", Mr Acton told him in a hushed voice. In the middle of the picture was a clearly recognizable moustache, and to one side and higher up, a human eye. There was also a large patch of just plain grease, and in the top right-hand corner a small doll, attached upside down by a drawing-pin. At other eccentricities of the same sort, Bobby blinked incredulously, and to him Mr Acton said:

"You understand? You realize what the artist wishes to do, his message to the world? With the powerful insight of genius he breaks up the order of appearance to show to us the underlying chaos that is the uttermost reality of things."

"Order back into chaos?" Bobby asked. "Yes. I see that. The aim, too, of that other great artist."

"Who is that?" Acton asked eagerly.

"Beelzebub," Bobby answered.

CHAPTER IV
"CRIME'S MERELY VULGAR"

THE REMARK was received in silence. No one seemed quite to know what to make of it, Bobby least of all. He had an impression that Mrs Findlay was going to say 'Shut up'. Instead she remarked:

"Beelzebub? One of the lords of sin, isn't he? I'm interested. You see," she went on, addressing Bobby directly, "I gave eighteen months to religion and found nothing. Now I'm going to give eighteen months to sin and see what sin has to offer."

"Now, Sibby," Charley Acton interposed, "you shouldn't talk like that before the police, you know."

"Don't be a fool," Mrs Findlay retorted. "I said sin, not crime. Crime's merely vulgar."

"I wish you wouldn't talk in that flippant way," Lord Newdagonby said. "It's not clever."

"It isn't, nor meant to be," Mrs Findlay answered coldly. "It's just a statement of intention. I've got to know myself, I must find out all my possibilities, experience all things, try all things. That's in the bible. Or how can I know what I am?"

No one answered this. But a kind of heaviness came into the air, an almost tangible oppression. Bobby, watching her closely, found himself wondering into what strange lands this passion to explore might not lead? He forgot his intention to leave at once, and he wondered, too, if just possibly this desire to know herself, to experience all things, might have brought her into danger of some sort or another? For that her father feared for her was, Bobby felt, quite certain. Mrs Findlay seemed to become aware of how strangely they all watched her. She said now in the same cold, deep voice:

"Is that so strange? Why? Isn't the need for experience the first of human needs? Isn't the first necessity for us all to know ourselves? And if religion can't tell us, why not apply elsewhere? How about lunch? I'd better see if there's any. It's getting time. Come on, Charley. You may be able to help."

"I could lay the table," Charley said helpfully. "That is, if you don't use too many knives and forks."

"We don't. Got to remember the washing up," Mrs Findlay told him. To Bobby, she said: "It'll give you a chance to talk to Loo about my improbable, possible, prospective murder."

Therewith the two of them departed, and Bobby turned to Lord Newdagonby:

"I shall, of course," he said, "make a full report of all this. I shall say that in my opinion all this odd business with the pearl necklace was an excuse to get me here for a private talk, and I think you did not expect Mrs Findlay to be present or for her to be quite so open. Murder is a serious subject to talk about before a policeman."

"You are very perceptive," Lord Newdagonby said, a touch of resentment in his voice as if he felt that in being so, Bobby was hardly playing the game. "Sibby is always so frank and outspoken. So honest," and this he said with now pride taking the place of resentment. But Bobby thought that it was not so much honesty that made Mrs Findlay so outspoken, but a kind of colossal egotism wrapped in which she felt above all criticism. "Honest as the day," Lord Newdagonby repeated, and then, and this time, just a little apologetically: "My only child. Possibly I fuss too much. She says so."

Bobby picked up his hat.

"Good morning," he said. "Unless of course you wish to make a statement."

"Oh, that sounds so very official," Lord Newdagonby protested. "It's only that there have been some 'phone calls."

"I have neither authority nor reason to question you," Bobby said. "If you have any cause to believe that any one is in danger of what Mrs Findlay called an improbable, possible, prospective murder, or if any threats have been made by 'phone or in any other way, please communicate with the Assistant Commissioner, C.I.D., Scotland Yard. Until then, nothing can be done. Good morning."

He spoke sharply, for he was convinced that, as he had told Lord Newdagonby, there had been an elaborate and rather silly scheme to bring him here and get information and advice, while at the same time avoiding any definite commitment or complaint. Quite possibly his lordship, relying on his rank and wealth, had expected to be able to overawe any mere police officer and get with ease what he wanted from him. Bobby's dignity was offended—how he put it to himself was 'the cheek of it'. He was already half-way to the door when Lord Newdagonby called him back.

"One moment, one moment, Mr Owen," he said. "Very likely it is all nonsense—meant for a joke perhaps. Sibby has some very foolish young friends. But there was a distinct warning that murder was intended."

"Murder? Of whom?"

"I didn't hear it myself," Lord Newdagonby went on. "Kitty took it. Miss Grange that is. She was rather upset. She said it sounded as if it was meant. Miss Grange is a relative—a rather distant cousin."

"Does she live here?"

"At present, yes. As long as she likes to stay. She is looking for employment at the moment. Quite unnecessary. She says she wants to be independent."

"She took this message then? Can you give me the exact wording?"

"More or less. It was that if we didn't take care there would be murder, as Ivor intended to 'do in'—that was the expression used—to 'do in' Sibby. Ivor is Mr Findlay, he and Sibby have been married a year now."

Bobby had a fleeting thought that from what he had seen of Mrs Findlay, any husband would probably want to murder her. But he put that out of his mind as officially inadmissible and said:

"Ivor Findlay? I think I know the name. Is he the Mr Findlay who was called the other day as an expert witness in the German patent case?"

"Yes. He is with Mack, Manners, and Marks. Well-known people. He acts as their scientific adviser. Charley Acton is one of their clients."

"Was there any suggestion why Mr Findlay should wish to murder his wife?"

Lord Newdagonby very clearly did not want to answer this question. Bobby remained silent and waiting. He had a trick of waiting that not only Lord Newdagonby but others too had found to be, in effect, an insistence on an answer that it was difficult to evade or to refuse.

"Oh, well," Lord Newdagonby said at last. "There has been some gossip I believe. Sibby's been going about a good deal with a Count Ariosto. He claims to be descended from the poet. Unluckily Sibby snubbed some of these press vermin—photographers—and the fellows have made a point ever since of taking snaps of her and the Count together whenever they can. Nothing you can take hold of, but very unpleasant, very suggestive. One week a snap of Sibby and Count Ariosto together. Next week Ivor and the fellow talking and underneath 'Heated argument?—what's it all about?' Things like that. As a matter of fact, that time it was racing. Ariosto was giving Ivor what he called a straight tip from the stables, and Ivor thought Ariosto was trying to get him into difficulties. Quite unnecessary. Ivor is always in difficulties with his betting. And then the straight tip turned out a success, and Ivor would have won some thousands if he had acted on it. He seems to have had a grudge against Ariosto ever since."

"Seems a bit illogical," Bobby remarked. "Not quite what you would expect from a scientist."

"Scientists," explained Lord Newdagonby, "are only scientists in the laboratory—outside it, they are rather stupider than other people because they have fewer everyday contacts—less experience."

"If you authorize us," Bobby said, "we'll try to keep an eye on the gentleman. I understand you to mean that Mr and Mrs Findlay are not on good terms?"

"Oh, no, no. I'm sure they're extremely fond of each other."

"No question of a divorce?"

"Dear me, no. I daresay either of them could—well, er, make out a case if they wished. But they are both extremely civilized people."

"You mean they don't attach any importance to primitive ideas about faithfulness to the marriage vows?"

Lord Newdagonby looked really taken aback, as if this were a most surprising way of putting things. It was a moment or two before he replied. Then he said:

"Well, obviously, vows can't be kept when—well, when they can't be kept any longer."

"Fortunately we needn't go into that," Bobby said. "I only wanted to get their attitude to each other quite clear. I have to try to decide how seriously these threats may be meant and if action ought to be taken."

"Besides, there's the money," Lord Newdagonby went on. "I settled a fairly large sum on Sibby when she married, and I also established a trust fund to produce a thousand a year for Ivor so long as they were married. He would lose that income if there was a divorce."

"Or a death?"

"Or a death," Lord Newdagonby repeated.

"A consideration," Bobby remarked. "Not many people are anxious to loss a thousand a year. What would happen to the money settled on your daughter?"

"Oh, that's her property absolutely. Entirely under her own control. Ivor always goes to her when he has lost more than usual on his betting, and she generally helps him out. Sometimes not, if he's been flirting worse than usual."

"Is it only flirting?" Bobby asked.

"Oh, well," said Lord Newdagonby, "as for that . . ." He left the sentence unfinished. Then he said with a sort of rush, as if he had only at last decided to bring out what was at the back of his mind: "Sibby told me immediately after the marriage that she had made a will leaving everything to Ivor."

"Yes," Bobby said thoughtfully. "Yes. I see. You called Mr Findlay a flirt, and I rather think you meant it was more than that. Is there any one person in particular? It's just possible there's some idea of forcing a divorce—forcing their hands so to speak."

"No, I don't think so. I told you they always seem very fond of each other. That's my impression anyhow. But not so to say—pedantic. No," he repeated, as if rather pleased with the word: "Decidedly not pedantic. The fact is, Ivor can't resist women. Nor they, him, apparently. He tries to be on kissing terms with every woman he meets. Some of 'em like it. Some don't. Kitty didn't."

"Kitty? Miss Grange?"

"Perhaps I shouldn't have said that. She came to act as his secretary, but she took offence at something and won't go near him now. He's apologized in the most abject terms. It hasn't made any difference."

"I think," Bobby said thoughtfully, "you told me it was she who took this 'phone call?"

"The first one, yes."

"There were others?"

"Two more, Sibby took one herself. And Mrs Jacks, our housekeeper, took the other. She was so startled she dropped the receiver and screamed for Kitty, but of course by the time Kitty came, whoever it was had rung off."

This seemed to dispose of one idea that had occurred to Bobby—that Miss Grange herself might be responsible for these mysterious 'phone calls. Of course, it was still possible it might have been some third person on her instigation.

"Will you give me Mr Findlay's address?"

"They live here. What used to be called the Royal suite has been fitted up as a separate flat with its own side entrance—the garden door once."

"The address of his firm?"

"Oh, that's Kilburn—17, Acacia Avenue, Kilburn. A private house they got hold of. Most inconvenient. They were bombed out twice and lost all their records. It's made things very difficult for them. Ivor finds Kilburn too far to go except when it's really necessary, so he uses a room he has fitted up somewhere in the attics here as a sort of office and laboratory."

"Does he see clients there?"

"Certainly not. I made that quite clear. I didn't intend to have a stream of the sort of cranks and semi-lunatics who infest patent agents coming here."

Just then the 'phone rang. Lord Newdagonby answered it. He listened and said in reply:

"Oh, very well, Kitty, if you want to. Try to be back as soon as you can. I can't get on till I have those books."

The door opened and Mrs Findlay came in, Acton trailing behind and still looking, or so Bobby thought, exactly like a little pet dog on a leash.

"There nothing for lunch," Mrs Findlay announced, "except a sole bonne femme. Mrs Jacks says she only prepared for Loo and Kitty. The rest of us will have to pig it at some cookshop or another. We might try the Ritz."

"Kitty," Lord Newdagonby told her, "has just this moment rung up to say she's lunching with Noel. Very inconvenient. I'm waiting for the books I asked her to get from the London Library. So there would be enough for you, Sibby, if you would care to share my sole bonne femme. One of Mrs Jacks's specialities, too. A most excellent cook."

Bobby thought he said all this rather wistfully, as if well aware that the last thing in the world Mrs Findlay would want would be to lunch alone with her father rather than at one of the smart resorts she had just described as 'cookshops'. Now her face lighted up suddenly.

"How about," she exclaimed, "all of us going to Noel's place in Jermyn Street? He generally gives you something decent to eat, and it would be rather fun to see how he and Kitty looked when they saw us all breaking in on their nice little tête-à-tête. Ivor, too. We would have to take him along."

"I thought Ivor never lunched," interposed Acton, and Bobby thought that this suggestion rather disturbed him, was in fact equally unwelcome and unexpected, as if possibly he, on his part, had been looking forward to a tête-à-tête—with Mrs Findlay at a guess. Acton went on in the same rather hurried manner: "He sent me a note last night to tell me what he's going to say about my everlasting razor blade. For him, most enthusiastic. He promised the formal report soon. I hope he's working on it now, only he will take on so many things he's always in such a frightful rush."

"Oh, another day or two won't hurt your precious report," Mrs Findlay answered carelessly. "If it's that awful row they had you're thinking of, we can take Mr Policeman along." This was said with a careless nod towards Bobby, much as if she thought he was there simply for her convenience. Bobby decided that he definitely disliked Mrs Findlay, who was saying now: "Besides, they can't very well start fighting in Noel's own restaurant, can they? Customers have to be respected."

"Is this gentleman you are speaking of on bad terms with Mr Findlay?" asked Bobby, who had been listening to all this with some interest, and was wondering if here there might be some clue to those three mysterious and slightly disturbing 'phone calls.

"Well, they nearly started fighting at the golf club," Mrs Findlay answered with a smile in which Bobby now found little charm. "Kitty's fault, the little fool. Ivor tried to kiss her. Common form with Ivor. He thinks that is what girls are for, and most of them think so, too. Especially when it's Ivor. But Kitty boxed his ears. Ivor says he had a headache for the rest of the day. And then Noel must take it into his head to make a fuss and tell Ivor all the things he would do if Ivor tried again. Ivor pretended to be awfully frightened, and said he was going to carry a revolver about with him for the future. Of course, he was only pulling Noel's leg, but it made Noel more angry than ever."

"Well, it's no use making things worse," Acton said. "No sense in dragging Ivor round there."

"I think it would be fun," Mrs Findlay persisted. "I'll ring Ivor and tell him he's wanted."

Instead, however of picking up the 'phone standing near, she hurried away.

"House 'phone," Lord Newdagonby explained to Bobby. "In the hall. It's all a journey up to those attics. Kitty and Mr Lake are more or less engaged," he added, "though Kitty says she hasn't made up her mind yet and they haven't known each other long enough."

Mrs Findlay came back into the room.

"I can't get him," she said. "It must be out of order, or he's taken the receiver off or something."

"Means he's busy that's all, doesn't want to be bothered," suggested Acton. "What about the Ritz?"

"Mr Lake is Noel, I suppose," Bobby remarked. "He keeps a restaurant?"

"No, it keeps him, and very nicely, too," Mrs Findlay interrupted. "He's head waiter or something."

"Now, now, Sibby," said Acton.

"Shut up," said Sibby.

"You know very well he's managing director," her father said rebukingly. "Biggest shareholder, too. They run this very expensive little place in Jermyn Street. The 'Isle du Lac.' And one or two others near Baker Street, I think, and another in the city."

"The same food at a quarter the price," remarked Mrs Findlay.

"But not the same wines," interjected Acton, this time with an air of smacking his lips over some agreeable memory. "Besides, Noel mayn't be there if he's lunching Kitty. He may take her somewhere else. What about the Ritz?" he asked.

"No," declared Mrs Findlay with emphasis. "I want Ivor, and I want him at Noel's place. Charley, you run up there and rout him out."

"No, thank you," answered Charley with unexpected decision, looking in fact now not at all like a little pet dog on a leash. "I don't know which is his room for one thing. Never been up there. I should only get lost in this beastly labyrinth of a place of yours. About a hundred rooms on each floor," he explained to Bobby. "Besides, Ivor can turn jolly nasty if he thinks he is being interrupted for nothing."

"Oh, very well, I'll go myself," Mrs Findlay said, apparently recognizing that this time Charley meant it. "You can pay for the lunch instead, Charley," she added as she left the room.

"Parting shot," Acton grumbled as she went off. "Five-shilling limit all right, but you don't get out of that place of Noel's under a pound—and then you have to watch your step." The conversation languished. Bobby was still wondering if, or where, those three mysterious warnings over the 'phone came into all this. He felt that behind it there was something ominous, menacing. He decided he would have to ask Lord Newdagonby a few more questions. Mrs Findlay came back into the room. She seemed excited, even frightened. Breathless, too, as if she had been running. She said:

"The door's locked. I can't get it open. I can't make him hear. I think he must be ill. I think I heard groans. I looked through the keyhole, and his chair's empty and he didn't answer when I called."

CHAPTER V
"THIS IS MURDER"

IN THIS GREAT old rambling house there were three separate stairways. Those generally called the garden stairs led from the garden door to the 'Royal Suite', now converted into a self-contained flat for the use of Mr and Mrs Findlay, and thence to the second floor, where they ended. Secondly there were the back stairs reaching from the basement to the attics and intended for the use of the servants, so that there might be no meetings on the main stairway between them and their employers, and so no chance of any whiff of broom or pail or dustpan coming between the wind and Newdagonby nobility. Thirdly, there was the great central stairway, all gilt and gold and marble. It was a really fine piece of work, ascending in a majestic double sweep, then joining again to rise to where in bygone days of splendour the Lord and Lady Newdagonby of the time had been wont to receive their guests. An imposing sight of an imposing era which was at least all glorious without.

Thence these stairs, though in less majestic manner, rose to the third floor and there stopped, since obviously those entitled to the privilege of this stairway could never wish to penetrate to the attic floor. That was solely the upper habitation of the lower world, though also used for the deposit of different kinds of lumber, including, as had recently been discovered, the famous correspondence with Voltaire, now in the British Museum, and still earlier letters from Tudor statesmen.

It was up this great central stairway that Lord Newdagonby, Bobby, and the others were now racing. Charley Acton was the first. He was setting the pace, and the others had trouble in keeping up with him. He had in one hand a poker he had snatched up from before the electric fire, tradition demanding that even if there was no coal fire, there should still be the customary fire-irons. Bobby and Lord Newdagonby followed, his lordship making unexpectedly good use of those very long, very thin legs of his. Mrs Findlay followed more slowly. She had rather the air of hanging back so as to let others arrive first. Her natural pallor had become intensified. Between the second and third floors they met a small, thin elderly woman in whom Bobby recognized the housekeeper he had seen before. She was, he supposed, the Mrs Jacks mentioned by Mrs Findlay. She looked surprised and slightly alarmed at this sudden hurrying bustle, and stood aside. Then when Mrs Findlay arrived and said something to her, she joined in it, bringing up the rear.

They reached the third floor, where this main stairway ended. From where he ran, behind Acton but in front of Bobby, Lord Newdagonby shouted.

"Stairs left. Turn left."

Acton obeyed. Lord Newdagonby was evidently beginning to feel the effects at his age of running up so many stairs so quickly. He paused for a moment to take breath. Bobby passed him and caught up Acton, following close behind him. Mrs Findlay and the housekeeper, Mrs Jacks, were at some distance. Up this final stretch of stairway Bobby and Acton raced alone. They reached the fourth floor. Acton still leading the way, they ran down a passage, lit by a skylight, doors on either hand, and then down another corridor at right angles to the first. At the end were three closed doors in a kind of bay, lighted by a side window. At the central one of these three doors, Acton threw himself with savage energy, trying to force it by aid of the poker he had brought with him. Bobby pulled him aside.

"This will be quicker," Bobby said.

He had in his pocket, as always, a pocket-knife that was really more like a small compendium of tools. He had some skill—quite unofficial—as a locksmith, and, as he had expected, the lock on this door was of the simplest description, little more indeed than a token lock. It was only the work of a moment to open it, while Acton stood fuming to one side. The moment it was open Acton tried to rush through, but Bobby held him back. Acton protested angrily, but Bobby took no notice and continued to prevent him from entering, standing the while himself quite still in the doorway, staring intently into this room, where a man lay crumpled on the floor.

"He's ill, a stroke, he told me, let me pass," Acton exclaimed, trying to push by Bobby.

"Not ill," Bobby said. "This is murder. Stay where you are."

He went across to where the stricken man lay, the handle of a knife sticking out between the shoulder-blades. Very gently he eased the position in which the body lay, but he did not attempt to remove the knife. Apparently there had been very little bleeding, and Bobby was afraid to draw out the knife for fear the bleeding should start. He did not think death had yet occurred, for it seemed as if there were a faint, occasional drawing in of breath. But he thought death was near. He became aware that Acton, still grasping his poker, ignoring Bobby's order to stay by the door, was bending over them. Bobby said to him:

"Is it Mr Findlay?"

"Ivor? Yes. What's . . . what's happened? . . . it can't . . . can't . . ."

His voice trailed off into silence. The dying man opened his eyes. Apparently the slight movement, the heard voices, had for the moment recalled his departing spirit. He said, quite loudly:

"Oh, you, is it? Why?"

"Who did this?" Bobby asked quickly.

Lord Newdagonby was there now, standing in the doorway.

"Good God, what's this?" he cried.

Acton jumped to his feet, jostling Bobby, nearly pushing him off his balance as he knelt.

"Keep Sibby out," he shouted. "Keep her out. There's been an accident. Don't let her in."

"Keep quiet," Bobby said, very angrily indeed. Bending nearer to Findlay, he said again: "Who? Who did this?"

But Findlay did not answer. He closed his eyes, he gave a great sigh and was dead.

Lord Newdagonby was in the room now. He had pushed before Acton, who, still holding his poker he seemed unable to put down, was standing by the door. To Lord Newdagonby, who was staring blankly, as if unable to believe what he saw, as if incapable of either speech or movement, Bobby said:

"Phone at once, for a doctor, for the police. Scotland Yard. I want help. Don't waste time. Be quick."

"But what's happened?" Lord Newdagonby said. "I don't understand . . . it's Ivor, and he's hurt?"

"I want help, I want a doctor," Bobby repeated. "Ring up Scotland Yard." But Lord Newdagonby only stood and stared as if still bereft alike of speech and movement. Giving up hope of getting help from him, and no doubt this sudden intrusion of grim murder into his quiet, ordered, scholarly life was sufficient reason for the apparent paralysis of movement that had fallen on him, Bobby called instead to Acton: " 'Phone for a doctor, Scotland Yard," he said. "Tell them I'm here and want help. Hurry."

Acton nodded, flung down the poker he had been clinging to so long, and rushed away.

To Lord Newdagonby Bobby said:

"Leave the room, please. I want no one here at present."

"This is my house," Lord Newdagonby protested.

"There's been a murder here, and I'm taking charge," Bobby retorted. "Please do as I ask. I want no one in this room, nothing disturbed, till I get help or till the doctor comes. Not that he can do much. Mr Findlay is dead."

Though he had spoken quietly enough, though he had given a glance behind him to make sure there was no one in the short corridor or passage leading to these three rooms, nevertheless Mrs Findlay, just round the corner where she had paused to stare after Acton's flying figure as he rushed by, heard him plainly. It was as if their tragic significance had lent to them some strange carrying power. Now she came hurrying, almost running.

"Ivor?" she called. "Ivor?" It was almost as if she expected him to reply and deny what she had just heard. "He can't be. Not Ivor, not dead," she said loudly, almost defiantly.

But the words died on her lips when she saw how her father, who had turned to the door as he heard her coming, how Bobby behind him, were looking at her. Lord Newdagonby took a step towards her.

"My poor child, my dear child," he said softly.

"Please tell Mrs Findlay what's happened," Bobby said to him. "Tell her everything possible is being done." He stepped back across the threshold. "And please remember I want no one here till help comes."

"Not Ivor, not Ivor," Mrs Findlay repeated.

Bobby closed the door, shutting them both out. With his back to it he stood there, silent and motionless, alone with the dead, the unforgiving dead. But if Bobby were still and motionless as the dead man himself, his eyes were active as his gaze travelled slowly here and there, regarding every object in the room with close, contained attention.

It was a large room, though its available space was lessened by the way in which its height diminished at one side to rather less than six feet. A result evidently of the slope of the roof above. Opposite, on the other side of the room, and running for two-thirds of the length of the wall, was a strong, plain wooden table or bench. On it stood various apparatus, to some of which Bobby could not even give a name. But he recognized an electric furnace, two sets of scales, a microscope, many flasks. At one end of this table stood two cages. One held two guinea pigs, busy feeding. The second cage was empty, the door open. He thought at first that the animals might have escaped and be at large in the room. But there was no sign of them, though he noticed that fresh food and water had been provided. On shelves standing against the portion of the wall not occupied by the table stood more flasks, glass containers, and other such scientific desiderata. Beneath these shelves was a cupboard, and opposite were two well-filled bookcases. Near one window—the room had two—was a small table bearing a typewriter. Close by was a large, comfortable-looking settee, well provided with cushions and rugs, as if used for an occasional rest or even perhaps sometimes for a night's repose if some experiment or test were in progress that needed close watching. In the middle of the room was a large, business-like desk. At it Findlay had apparently been sitting and working when attacked, and near it he had fallen. On it lay a confused litter of papers of one sort or another. Whatever Findlay's scientific qualifications, he evidently had little idea of system in dealing with his papers. His fountain pen lay there, uncapped, as if it had fallen from his hand as he was using it, but there was no trace of any writing he could have been engaged on.

"It was some one he knew," Bobby reflected, trying to reconstruct the scene in his mind. "Came up behind. Findlay took no notice, or possibly glanced over his shoulder just in time to see the knife coming. Was he writing something? Was that something what he was killed for?"

Useless questions. More must be known before any theory could be formed. Heavy steps approaching told Bobby that help was at hand. He opened the door. Police and doctor had arrived together. Not that there was much the doctor could do, except to agree that life was extinct and to express a somewhat hesitating opinion, based on the condition of the blood in what bleeding had taken place, that the wound had probably been inflicted somewhere about eleven, but with a wide margin of error. Bobby had already noticed that the dead man's wristwatch, broken in the fall, showed five minutes to eleven. The doctor was very pleased at this proof that his estimate had been so nearly exact, and he did not at all approve of Bobby's remark that he would have to try to ascertain if Mr Findlay was careful to keep his watch at the correct time. Accepting eleven or thereabouts as the hour of the attack, this meant, Bobby reflected, that it had taken place just about the time that he himself had arrived here on his visit to Lord Newdagonby.

By now, all the usual routine was in full swing. Photographs were being taken, sketches made, measurements recorded. The finger-print expert was scattering his powder on everything available. The knife used in the murder was being examined. It was an ordinary kitchen knife, but it had evidently been sharpened in readiness for the deadly work for which it was intended. At the moment it was being tested for finger-prints. Bobby had also made sure that the electric furnace had not recently been used, and no useful clue destroyed in it.

He now remained standing aside, watching quietly while all this was going on. Chief Inspector Simons, known irreverently to his subordinates as 'Ju-ju', because his first name was Julian, had arrived, and was officially in charge. Bobby's presence was officially purely accidental, and his function was supposed to be confined to the receiving of reports and a general overall direction. Not that any one who knew him or his record really expected he would confine himself to that unexciting part. As a matter of fact, Simons was glad enough to see him there. A difficult case, Simons was saying to himself, and he would probably be glad of any help. Besides, he knew Bobby was always very willing to give full credit, even generously full credit, to all his assistants. Presently Simons came across to him.

"Ordinary kitchen knife," he said. "No dabs. Been wiped most likely. One thing I noticed. There's a pad of paper been pushed in to keep the handle firm. But it does look as if the handle had been loosened on purpose, not just from being used. In a way that might happen easily enough, only there's no scratch or anything like that on the blade. I don't suppose it means anything."

"No," agreed Bobby, taking the knife and examining it closely. "Probably not. Better remember it, though, and just as well you noticed it. Have you the paper pad?"

"Not much good," Simons answered, producing it. "Looks like it had been part of a restaurant menu."

"Oh, yes," Bobby said, interested. "Take care of it. There's a Mr Noel Lake, who seems to have been on bad terms with Findlay and who keeps a restaurant."

Simons whistled softly.

"Restaurant, eh?" he said. "And kitchen knife and all? In a way, that smells. Smells," he repeated. "Know what the bad terms was about?"

"Woman," Bobby answered briefly. "But we mustn't jump to conclusions," he added. "Better begin asking questions, hadn't you? I should think you could leave your men to get on by themselves now."

Simons surveyed his busy staff with that doubtful air some seniors are apt to assume towards their juniors. However, he agreed that just possibly they might be trusted now to finish their work without making too many bloomers. Bobby suggested, too, that it might be as well to begin by having a look round the rest of this attic floor, and again Simons agreed.

"You never know your luck," he remarked. "In a way, that's my motto."

CHAPTER VI
"IN A WAY, THAT'S FUNNY"

ON EACH SIDE of this room the dead man had occupied was another, much smaller. The doors of both these rooms were locked, and Simons sent one of his assistants to find Mrs Jacks and get the keys.

While waiting for them, he and Bobby began a quick examination of all the rest of this attic floor. Mr Acton's estimate of a hundred rooms to each floor was something of an exaggeration, but both Bobby and Simons were soon inclined to regard it rather as an understatement than otherwise, so unending did appear to be this twisted, twining labyrinth of passages and corners and alcoves. Some of the rooms were still furnished, left as they had been when at the beginning of the second world war domestic staff had grown smaller and smaller and finally vanished—as it turned out, for ever. But that had not been realized at the time, and each room in turn as it had been vacated, as footmen turned into guardsmen and kitchen maids into munition workers, had been kept ready for the days when the footmen and the maids would come again into general circulation.

Now in all these rooms dust and cobwebs reigned, and nowhere was any trace of recent use. Others of the rooms were quite empty, and had clearly been so for years. Others again had been used merely for storage, and contained great piles of old furniture, of boxes, of odds and ends, of all sorts and kinds, all again thick with dust and evidently untouched and unvisited for many a long day.

"Enough stuff to set up half a dozen second-hand dealers," commented Simons, as he and Bobby made their swift survey of this tangle of rooms, cupboards, corridors, and so on.

Though they hurried as much as they could, it was some considerable time before they got back to their starting point, satisfied there was nothing on the attic floor to throw any light on what had happened. Waiting for them was the constable sent to find Mrs Jacks and obtain from her the keys of the two locked rooms, the only rooms indeed so locked on the whole floor. He reported now that Mrs Jacks had promised to look for the keys, but was not sure where they were. Simons sent him off again to see if she had succeeded in her search. He was soon back, bringing her with him. Apologetically she explained that she had been unable to 'put her hand' on them. Poor Mr Findlay—here she showed symptoms of tears—had had them. He wanted the rooms kept locked so as to be sure they remained empty and available for his own use, if necessary. Mrs Jacks could not, she said, remember clearly, but she thought he must have kept the two keys in his own possession. They would be most likely somewhere in his room, poor gentleman.

"Room been gone over thoroughly," Simons said. "No sign of any keys."

"Well, then, I don't know," Mrs Jacks said. "Perhaps they're somewhere in their flat downstairs. But there can't be anything in those rooms. I swept them out myself when Mr Findlay's room was being got ready, and there's nothing in them, nothing at all."

"Oh, well, never mind," Bobby said. "If they've been kept locked, no one can very well have been in them."

"Oh, no, no one could," Mrs Jacks agreed, apparently a little startled by the suggestion. "I wouldn't like to think it," she added with a frightened glance at the two closed doors, as if wondering who or what might be lurking behind them.

"Oh, we didn't think the murderer might be hiding there," Bobby assured her smilingly.

Mrs Jacks seemed inclined to continue the conversation. After all it is not every day that one gets a murder in one's own home to chat about. Not surprising she wanted to talk and even to ask questions. Bobby, however, got rid of her quickly and with decision, and when she had gone suggested to Simons that it might be as well to have a look and make sure the rooms were as empty as they were said to be. He did not think, he said, that the locks would give much trouble. Simons seemed a little puzzled.

"You don't really think," he said hesitatingly, "there may be something there?"

"Not a chance in a thousand," Bobby answered. "But it's always a good rule to see for yourself. What's really in my mind at the moment is whether it would be at all possible for any stranger to get into this great barracks of a place without being noticed and hide. You see, if that's possible, it widens the field enormously. Otherwise the murderer must apparently be one of these people. A hundred to one that's the case, but we've got to consider everything, and I should say you might camp out up here for long enough without being spotted."

Simons didn't look as if he much appreciated this suggestion of a possible widening of the field of inquiry to such an almost unlimited extent. Bobby was already at work on one of the locked doors, and as the lock here, too, was of simple construction he soon had it open. Within they saw only bare walls, bare floor, uncurtained windows, cobwebs everywhere draped like curtains, everything thick with dust. Simons was much relieved.

"No one been in here for donkey's years," he declared.

Bobby agreed. He closed the door, shot the bolt of the lock again, and turned his attention to the door of the second locked room. "Oiled recently," he remarked as he started work. Soon he had it open. There again, blank walls, bare floor, thickly draped cobwebs, dust that seemed immemorial.

"Same as the other," Simons said. "Nothing but dirt and cobwebs."

"Nothing else," agreed Bobby, "but plenty of it. Didn't Mrs Jacks say she had both rooms swept out when Findlay established himself up here a year or so ago?"

"In a way," Simons said doubtfully, "in a way, it does rather look as if there was more than a year's growth of cobweb and dust, especially cobwebs in the ceiling corners. Perhaps they didn't sweep up there though."

"Perhaps not," Bobby agreed again. "But more than a year's dust on the floor, I think. Have another look at the floor."

Simons did so, stared, then gave his low whistle he kept for special emergencies or surprises.

"Does look like there's been some one walking quite often straight across to the wall opposite. Sort of path in the dust it looks like."

"So it does," said Bobby, still in agreement.

In fact, across the floor, through the dust that lay on it so thickly, showed a faint trail or path leading from the door where Bobby and Simons stood to the wall, the party wall separating this room from that in which Ivor Findlay had worked and died.

"What beats me," said Simons as they stood there, looking and thinking, "is what's the idea? Straight over to a blank wall and back again. In a way, that's funny."

Bobby went across to the wall opposite, to the spot where this trail in the dust seemed to end. From the doorway Simons watched intently, puzzled, but obedient to a slight gesture Bobby had made, asking him to stay where he was for the moment. He saw Bobby stoop and put an eye close to the wall, then straighten himself and move cautiously and sideways along the wall, examining it carefully all the way. Presently he stooped again, and again pressed one eye to the wall. Then he returned to Simons, waiting in the doorway.

"Your turn now," he said. "You have a look."

Simons, who by now had guessed what to look for, obeyed and then came back.

"Two peepholes in the wall," he said. "Some one been keeping watch. Two peepers, one hole for each. What for?"

"Not necessarily two peepers," Bobby said. "Between them, the two holes give a sight of the whole room. With only one hole the view would have been partial. A thorough job."

"Well, who? Well, why?" Simons asked. "Even if Findlay's work was confidential, no one could get much idea of it by peeping through a spy hole."

"No," said Bobby. "That's quite clear."

"Could it have been Mrs Findlay?" Simons suggested next. "Keeping an eye on hubby? Had he a pretty secretary?"

"There's Miss Kitty Grange," Bobby answered. "She seems to have been working for him till recently, when she slapped his face and retired."

"Oh, well, in a way," Simons said, feeling his theory proved up to the hilt, "that's what I was thinking. Pretty girl?"

"I haven't seen her yet," Bobby answered. "She is one of the family apparently—some sort of cousin, I think. She is engaged to the Noel Lake I told you of. His row with Findlay was about her."

Once more Simons emitted his characteristic low whistle.

"Getting somewhere," he declared. "Mrs Findlay guessed what was up, and thought she would make sure. Eh?"

"Mrs Findlay is a tall woman," Bobby said. "About five feet eight or nine. Those spy holes suggest some one not much over five feet."

"Mrs Jacks," Simons suggested at once. "She's about that. She might be in Mrs Findlay's pay?"

"A possibility," Bobby agreed. "Though I don't much think that sort of spying is in Mrs Findlay's line. Worth thinking about, though. But if it's Mrs Jacks, no wonder she was so anxious to tell us the rooms must be empty and she couldn't find the key she most likely had in her pocket. Do you think it might be as well to look up Mrs Jacks's background?"

"I'll put it in hand at once," Simons promised.

They left the room then, Bobby carefully fastening the door again so that there might be as little as possible to show the room had been visited. Simons said he thought he had better see how his boys were getting on. The routine work was nearly finished. The finger-print expert had found various 'dabs' and some evidence that here and there objects had been recently wiped, since on them was none of the dust to be found elsewhere. He had discovered one very clearly marked set on Findlay's desk, opposite where he sat. A woman's prints, the 'dabs' man said, and Simons was very interested. So was Bobby.

"Have to be identified," declared Simons emphatically.

"Not so easy," said the dabs man with some resentment. "We aren't allowed to take 'dabs' from people without their consent. Why not? Why should any one object unless they've their reasons? These dabs prove a woman's been in here this morning, don't they? Well, then, why can't we ask all of 'em in the house to let us take their prints, and see they do?"

"That's right," agreed Simons, and Bobby suggested they had better ask Mrs Jacks if the room, and more especially the desk, had been dusted that morning.

He and Simons descended therefore to the ground floor and found Mrs Jacks busy serving Lord Newdagonby with his almost-forgotten 'sole bonne femme'.

"The poor gentleman's got to eat, murder or no murder," she explained.

In answer to their questions she was emphatic that Mr Findlay's room had been dusted and cleaned as thoroughly as possible that morning. Mr Findlay, poor gentleman, had been that particular about his things being moved or so much as touched. Consequently, the task of keeping the room clean and tidy had not been easy, and Mrs Jacks had generally seen to it herself, rather than allow the daily woman to go in. As it happened she was emphatic in remembering clearly that Mr Findlay's desk had been unusually clear of papers that morning, so she had been able to give it a good rub over.

"There's some reason to think he had a visitor during the morning, some time before the murder," Bobby remarked. "Some time before eleven, that is. We think Mr Findlay must have been killed about that time."

"Oh, no," Mrs Jacks answered at once. "It must have been after that. I heard his typewriter going about a quarter or twenty past or thereabouts."

CHAPTER VII
"GUINEA PIGS?"

TO THIS STATEMENT, Mrs Jacks adhered resolutely. At first she had though t it was Mrs Findlay, who sometimes used her husband's typewriter. But now she wasn't so sure, because

Mrs Findlay wasn't so very proficient in the use of the machine and this had been a rapid typing.

"Like the way Miss Grange does, only not so fast as her," said Mrs Jacks.

Also she was certain she was not mistaken about the time. She had been watching it carefully. A rumour had reached her that grape-fruit would be on sale at a neighbouring shop at half-past eleven. The shop was about five minutes' walk away. She was intending therefore to leave the house between twenty and twenty-five minutes past the hour so as to make sure of being at the head of the queue. In this she had succeeded, she had secured her grape-fruit and had returned home. No, she had no idea how long the typing had continued. All she knew was that typing was going on at, or a minute or two later, than eleven twenty.

Simons asked next if she thought it possible for a stranger to get into the house without being noticed. Mrs Jacks replied firmly that, now he had said that, she would never sleep easy in her bed again, not in this house, and she would give notice immediately. Pressed to give a more relevant answer she agreed that the lock of the back door was out of order, and that it was seldom bolted during the day. She supposed it would be possible to open it and just walk in, and it was a wonder that not only the poor gentleman, but all of them, had not wakened up one morning all murdered in their beds. It set her all of a twitter just to think of it. Oh, yes, of course, the door was always bolted at night. She saw to that herself, as soon as it was dark in fact. She supposed also, when Simons made the suggestion, that a ring at the front door would have drawn her to answer it, so leaving the coast clear in the basement to which the back door gave access. And once inside, in this great barracks of a place, it would be easy enough to avoid observation. But the garden door, opening on the stairs leading to the flat or suite occupied by the Findlays, had a Yale lock, and so was quite secure.

This talk with Mrs Jacks had taken place at the foot of the great central stairway. As she seemed to have no more to tell, she was asked to show them the room that had, on request, been set aside for the temporary use of the police so long as they remained in the house. It was small and bare, and chill with the chilliness that comes of long disuse. Already it was occupied by a constable who was also a skilled shorthand writer, and who at the moment was busy trying to sort and arrange a pile of material, documents of one kind and another and so on, that had seemed to require closer examination. Mrs Jacks hoped the room would do, a faint suggestion in her manner, that anyhow it would have to 'do', and in any case too good for them. So Bobby said politely that it would 'do' very well indeed, and did Mrs Jacks think they could have a few minutes' talk with Mrs Findlay? Mrs Jacks said she would tell Mrs Findlay and retired, and when she had gone Simons said:

"What do you make of that story about the typing, Mr Owen? Can we accept it, or is she lying?"

"Why should she?"

"Well, if she did it herself . . ." Simons suggested. "You know I don't like those peepholes. They smell."

"They do," agreed Bobby. "But what of? No proof that it was Findlay who was typing. It may have been the murderer."

"Well, in a way," Simons admitted, though a little taken aback by a suggestion that had not occurred to him. "But is that likely? Could any one sit down calmly to do a bit of typing with the man he had just put a knife into dying a few feet away? No jury's going to take that without a lot of evidence."

"No jury will ever take anything without a lot of evidence, and quite right, too," Bobby answered. "But no murderer is likely and nothing he does is likely. Our worst headache."

"Findlay's watch stopped a little before eleven," Simons pointed out. "We mustn't forget that."

"Oh, no, very important," Bobby agreed. "A scientist like Findlay would be likely to keep his watch right, I should think. You might ask about that perhaps."

"So I will," Simons said. "You remember that the doctor put a little before eleven as the time of the attack?"

"What's bothering me most at the moment," Bobby went on, "is those guinea pigs, and do they mean anything?"

"Guinea pigs?" Simons repeated. "Why guinea pigs?"

"Two in one cage," Bobby said. "Both quite lively. Another cage empty, but provided with fresh food and water."

"Scientific blokes are always experimenting with guinea pigs," Simons reminded him; and, before Bobby could once more express agreement, Mrs Jacks returned with a message that Mrs Findlay was still at lunch but would not be long.

Bobby, not too pleased, said he hoped that 'not too long' would prove to be very short indeed and would she please say so to Mrs Findlay. Then he asked Mrs Jacks if she knew anything about Mr Findlay's guinea pigs.

"He got them a week or two ago," she explained. "He wanted them for his work."

She added in reply to other questions that she cleaned out the cages and gave the animals food and water every day. She had done so that morning as usual, and she looked both surprised and puzzled when Bobby remarked that one cage was now empty. Each cage had had its usual two occupants that morning, and she had no idea why one was now empty. Probably Mr Findlay had got rid of its former occupants for some reason. She hoped they hadn't managed to get loose, and weren't now wandering about the house somewhere. She seemed to have a vision of a house overrun with guinea pigs, and added that what with one thing and another she didn't know where she was.

With that she retired, promising to deliver to Mrs Findlay Bobby's message that he hoped 'not long' would be 'very soon'—a message Bobby suspected would be delivered, if at all, in very modified form. As soon as she had gone Simons said very discontentedly:

"I call that pretty cool. Husband just been murdered, and she doesn't want to be disturbed at lunch. You've seen her, haven't you? What did you make of her?"

Bobby said thoughtfully that she had given him the idea of one who had, so to say, lost herself in the difficulties of life and had not yet decided how to meet them. A restless, questioning personality, one wanting to explore everything, including herself, but not certain how to do it.

"A difficult job, anyhow," Bobby commented.

He added that quite possibly all that might be a mere façade. He was inclined to suspect that behind it all lay a tendency to hysteria. What hysteria was, he said, he didn't know, but he agreed rather gloomily with Simons's remark that hysteria was apt to show itself in a tendency to sudden outbreaks of violence.

"Suspect No. 1," declared Simons with emphasis. "Any trouble between her and Findlay?"

"Lord Newdagonby made rather a point of their being very fond of each other. Said they got along excellently, only with the sort of easy tolerance that doesn't much mind a little laxity on either side. Fashionable idea to-day. People like to call it being unpossessive."

"What's a little laxity mean?" Simons asked, and when Bobby did not answer, he added: "I've heard all that before. But there's a breaking point."

"Yes, I know," Bobby said gravely.

He was thinking of Mrs Findlay's declaration that she was going to give eighteen months to sin as she had given the same time to religion. Was that merely idle talk, a pose to impress, or had it meant something? It was to be remembered that she had spent eighteen months in a sisterhood, taking her share in work and routine as if by them fully satisfied. But she had walked out at the end of her self-appointed period of trial after telling a horrified mother superior that she found nothing satisfying in religion and now was going to seek for satisfaction in what she called 'sin'. And what had 'sin' meant to her? Was it all mere bluff and silly chatter? Or something else? She had, Bobby remembered, drawn a distinction between sin and crime, the latter being merely 'vulgar' according to her. But Bobby knew that the boundary between the two could easily be crossed, indeed probably had to be crossed sooner or later.

Conversation languished. Bobby was deep in thought. Simons was devoting himself to the pile of documents removed from the dead man's desk. More immediately important, both men were also occupied with a supply of sandwiches sent in by Simons's forethought from a neighbouring snack bar. Abruptly Simons said:

"Husbands and wives—you've got to face it. They do each other in at times. You can't stand each other, but you can't separate. Tied up in a way and can't get loose. Except this way."

"A philosophy of marriage," Bobby remarked.

"I didn't mean anything like that," protested Simons, slightly alarmed.

"We must keep our minds open," Bobby said. "Many possibilities."

He applied himself to the sandwiches again, and presently Mrs Findlay appeared. She showed little outward sign of emotion, though Bobby noticed that her make-up had been recently renewed and seemed to have been applied with a certain nervous haste. He did not think her lipstick was often splashed on like that. Those small, deep-set, restless eyes of hers showed no trace of tears. They were partly hidden by half-closed eyelids as before, and all her movements were slow and controlled as if she felt she had to be careful lest they should slip beyond restraint.

Simons began with a few words of sympathy. She waved them aside impatiently and haughtily.

"Never mind that," she said. "My husband has been murdered. Your duty is to find the murderer. You want to know if I can help you. I don't think I can. I don't know of any one likely to want to kill Ivor, or of any reason why they should."

Simons explained that this was to be only a brief preliminary talk. Later they would ask her to make a full statement. At present their object was to know if she could tell them anything of immediate importance. Did she know of any caller Mr Findlay was expecting, and when had she herself seen him last?

"Well, we had breakfast together," she answered, "and then he went upstairs to work as usual. He never saw any one

here. Father only let him fit up a room for his work if he promised not to see clients in it. Father said he wasn't going to have
half-cracked inventors swarming all over the place, and Ivor
didn't want either. He had a perfect craze for privacy and secrecy—of course, a patent agent's work is secret, confidential,
but Ivor was rather silly about it. He nearly bit my head off last
week when I asked him what he wanted guinea pigs for. And
privacy! He would shout the roof off at the least interruption."

"Two guinea pigs seem to have disappeared," Bobby remarked.

"Have they?" Mrs Findlay asked. "I suppose he had done
with them. I think you may be quite sure no one was here
this morning. I've asked Mrs Jacks. She says she's sure no
one's been."

"Mr Findlay didn't say anything to you about expecting any
visitor, did he?"

"Oh, no. I think you may be perfectly sure he had no visitor
to-day—except his murderer."

"That rather suggests it must have been some one in the
house," Simons remarked.

Mrs Findlay's small, restless eyes grew steady for once as
they fixed themselves on Simons in a long, unblinking stare.
For a moment or two she was silent. She said:

"Naturally." Then she was silent again. The two men were
watching her, but she had removed her gaze from Simons and
seemed lost in sombre meditation, her eyes veiled as it were
in thought. They waited. She went on: "But I don't believe it.
Your business to find out. But it wasn't me or father or Kitty or
Mrs Jacks for that matter. Why should we? Well. Well?"

"Can you tell us what you did after breakfast?"

"I was busy about the flat. There's plenty to do. I've only a
daily woman. She comes about nine, except when she doesn't
come at all. We gave both rooms a thorough turn out. There's
only two—bedroom, sitting-room, and the bath and kitchen. I
left her to finish, and went out about half-past ten I suppose.
I got back about twelve, I think, and I hadn't murdered Ivor
in the interval. Mr Owen was with my father when I got in. He

was very worried about those 'phone messages saying I was going to be murdered. Now it seems Ivor was meant, not me at all."

"You can't throw any light on these messages?"

"No. I never took them very seriously. Father did, but I didn't. I thought some one was trying to be funny."

"Can you say exactly where you went and what you did when you were out between half-past ten and twelve?"

"No. I was shopping. I wanted some silk thread, and I couldn't find what I wanted. I went into two or three shops to ask. I don't suppose they'll remember. They are probably asked half a dozen times every day. Then I came home, and on the way I met Mr Acton, and he came with me. He was very pleased about a letter Ivor had sent him, and he wanted to ask him about it—it had to do with a new razor blade Mr Acton means to put on the market. That's all. If it's an alibi you're fishing for, I can't give it. I could have come back, I suppose, let myself in, slipped upstairs, murdered Ivor, and gone out again. Only I didn't. And if I had I shouldn't have taken the opportunity to do any typing."

"You've heard about that?" Bobby asked quickly.

"Mrs Jacks told me," she answered.

"I understand," Simons went on, "that you haven't been in Mr Findlay's room this morning?"

"I said so, didn't I?" she answered, staring at him. "Yes," she repeated, that long gaze of hers never changing or faltering, "I've told you so once already."

"Because," Simons said steadily, and yet with a certain unease as if he had to fight against the almost hypnotic power of that slow stare, "because there's finger-prints on Mr Findlay's desk. Mrs Jacks says she dusted and polished the desk this morning, so the prints must presumably have been made this morning. They may be the murderer's."

Mrs Findlay was smiling now, that haughty, remote smile of hers, as of one infinitely amused at the proceedings of some small creatures she was watching from afar.

"I don't think," she said, "I should pay too much importance to that. Mrs Jacks is an excellent cook, and my father wouldn't part with her on any account. But she hasn't much idea of housework. She would think she had done all that was needed if she gave Ivor's desk a whisk with a featherbrush and put a dab of polish on one corner. If she did even that much. She could easily say and think she had thoroughly polished a floor—or a desk—when she had done no more than give it a dab here and there—if as much."

"Possibly you wouldn't object," suggested Simons, "to letting us take your prints? It would be a help—avoid any chance of confusion."

"I should object very much," Mrs Findlay replied at once. "I've told you already it can't be mine unless I made it yesterday evening. I was up there then."

"I am sorry you feel like that," Simons said gravely. "I hope you will change your mind."

"You will get as many finger-prints of mine as you like in our flat," observed Mrs Findlay, and now there was a kind of secret irony in her manner, even a secret amusement. "At least unless we destroyed them all cleaning this morning. I think you've taken possession of the flat, haven't you? Mrs Jacks tells me there's a policeman outside. I don't know what right you have to do that."

"The right of police officers investigating a brutal murder," Bobby interposed sternly. "Mrs Findlay, don't you think it would be wise to be a little more co-operative? Surely you wish the murderer of your husband to be found?"

"Will that give him back to me?" she asked; and for a moment Bobby almost thought a touch of emotion disturbed the haughty calm she had hitherto shown.

But he was not sure; and if any such sign had in fact been momentarily visible it vanished again immediately. Simons said:

"It's of no consequence. I just thought it might help if we could be sure whose they were."

"A little unfortunate," she observed, "that we happened to give the flat such a thorough doing out this morning."

"Of course, you couldn't foresee what would happen," Bobby remarked, watching her closely.

"No, indeed," she answered, and she gave no sign of realizing that his remark might carry any underlying implication.

"We think it is probably a woman's," Simons said.

"I'm not the only woman in the house," she answered. "There's Mrs Jacks. She was there this morning. There's the charwoman—and Kitty Grange as well. She might have ventured in when she knew Ivor had a letter about her fur coat."

CHAPTER VIII
"IT'S ONE SHE WANTS TO SELL"

When she had said this Mrs Findlay got up to go, as if she considered the interview closed. Bobby had other ideas.

"One moment, please," he said. "Why do you use the expression 'ventured'?"

"You know, don't you?" she retorted. "Didn't father tell you Kitty had had a row with Ivor? What's the sense of asking when you know?"

"For one thing, to be sure what you know," Bobby told her sharply. "For confirmation, for another. For a third, I am sorry you have not given an impression of being very willing to help."

"I can't help your impressions," she said, using again that coldly haughty tone of hers, and again she turned towards the door.

But Bobby still made no corresponding gesture.

"I have to ask you this, Mrs Findlay," he said. "Did you resent the attentions Mr Findlay seems to have been fond of paying to other women?"

Her eyes grew uncertain and wandering again. It was as though she were asking herself the same question and was not sure of the answer. A moment or two passed, and then she replied with the simple monosyllable:

"No."

"Thank you," Bobby said. "You spoke of a fur coat in connection with Miss Grange?"

"It's one she wants to sell," Mrs Findlay explained. "What about it? It's part of a small legacy from an aunt of hers who died a few months ago. She meant to keep it at first, and then she thought she had better sell it and she's been asking all of us if we knew any one who might want it. Ivor had a letter this morning from a friend of his he had mentioned it to, and he asked me to tell her."

"Did you?"

"Yes. Of course. Why not?"

"What did she say?"

"Oh, got on her high horse at first, and said she didn't want to have anything more to do with Ivor after the way he had behaved. And then she asked if I knew how much the offer was. I didn't. I didn't ask, and Ivor didn't say, only that if she wanted to know about it she was to ask him, and to be quick, because it was some one going abroad soon and couldn't wait." She paused, as if in thought, and then said slowly: "A kind of blackmail. To bring her to heel. A kind of blackmail," she repeated; and again let the word drop slowly from her lips, as if for her it had a kind of hidden significance.

Once more she turned towards the door, and this time Bobby rose to open it for her. He did not think it wise to question her further just then. Simons looked disappointed. He had thought she ought to be pressed much harder, but that was something Bobby never did—not at least until he was fairly sure he had all the information he was likely to get voluntarily. As he closed the door behind her, Simons said with disapproval.

"That's a queer bird if ever there was one. Takes the murder of her husband just the same as if he had come home a bit tiddley."

"I don't pretend to understand her," Bobby said. "Difficult anyhow when I'm pretty sure she doesn't understand herself.

Searching, and doesn't know what she's looking for or wants to find."

"Notice the way she said 'blackmail'?" Simons asked. "In a way, sort of rolled it in her mouth, like it was a bit of sugar candy. At least, that's how it struck me."

"So it did me," Bobby agreed. "It may have been meant for a hint. I don't much think so myself. I don't think she's a lady who deals in hints. Giving orders is more her line. Have to remember it and look out for any signs. But Findlay was a betting man apparently, and betting's a good cover for any eccentricities in a banking account."

"That may be why he was a betting man, if he was playing the blackmail game. Nothing so far to show it though," Simons remarked, and Bobby nodded an assent.

"She's a clever woman," he remarked. "She countered that finger-print business very neatly."

"You think it's hers?"

"Oh, yes, certainly. Which means that she was in her husband's room this morning, but doesn't want to admit it. She put it across that Mrs Jacks was careless about her tidying and could very well have never given Findlay s desk any thorough dusting. And then she let us know it was no good trying to get her prints in the flat upstairs, because it had a thorough doing out this morning."

"I'll get her dabs all the same," Simons declared.

"Not much use, I wouldn't bother," Bobby told him. "All right to have them if you get a chance, of course. Supporting evidence if identity of time and place can be established, but no more. You would never get any jury to worry about a wife's dabs on a husband's desk. We've got to know a lot more about their attitude to each other. Affection or something stronger?"

"I don't think," interposed Simons.

"One can't be sure," Bobby said. "Dislike or something stronger?"

"That's more like," Simons interposed this time.

"Don't be too sure," Bobby repeated. "Or else mere indifference? But she's a woman of strong feelings. I think. I think," he repeated and then corrected himself: "No, I don't think anything," he declared. "Too soon."

There was a tap at the door and a constable appeared, escorting a small, fair, rather scared-looking girl, probably not much more than some twenty years of age.

"Miss Kitty Grange?" Bobby said, rising to move forward for her a chair she accepted with a slightly relieved air, a little indeed as if she had been rather inclined to expect handcuffs instead.

"It's so dreadful," she said with a little gasp as she seated herself. "I can hardly believe it's true. Can you?"

"Unfortunately we have to," Bobby said; and left the routine opening questions to Simons while he listened and watched and tried to decide what part, if any, Kitty might have played in the tragedy. Not a pretty girl, he thought, except in so far as all young girls are pretty. Her features were too irregular, her mouth too large, her light-brown hair a trifle dull with little sparkle showing. Her best feature was her complexion of cream and roses that, he thought, owed 'all to God'. He noticed, too, a certain natural instinctive grace even in the few movements she made in accepting the chair he offered, and again in her poise as she sat bending forward, her hands held in front of her and nervously clasping and unclasping each other. She was answering Simons's questions clearly and simply but very plainly with effort and a sense of strain. When Bobby offered her a cigarette, thinking it might help to soothe the very natural agitation she was showing, she shook her head and said, "Oh, no, thank you," in a slightly shocked tone, as if she thought it would seem heartless to smoke cigarettes in the shadow of such dreadful happenings.

Describing her movements that morning, she explained that she had started out early, about ten, and had gone to the London Library to get some books Lord Newdagonby wanted. Two, and the two specially required as it happened, were not available at the moment, but the librarian had promised to try to have them for her by afternoon, if she would return then. If necessary, since Lord Newdagonby was a generous supporter of the library, he would buy a copy of the one specially asked for, though he might have to send for it to Paris, and that would mean delay.

"It's a French book, not the English translation," she explained. "About existentialism."

"What's that?" Simons asked. "Exist—" he began and gave it up.

"The latest philosophic fad," Bobby explained. "There's a book about it they're advertising a lot—'Existence is Originally Absence'."

"That's the one," Kitty said. "Only uncle wants the French edition. 'L'existence de l'homme est originalement absence'. Luckily I got all the books Sibby—Mrs Findlay—wanted. There isn't any run on books about Byron."

"Byron?" repeated Simons. "Oh, yes, I know—'Roll on, thou dark and deep-blue ocean, roll.'" He looked quite pleased with himself, evidently thinking he had kept up his end very well. "Very fine," he commented. "There's a film, isn't there? 'The Bad Lord Byron.' Did you bring Mrs Findlay's books back here, Miss Grange?"

"I thought I would leave them till I went to the library this afternoon," Kitty answered.

"'The Bad Lord Byron'?" Bobby remarked. "A much more popular title than 'The Good Lord'. Some one or another being bad seems so much more attractive to some people than being good," and then he saw that Kitty was looking at him with a kind of terror showing in her grey and startled eyes. "You've noticed that?" he asked her, and when she did not answer, he said: "I'll have to try to see that film some day."

Simons managed to keep back with some difficulty a strong protest trembling on his lips. Only respect for Bobby's senior rank as a 'commander' prevented him from saying something very severe about not wasting time on film chat. He turned the questioning to the relationship existing between Findlay and his wife. Kitty began to hesitate, showed some embarrassment, but insisted that there had never been any quarrelling or any sign or suggestion of ill feeling. When Simons tried to press her, she began to get angry. Her clear grey eyes began to sparkle, and her soft cheeks first flushed and then paled again. Bobby observed these symptoms with interest. Was it not Balzac who had remarked somewhere that between an irritated angel and an angry tiger, he would prefer to meet the latter? Certainly this young woman had a considerable temper of her own, once it was roused.

"I don't think you ought to ask things like that," she was saying now, "and I'm not going to answer them. I don't like tittle tattle, and I don't repeat it."

"It's hardly that, Miss Grange," Bobby interposed. "It's an attempt to get the background clear. If we don't, we can get all sorts of wrong impressions instead. For example, we are told you felt you had reason to complain about Mr Findlay and that Mrs Findlay knew. Would that have caused any kind of quarrel between them, do you think?"

"I'm sure it wouldn't," Kitty responded. "Sibby never seemed to mind anything of that sort. Ivor was like that with nearly every one, and Sibby only laughed. Only I never thought he would dare with me," and again the grey eyes began to flash their danger signal.

"I think you boxed his ears, didn't you," Bobby asked smilingly, "and told him you would never speak to him again?"

"I told him just what I thought," Kitty admitted. "I told him I would never have anything more to do with him, and I won't."

"Mrs Findlay didn't take it very seriously though," Bobby commented. "They've not been married very long, have they? Are they still in love with each other?"

This was the question over which, when put to her in another form, Kitty had hesitated before. Now she hesitated again and then said:

"I think it was chiefly on Sibby's side. He told me once she had practically blackmailed him into it, but I don't know what he meant. I expect it was only talk. You couldn't always believe him. Sibby says she thinks you believe she did it. That's only silly. Because it really was her doing—their marriage, I mean.

She had made up her mind she wanted him. She told me so. And she had him, so why should she kill him?"

CHAPTER IX
"AM I UNDER SUSPICION?"

AT KITTY's reference to 'blackmailing', Simons had looked up quickly and then had glanced at Bobby. But Bobby showed no sign of having noticed the word. He began to ask about the fur coat Mrs Findlay had mentioned, and Kitty said, yes, she had one she thought she would like to sell, and she had been making inquiries among her friends to see if she could hear of any likely purchaser.

"It was a good offer Mr Findlay got for you, wasn't it?" Bobby asked.

Kitty thought it was. She had been told she ought to ask £80. But this offer was for a hundred and one guineas. No, she didn't know the name of the person making the offer.

"Didn't you ask Mr Findlay?"

"No, I didn't want to. Mrs Findlay didn't know. She said I had better run up and ask Mr Findlay, but I wasn't going to. I told him I wasn't ever going to speak to him again if I could help it, and I didn't mean to. And I wasn't going to his room either."

Bobby asked a few more questions on other subjects, and then said he hardly thought they need trouble her any more just then. Later she would have to be asked to make a full and formal statement. But at present they were only trying to get it all straight in their own minds so as to have a better idea of how things stood. He got up to open the door for her, and on the threshold she paused and said a little nervously:

"Is it true what they're saying about its being a kitchen knife?"

"That was what was used," Bobby answered gravely. "Why do you ask?"

"It's what they are all saying," she answered. "I don't see that it matters. There are lots of them about. You want them if you're doing any cooking. I've been using one for opening uncle's letters."

"Quite a rise in the world," Bobby remarked. "From kitchen to study. The upward lift?"

"It just happened to be there," she answered.

She went away then, and Bobby sent the constable in attendance to find Lord Newdagonby and ask for the favour of a few moments' talk. The constable departed on his errand, and Bobby went back to his seat by Simons, who had now a very puzzled and worried air.

"What's all that mean?" he asked. "I mean, about blackmailing Findlay into marriage. Or was it the other way round, and was it him blackmailed her? Rich woman, isn't she?"

"Oh, yes," Bobby agreed. "Lord Newdagonby seems to be in the millionaire class or thereabouts, and he is evidently very fond of her—his only child."

"Money don't come into it, then," Simons said.

"Money has a way of turning up everywhere," Bobby replied thoughtfully. "Though I don't yet see where it comes in this time. Besides, a blackmailer generally goes for money, not for marriage. You can always demand another good fat cheque, but not another wife. Still, it's a possibility."

"Must be some reason for all this talk of blackmail," Simons grumbled. "And what did that girl mean by talking about kitchen knives and telling us she had been using one to open letters? Sort of a hint that his lordship might have nipped upstairs and done it?"

"Well, as far as that goes," Bobby suggested, "it implicates her as much as it does him."

"Passing the buck," Simons said. "In a way she's a deep 'un. That's my idea."

"Girls always are," Bobby said. "A boy's thoughts may be long, long thoughts, but a girl's are deep, so deep she often doesn't know herself what they are. Something more to remember. And that fur coat. Does that come in? She's got no money apparently, looking for a job. Also apparently she's half-engaged to a man who runs a restaurant—the Isle du Lac, very expensive. Is he hard up, and does she want the money to help him? Only an idea. But this chap had a bad row with Ivor Findlay over the way he had behaved to her. Restaurants and kitchen knives. I wonder if she's afraid we may suspect a connection?"

"Well, there could be, in a way," Simons reflected. "Could be," he repeated.

"We shan't have to forget him," Bobby said thoughtfully.

"There're those 'phone calls," Simons went on. "You didn't press her about them?"

"Keep them in the background for the time," Bobby advised. "Something may be said to give us a line. They're an odd feature," and then the door opened to admit the thin, elongated form of Lord Newdagonby.

Bobby rose to greet him and to push forward a chair. He murmured something about understanding they wanted to see him, folded himself up as it were to take the chair Bobby offered, and apologized for having so little to tell them.

"As you can imagine," he said, "I feel terribly shaken—terribly. I can still hardly believe it's real, I half-expect to wake up in bed and find it is all some dreadful nightmare. One reads of these things in the papers, one doesn't expect them to happen in one's own house."

"They always happen in somebody's own house," Bobby said.

"Quite so. That is what it is so hard to realize. Like being knocked down and killed by a car. One knows it happens, but one doesn't expect it. One thing I must ask. My daughter seems to think you suspect her. I should be pleased to receive your assurance that such a preposterous idea had never even occurred to you."

"We always have to explain," Bobby answered, "that it is routine to suspect every one till we have established their innocence. Any person for whom identity of time and place can be shown is possibly guilty. We try to eliminate them one by one till at last only one possibility remains."

"Even when there is no suggestion or possibility of any motive?"

"Strictly speaking," Bobby explained, "it is not necessary to establish motive. Our business is with facts, not motives. Motive is, of course, very often the essential pointer, but not always. Not that we forget the old saying: 'Who benefits?' "

"May I suggest that what you call identity of time and place applies as much to me as to my daughter?" Lord Newdagonby said with great severity. "More so indeed. Mrs Findlay was out at the time of the murder. I was in all morning."

"We have not overlooked that fact," Bobby answered calmly.

Lord Newdagonby gave a little gasp and then sat upright, straightening that long, thin body of his till even as he sat he seemed as tall as any ordinary man.

"Do I understand," he demanded, his two small eyes very bright and angry on each side of that enormous nose of his, "do I understand that I . . . I . . . am I under suspicion?"

"In a provisional sense only," Bobby assured him. "May I take it you are willing to answer a few questions we should like to ask you—provisional questions only, of course. All we are trying to do at present is to get the situation as clear in our minds as may be possible."

Slowly Lord Newdagonby relaxed his upright position, shutting himself up as it were on himself. Bobby watched the process with interest. He was inclined to think that if only his lordship had been born in another sphere of life, he might have earned quite a good weekly wage as the 'boneless wonder' or the 'living skeleton' in any travelling circus. Irreverent thoughts no doubt about a member of the British peerage, even though peers are no longer what once they were.

"I confess," Lord Newdagonby said slowly, when at last this folding-up process was complete, "I had never expected to figure as a suspect in a case of murder. And the fact that I could have no conceivable motive is wholly immaterial, I understand?"

"Facts come first," Bobby repeated. "Obviously, if we knew of a motive, any strong, compelling motive, it would be important. Very important. But we don't. Need I remind you that identity of place and time applies to several other people? And it's quite possible apparently that some one else could have slipped into the house unseen and got away again without any one knowing."

"Very good," Lord Newdagonby said with a meekness his angry little eyes and flushed cheeks in no way confirmed. "I am suspected of murder. In that case I am presumably a liar as well. So why ask questions to which, by hypothesis, you can only expect untrue replies?"

"I am sorry your lordship takes it like this," Bobby said formally. "We had hoped for more willing co-operation. We recognize that our suspicions are unfounded in all cases but one, and where they are unfounded we hope to receive the utmost help. Even if only for obvious self-interest. It would help us, for example, if you would tell us everything you can about Mr Findlay, how long you have known him, if you know of any enemies he may have had, if you approved his marriage with your daughter. Anything at all, in fact."

"Well, Ivor Findlay was the son of one of my tenants—very old tenants," Lord Newdagonby answered after a pause. "Findlays have held the same farm as far back as our records show. There is a story one of their ancestors and one of mine were taken prisoner together at the battle of Shrewsbury and executed on the same scaffold—my ancestor beheaded and theirs hanged. Not much difference all said and done, I suppose. But such a long connection is of interest, and when old Mr Findlay died, leaving a young widow and a child, I helped with the boy's education. He turned out a clever lad, won scholarships, I helped, he went to Oxford and did very well. He came to the house occasionally and met Sibby. I didn't notice that they showed much interest in each other at first, and I admit it was a considerable surprise when Sibby told me they were engaged. I don't say her choice would have been mine. I did to a certain extent remonstrate with her. But she had made up her mind. Nothing I could do, even if I had wanted to. Ivor was in a position to support her, and then I had no real reason to object. I made suitable provision for them."

"Thank you," Bobby said. "There seems to have been some gossip that it was chiefly your daughter's doing. In fact, there seems to have been a story that he complained he had been bullied or blackmailed into the marriage."

"I think you may safely disregard that," declared Lord Newdagonby. "Merely malicious gossip."

"I see. There was no previous entanglement on Mr Findlay's side with any other woman?"

"Certainly none that I know of. Are you thinking that some such woman may be the murderer?"

"A possibility we have to consider," Bobby replied once more. "We are so much in the dark, we have to grope everywhere for a clue. You mentioned a Count Ariosto, a friend of Mrs Findlay's. Can you tell us anything about him."

"Not very much," Lord Newdagonby answered, this time looking a little amused. "A harmless little Italian, I should say. He lives here and visits Italy in the summer. Very good manners, a gentleman and an aristocrat, but not much money I think. I have only seen him once or twice, but that is my impression. It is true there has been some silly talk going on as I told you. But that's all."

"You don't think there's any possibility that he may have hoped to marry your daughter himself, and that he may have felt he had been cut out by Mr Findlay with a quarrel as a result?"

"It seems to me rather a far-fetched idea," Lord Newdagonby answered. "There may be something in it, I suppose. I don't know."

"Do you know his address?"

"The Bliss Hotel, Mayfair Square, I think. But he is often away I understand. Much in demand at week-end parties. Excellent bridge player. All the social tricks in fact. Sibby told me once he was the answer to the week-end hostess's prayer."

"Doesn't sound much like a murderer, I admit," Bobby said. "Oh, by the way, we are trying to trace the weapon used.

A kitchen knife you remember. I'm told there was one in your study. Is it there now, do you know?"

"I really haven't the least idea," replied Lord Newdagonby. "There was one, I know. I used it for a time for opening letters. So did Miss Grange. Did she mention it?"

"She told us there was one there she had been using," Bobby answered. "Perhaps some one took it back to the kitchen. Do you know how it got to your room?"

"I think I brought it up myself without thinking once when I had been in the kitchen helping to peel the potatoes. Mrs Jacks was away, and Sibby was doing the cooking. She likes to do a little cooking occasionally. I wanted to help, but she packed me off as being more bother than I was worth." Lord Newdagonby smiled tolerantly. "She bullies her old father shamefully," he complained, and plainly enjoyed the fact. "Is this knife," he went on, "the one I'm supposed to have used? I must say you distribute your suspicions very impartially. Now I come to think of it, I believe the last time I saw the knife you've talked about, Mr Acton was using it to sharpen a pencil. I remember now his remarking that he had lost his penknife. And he's been rather dancing attendance on Sibby just recently."

"Yes, I noticed that," Bobby said, and added slowly: "Was that in any way a cause of ill-feeling?"

"Out of the question," Lord Newdagonby replied sharply, so sharply indeed as to convey a faint suggestion that perhaps he was less certain than he wished to appear. "I told you—Sibby and Ivor had complete confidence in each other. Complete."

"I was thinking," Bobby explained, "of possible ill-feeling between Mr Findlay and Mr Acton?"

"None that I know of. Most unlikely," Lord Newdagonby still insisted. "If there was anything of the kind, it must have been about something else. Business perhaps. Ivor did say something once about a snag in the manufacture of the razor blade that Acton has on hand. But if there was some sort of quarrel it might be over any trifle. Ivor did tread on people's toes at times, and didn't care if he did. And then his flirtations.

They weren't always understood. I must say I never saw or heard anything to suggest any kind of ill-feeling on either side."

"Thank you," Bobby said; and explained as he had done before that this was only a preliminary talk, and that a formal statement would be taken later on, when possibly they might be able to see their way more clearly.

CHAPTER X
"IT'S EVIDENCE"

"I DON'T LIKE that old geezer," was Inspector Simons's comment when Lord Newdagonby had retired and they were waiting for Charley Acton, the next on their list to be interviewed. "In a way, not quite human, him and his Exist—what was it?"

"Very human in one respect at least," Bobby remarked. "He is devoted to his daughter. Not much he wouldn't do for her."

"Meaning—?"

"Meaning no more than that," Bobby answered. "I do think he wouldn't stick at murder if he were pushed to it and he thought it necessary for her happiness. But there's nothing to suggest it. I agree he seems entirely without inhibitions, as our intelligentsia say admiringly, though less admiringly when a gentleman also without inhibitions burgles their flat."

"Notice," asked Simons, "how all of 'em drop hints about some one else? Sort of 'Not me, but what about the next man?' Mrs Jacks hears typing—"

"If she did, if that story's true," Bobby interrupted. "No confirmation. Mrs Jacks isn't complicated, but I don't know that I like her any better than you like Lord Newdagonby."

"It's evidence, what she said," Simons insisted. "And took care to tell us Mrs Findlay used the machine sometimes. Then Mrs Findlay talks about Miss Grange's fur coat, and drags it in that Miss Grange don't like Findlay, but might have been in his room this morning all the same. Miss Grange comes along and tells us there was a kitchen knife, like that used in the murder, Lord Newdagonby had in his room. Passing the buck? And his lordship hints at something new—business quarrel. Passing the buck again? And now I'm wondering what Acton's pointer will be?"

Before Bobby had time to make any comment, Acton appeared. He, too, was plainly highly nervous and ill at ease. His hands were shaking, he kept moistening dry and parched lips with the tip of his tongue, and his face was of an almost ghastly pallor. Natural enough of course. No one can be expected to retain complete calm when brought face to face with a sudden and brutal murder. Bobby uttered a few words of sympathy, to which Acton responded grateful] y.

"A very great shock," he said. "An old friend and a very close business associate. A terrible loss—and not only as a friend. Only this morning I had a letter from him to say he was ready to start making his report on my everlasting razor blade. Enthusiastic about it, and now I shall never have it."

"There will be his notes, won't there?" Bobby asked.

"I'm afraid not," Acton answered. "I can't say for certain of course, but Ivor had his own methods. Secretive. He would never allow any one there when he was working. He would make the most thorough investigation of anything he was testing, and only when he was thoroughly satisfied would he begin to set down his conclusions. Now everything will have to be done all over again."

"But you have a letter from him, haven't you?" Bobby remarked.

"Oh, yes, yes, there's that," agreed Acton, brightening perceptibly. "I had forgotten for the moment. I can't think of anything but this dreadful business—so inexplicable. Why should any one want to murder poor Ivor? Possibly my American syndicate will be willing to go ahead on the strength of his letter. It's a big thing. Big money required. We want to start factories all over the world so as to get a good start."

Bobby remarked that an everlasting razor blade would certainly be a great convenience. Did Mr Acton mean really everlasting? So Mr Acton smiled and admitted that 'everlasting' was perhaps in the nature of an advertising slogan. But it did mean at least twenty-five years. The idea was to stamp the date on every blade and replace free of charge any whose edge showed the least sign of wear in less than that time.

"All the same," continued Mr Acton very earnestly, "on the basis of our tests I should be prepared to guarantee a century of use—a full century."

"Well, sir," said Simons, much impressed, "you've certainly got something there."

"A hundred years is a long time," Bobby observed. "I'm wondering how you arrive at it?"

"I fixed up a gadget," Acton explained. "It kept three blades in action continuously day and night for six months. I agree that by the end of that time the edges were the worse for wear. But still usable. I tried them myself. Now the time a razor blade is actually in use while shaving isn't very long. Say five minutes—at the most. I calculated that in six months there are something like a quarter of a million minutes or about fifty thousand shaving periods of five minutes each. But in a century there would only be a little more than somewhere between thirty and forty thousand shaves required from each blade, allowing about one shave a day. Which leaves a good margin."

"Yes, so it does," agreed Bobby. "Your slogan could be: 'It'll be all the same in a hundred years.'"

Acton expressed high appreciation of this suggestion. When the company was floated—'Everlasting, Ltd.', and didn't Mr Owen think that an excellent name?—he would make a point of seeing that Mr Owen was sent an initialled application form. The capital would be a million in each of the three divisions of the world—the American, the European, and the Pacific. He even hoped his razor blade would penetrate the iron curtain, though probably the Russians would claim that the invention was the unaided work of Russian scientists. The profits should run to at least twenty per cent. Bobby said it made his mouth water, but unfortunately mere policemen, struggling along on a wholly inadequate, entirely ridiculous salary, had no money to spare for investments, however promising. Acton said in that case he needn't put a limit on the initialled application form he would still see Bobby received in due course. He had had to put a limit on the form to be sent to Findlay, because Findlay had hinted at applying for a very large allotment, up to fifty thousand of the one-pound shares contemplated.

"Poor old Ivor," said Acton with a kind of sorrowful disapproval. "Just like him. A born gambler. If he thought he was on a good thing he would back it to the limit. He was stagging of course—meant to sell part of his allotment and use the profit to pay for what he kept. I wasn't going to have that. His gambling was his own affair, but not with my company. I told him he could have priority for five hundred, but after that he would have to take his chance. I'm afraid he didn't like it."

Simons, who had been listening to all this with great interest, said rather longingly that it sounded jolly good—twenty per cent was a lot better than the two and a half you got from the Post Office.

If a hint had been intended, it passed unnoticed, and Bobby remarked that Lord Newdagonby had said something about a 'snag' Findlay had talked about. Would that refer to the limit on the suggested priority allotment application?

"I shouldn't think so," Acton said, looking puzzled. "Snag? Oh, perhaps the poor chap meant my refusal to take out a patent. Ivor argued people might think that suspicious—lack of confidence possibly, though I don't know why. He and I got quite heated. But if you take out a patent you have to give details, and that means telling all the world the lines you are working on. I prefer to keep my process to myself, at any rate for the present. I don't want every one everywhere working on my lines or using my idea to get ahead of me. This is going to be a big thing, Mr Owen. It's going to be one of the biggest things ever. You see, the process should be applied in time to every kind of edged tool—not yet, but in time. At present there is a certain brittleness that wouldn't stand up to heavy strain. But I shall get over that in time. Yes," he said slowly, "yes, in time, a little time. I'm on the track, and a little time, that's all I want. And then—and then—"

He drew a long breath and was silent. He seemed to be no longer aware of their presence, he had a rapt and far-off air, it was as though he had lost all touch with his surroundings, and in his eyes there shone a light, a distant light. Bobby looked at him curiously—a man held, lost, absorbed in his own vision, oblivious to all else. So, Bobby thought, must others have looked—James Watt, for instance, when the idea of the separate condenser to preserve steam came to him, or Archimedes in that hour when he cried 'Eureka'. Bobby coughed softly to bring Acton back to a sense of his surroundings. Then he said:

"Mr Findlay thought it would be wiser to patent the invention?"

"We had quite a row about it. He was most insistent. I had to tell him plainly it was my invention, my process, and it was going to be my decision. I said he was going a long way beyond his province as scientific adviser."

"What did he say to that?"

"Oh, just went on grumbling. I'm afraid I rather lost my temper. I remembered an appointment and took myself off. But I think he was beginning to see what I meant."

"You speak of your process as being secret. It wouldn't be secret from him, I suppose. Did you think there was any risk of—well, his using his knowledge for his own benefit, taking out a patent on his own, for instance?"

"Dear me, no," Acton answered, and laughed outright. "Poor old Ivor was a gambler. He was always running after women. He wasn't too scrupulous about money or some other things either. If he borrowed anything, half a crown or a hundred pounds, you were never likely to see it again. But when it came to his work, a sort of—well, I don't know how to put it. A sort of Sir Galahad of science, if you see what I mean. He would never swerve by a hair's breadth from what he believed. A split mind, you might say, or a split conscience if you like. One, about science, anything to do with his work, well, that was sacred. Anything else, well, that was different. Truer to say, that there he had no conscience at all."

"Thank you," Bobby said. "We had rather gathered as much, but you've put it very clearly. A great help. You see, we want as clear a picture of Mr Findlay as possible. We have to fit him into a background of murder. There is another point where you can help us perhaps. Mr Findlay seems to have got along very well with his wife, and yet we have information that it was she who pressed for their marriage. In fact, the expression has been used that she blackmailed him into it."

"Blackmailed him?" Acton repeated. "How could she? I never heard anything of that sort before. Just silly, I should say."

"Lord Newdagonby," Bobby went on, "also said that though Findlay ran after women, he and his wife allowed each other a good deal of latitude in such matters. In short, that they had towards each other what he called a highly civilized attitude. Very nice, no doubt, but in such matters, to use the same expression, the highly civilized attitude sometimes changes very quickly into a highly primitive one. That is our experience. Under the skin of the highly civilized, the primitive emotions may still be there, still break out on occasion."

But Acton shook his head, and he was smiling as he replied:

"Divorce perhaps, but not murder. Besides, Ivor is the victim himself. If you're thinking of Sibby, Mrs Findlay, I should call her a cold-blooded bully. There is something about her that does dominate people. She is fascinating by the sheer force of her entire devotion to herself. But murder is entirely outside the range of her absorbing interest in herself and what she calls the human need for experience. Far too intense to allow any room in her for passion. That is, if you really mean you are suspecting her."

"Only in the sense that we are suspecting every one on the spot," Bobby explained, as he had explained so often before.

"Well," retorted Acton, and he spoke with emphasis, "all I can say is that suspecting Sibby is merely silly—if you don't mind my saying so. Any one else perhaps, but not Sibby. It doesn't fit."

"I think you yourself have been very friendly with her?"

"Oh, I would hardly say that," Acton protested. "I certainly felt the impact of her really tremendous personality. We have a common interest in the new developments in art and poetry. We are both founder members of the Uttermost Club. But that's all." He smiled again, and a little shyly, said: "You see, I'm unique in a way. I get teased about it. But I do happen to be rather fond of my wife and the kiddies—I've two. Ivor knew that all right. Not that I think he would have worried even if he had thought that Sibby and I were flirting—or more. We weren't anyway. He was far too vulnerable himself. I believe that was why he was so fond of keeping his door locked when he was supposed to be working. If you called to see him, it was always in the flat. You knew a suite upstairs has been converted into a self-contained flat for them? Separate entrance and all. The garden door it used to be. I happen to know that sometimes he would give his lady friends a key to the garden door so that they could slip up to him in his room in the attics without any one knowing."

"If that's so," Bobby said, "it widens the field immensely. It would mean that somebody no one knew anything about may have been there this morning and got away again unseen. Are you sure?"

"Count Ariosto showed me one once—a key I mean. A woman had given it to him. She said she had it from Ivor, but she didn't want it, and would he give it back to him."

CHAPTER XI
"IT'S VIVISECTION"

"WELL, HE GAVE us his pointer all right, didn't he?" grumbled Simons when presently Acton had departed, not without expressing very earnest wishes for the discovery of the culprit. "His Italian Count and a key to the garden door! Passing the buck. They all do it. What about all of them being in it and trying a sort of merry-go-round to keep us all busy?"

"It might be that they all want to help and all have their own ideas," Bobby remarked. "There never is a case of murder but we get suggestions by the dozen. Quite refreshing to meet some one who admits he is happily married. Terribly out of date, though."

"There's plenty that are," objected Simons, who, however, seldom read the more advanced periodicals, and had never attended a cocktail party in his life. "What next?"

Before Bobby could reply, the question was answered by the appearance of the constable on duty to say that a Count Ariosto—visiting-card produced—had arrived. He described himself as a friend of the family and explained that he had just heard what had happened. But he simply couldn't believe it was true, and so had come at once to inquire.

"Very excited like," said the constable, and added, in tolerant explanation: "Foreign gent."

Bobby said they would see the gentleman at once, and Count Ariosto appeared. He was of a youngish middle age, smartly dressed, a little too smartly perhaps, good looking, with large, black, flashing eyes and prominent, well-shaped features, including the typical Roman nose. He walked badly, with a kind of quick, hurried shuffle, as though in haste, and with gestures as eloquent as his words, he expressed his horror, his bewilderment, his distress.

"A lady," he said, "whom I revered for her gracious personality, her intelligence, her charm. That she should meet so terrible an end, it is inconceivable, it is inexplicable. At first I could not believe it. I hurried here to be reassured. But it seems it is actually so."

"What lady do you mean?" Bobby asked, while Simons gaped with open mouth and eyes. "There has been a tragedy here—apparently a murder. But not a woman."

"Not—not a woman," Ariosto gasped. "Not Sibby Findlay—I heard . . . I understood . . . who is it then?"

"Her husband—Ivor Findlay," Bobby answered.

"Oh, Ivor," Ariosto said blankly. "Oh," he repeated. "A great relief," he muttered, but he did not look it. He began to mop at his face with his handkerchief. "Such a dear friend. . . ." He subsided into a silence of what seemed complete bewilderment. He made an effort to recover himself. He said: "You mean Ivor has been murdered? It is impossible, even more impossible. But who . . .? . . . why . . .? It is incredible. Ivor, not Sibby?"

"Mr Findlay, not his wife," Bobby repeated. "As to the who and the why—well, that's what we mean to find out. It might help if you would answer a few questions."

Count Ariosto—his first name was the very English one of Tom—expressed his entire willingness to give all the help he could. He still seemed, however, lost in a kind of haze of bewilderment. Nor was it easy to keep him to the point, though, as the questioning went on, he seemed to recover his balance. Of Italian descent and claiming an Italian title, he had been born in England of naturalized parents, and so was a British subject by birth. Both his parents were dead. His father had never used his title of Count—"he was a poor man, he did not like to swank", Ariosto explained in parenthesis—but for his own part he had not wished to let it lapse and then his circumstances had greatly improved.

"Our family is one of the oldest in Italy," he explained. "Not like the Colonna perhaps, but very, very old. Our pedigree goes right straight back to the poet. You have heard of the great Ariosto?"

Bobby said he had, though unfortunately he was not well acquainted with his work, and the Count went on to explain that he still kept in touch with his Italian relatives. Every summer he went to Italy and always paid them a visit.

"Alas! they are ruined," he informed his two listeners. "They were always poor. Now they are ruined. The war. They have nothing. But then to-day, we are all poor, all ruined. Me also. So what would you?"

Bobby asked what was Count Ariosto's profession. Ariosto replied that he was a financier. Bobby remarked that that was a difficult occupation for a poor man. Financiers were generally wealthy unless they were bankrupt. Ariosto became voluble.

It began to appear that what he really meant was that he speculated on the Stock Exchange.

"Oh, but cautiously, so cautiously," he protested. "Not like our poor Ivor. I do not put on my shirt when I buy, as Ivor does with his horses, and I sell as soon as I see a profit. No one ever went bankrupt by taking a profit," he added, quoting one of those wise maxims current in a market that seldom pays them any attention in practice.

He had been fairly successful, he admitted. Some of his profits he had invested in the Hotel Bliss, where he lived when he was in England. He let drop, however, that he was often invited to spend his week-ends at the country houses of his many wealthy and well-known friends. It was at the bridge table at these week-ends that he had first met his dear friend, Mrs Findlay. Impossible, he declared, to imagine his relief when he heard that the story of her death was false. Yes, indeed, an inconceivable relief.

"How close was your friendship with her?" Bobby asked. "Was there anything in it to cause trouble between her and her husband? Did he ever show any sign of resentment?"

Ariosto protested vehemently, and with every appearance of genuine surprise at the question, that there never had been any reason or appearance or hint of the faintest suggestion of any such feeling. Sibby Findlay and himself had been merely bridge-table friends.

"Our play fitted," he said. "We did well together—so well indeed that sometimes it was not liked when we cut together. That is all. Nothing more," he declared with emphasis. "My God, no."

This last expression broke out with such vehemence that Bobby glanced up quickly and Simons stared. Ariosto did not notice. He gave the idea of being lost in thoughts that were not too pleasant.

"You see," Bobby explained, "our information is that both the Findlays were rather free and easy—tolerant in the modern manner—with friends of the opposite sex. But people may be tolerant outwardly and less so inwardly, and their tolerance may break down rather suddenly."

Ariosto protested again that he knew nothing about that. Jealousy was out of date, wasn't it? Certainly he had never seen or heard of any sign of it. Never. Sibby Findlay had many friends—well, acquaintances. People were afraid of her. She was in fact an extraordinary woman. She gave somehow the idea that she was the surgeon and you the patient on the operating-table. Vivisection. That was it.

"How do you mean—vivisection?" Bobby said, puzzled by this description.

"It is not to be explained," Ariosto answered slowly, and he seemed worried, even afraid. "A woman compels by her beauty, her charm, her—her womanliness. It is her right, and how gladly we others yield. It is for us a duty and a joy. In the desert, when I was serving with the Eighth Army"—this was said with a not altogether unconscious touch of swagger—"we would queue up merely to peep at a woman pouring out tea. But when all she shows is a kind of cold curiosity—ugh, it is against nature. Against nature," he repeated, almost shouting now and raising both hands in the air as if in universal protest.

"You called her your friend," Bobby remarked.

"It is better than to call her your enemy," Ariosto answered, and there was little of friendliness in the tone he used.

"We have it suggested," Bobby went on, "that it was she who wanted the marriage with Mr Findlay. In fact, the expression 'blackmailed him into it' has been used."

The effect of this on Ariosto was unexpected. He jumped to his feet, began to speak, then changed his mind, and sat down again. He seemed suddenly oblivious of his surroundings, as if lost in what was apparently a mixture of surprise, bewilderment, and fear. Once again he opened his mouth to speak, and once again he changed his mind and was silent. Bobby said: "Well", and Ariosto suddenly became voluble.

"If it was that, if she blackmailed him, too," he burst out, "why did she kill him? But why should she? The dead are safe, she had no power to impose her questioning on them. If he had killed her, yes, that would make sense. But it is not so. No? You are not having me on?" This time there was an unmistakable note of disappointment in his voice, rather as if there had remained with him a lingering hope that it really was Mrs Findlay and not her husband who had been the victim. He went on: "When I heard what had happened and it was Sibby, I thought: 'Ah, then, it has come, with one she has gone too far, and now one has freed himself'."

"You thought she had been blackmailing—?" Bobby began, but Ariosto interrupted him.

"No, no, not blackmail in your sense, in the police sense. No," he explained. "It was her probing, her trying to find out, to push you along so as to see what you would do. It could become past bearing. And always bad, bad things, because if it was something not bad, then it was not interesting."

"Was it like that with you?"

"Ah, no," Ariosto protested. "No. I do not stand for that, and then it was I who had a hold on her, for there was no one who could play bridge with her as I could, and I said to her: 'If you do not stop this trying to poke into my inside, listen, I play no more with you. You understand?' After I had made that plain I had no more trouble. None."

"Was she so fond of bridge as all that?" Bobby asked.

"Ah, no. No. But at the bridge table people show themselves, and that is what she wanted. To pry into them, and then when she knew their weak points, she could play upon them. Experience she called it. Getting to know. Bah." He almost spat in the rush of his angry recollections. "So when I was told, I thought that a slave had revolted—the rabbit turned on the snake, the guinea pig on the vivisector. Do you understand how that could be? All suddenly."

"Oh, I think so," Bobby answered, though indeed it would have been more truthful to reply that the greater his experience became, the less he understood how, in the tangled minds of men, one motive among others could suddenly and violently become imperative.

"But it is not like that," Ariosto went on, much as if he were talking to himself rather than to them. "It is the poor Ivor, it seems. Why? Ivor no one took seriously, no one was troubled by him. He was not serious. Oh, in his work, that was different. There he was solid, firm as a rock. But in other things, a trifler, a nothing. No woman was ever deceived by anything he said, no man cared what he said for that matter. It was always, 'Oh, it's only Ivor'. A butterfly."

This was said with a half-amused, half-tolerant contempt that in its turn amused Bobby, since it was a verdict passed by a man whose chief contribution to life seemed a flair for Stock Exchange speculation and a gift for bridge and social chatter, on a man of solid professional achievement and scientific repute. However, there were more serious matters to be considered than Ariosto's standard of values.

"Our information," Bobby went on, "is that Mr Findlay would on occasion give his lady friends a key to what is called the garden door here, so that they could slip up to his room on the attic floor without any one seeing."

"But how should I know?" Ariosto demanded. "It may be so. It would be secret between them, they would not be likely to tell others. I don't know. How was the murder committed? Was it poison? or shooting? or what?"

"He was stabbed in the back with an ordinary kitchen knife," Bobby answered. "By some one who knew where to stab to the best effect. Some one who had been in the army perhaps, where a man was taught the best and quickest way of killing."

"Every one has been in the army," Ariosto remarked. "A kitchen knife? Nothing to do with me, I have nothing to with kitchens, only what comes out of them—when you can get it."

"Yes, that's sometimes the trouble, isn't it?" Bobby agreed, and went on: "Another thing we have been told is that on one occasion a lady gave you a key and asked you to return it to Mr Findlay. If that was so, and if it was the key to the garden door, it would mean that you could get up to his room without being seen at any time you wanted."

"But it is not true," Ariosto protested angrily. "It is absurd. It is ridiculous." His protests ended abruptly as he saw how quietly and steadily Bobby was regarding him. He became silent, he seemed as it were to shrink into himself: "You do not mean," he asked in a very small voice, "that you—you—suspect . . ."

His voice trailed off into silence, and Bobby said very amiably:

"So far we have no reason to suspect any one person in particular. Let's get back to the key to the garden door. It may turn out to be also the key to the murder. We have a clear statement that a lady did once give you such a key and asked you to give it back to Mr Findlay."

"I remember now," Ariosto admitted reluctantly. "What about it? I did not know what the key was. I did as the lady asked. Naturally. Why not? It was not in my hand more than two minutes. That is all."

"Who was the lady?"

"I do not know, I never knew," Ariosto insisted with more of the gesticulation that became more frequent and more pronounced at his nervousness increased. "It was at a cocktail party. At a cocktail party it is not necessary to know each other—very often you do not even know your host."

"Who was he that time?"

"I have no idea. Very likely I never knew. Besides, I do not remember what cocktail party it was—one goes to many. One forgets. It is absurd, indefensible—"

Bobby cut short protests which threatened to become an excited flood of anger and incoherence. He asked some more questions, but failed to secure any more definite information, and when he asked for an account of Ariosto's movements that morning, all he learned was that Ariosto had been for a stroll in the park.

"One often meets a friend there," Ariosto explained.

That morning, however, this had not happened, and Ariosto was then allowed to depart, further protestations of entire innocence having to be suppressed with the firm assurance that there were at present no grounds for bringing any charge against any one. But this had to be coupled with the admission that no one as yet could be considered entirely cleared. Not even one so palpably innocent—innocent with an innocence comparable only to that of a new-born babe—as was Count Ariosto, and so that gentleman had to retire, unconsoled and uneasy. His rather curious, quick, shuffling sort of walk gave him as he went an odd resemblance to an agitated duck.

"Flat feet—bad, too," Simons remarked, and Bobby nodded in thoughtful agreement.

CHAPTER XII
"SHE WANTS TO BE WICKED"

"WELL, ONE THING," Simons remarked as the door closed upon the shuffling, hurrying figure of a retreating Ariosto, "that's about the only time there hasn't been a try on at passing the buck." Bobby, deep in his own thoughts, made no comment. Simons, who knew all about Bobby's ways and habits, added slyly: "Bit suspicious, don't you think?"

"I wouldn't say that," Bobby answered, rousing himself from his meditations. "I fancy Ariosto was too flustered at finding he might be a suspect to think about anything else."

"Admits he had a key to this garden door of theirs," Simons remarked, "and only his own word for it that he passed it back to Findlay. And he doesn't know who the lady is he got it from, so we can't check up on that either. Isn't getting us much further forward, is it?"

"Oh, I don't know," Bobby answered. "Anyway, we're getting a very good build-up of the Findlay background. A lot of interesting facts, but wholly disconnected at present. It's going to be a job to sort out what is relevant from what isn't. And still more of a job to be sure where Mrs Findlay comes in. We come across some queer customers from time to time, but I've never before met any one quite like her."

"Going to give eighteen months to sin, but crime's vulgar," grunted Simons, who had had this phrase repeated to him. "Well, I ask you," he said with a gesture of hopeless resignation. "Crazy talk. Only talk? Or is it more?"

"That's what we've to be sure about," Bobby told him. "The one thing I am sure of at present is that it does mean something, and something pretty nasty. But as to whether it means murder, I don't know."

"Oh, well, I suppose we've got to sort it out," declared Simons, still more hopelessly resigned. "What next? There's this Noel Lake bloke. We haven't seen him yet."

Before Bobby could answer, the constable on duty at the door reappeared. The man on the beat that morning had sent in a report. He had gone off duty at two p.m., and had not heard of the murder till later. Now he had rung up to say he had seen a car parked in the narrow opening from which access was obtained to the garden door. A complaint had been made that it was blocking the way through to what had originally been the Dagonby House stable-yard and mews, now in the occupation of a somewhat mixed community. Complaints of this nature had been made before. Mr and Mrs Findlay had been communicated with, and both had promised to see it didn't happen again and also to warn their friends. This car, however, was not theirs. As it was unoccupied he had taken a note of the number, and was waiting for the owner to appear when he was called away to attend to a collision elsewhere between a taxi-cab and a private car. He had given his station sergeant the number of the obstructing car, and its owner was being traced. The hour noted was some thirty minutes or so before the estimated time of the murder.

Bobby remarked that this might be important, and Simons went to ring up the station sergeant and ask if the owner of the car had yet been identified. He came back almost at once with a name and address, that of a Mrs Ida Tinsley, Topper Court, N.E. 1, and Bobby and Simons both had at once the same idea that this might possibly be the lady from whom Ariosto was said to have received a key to the Dagonby House garden door.

So Bobby said that was where they would have to go next, only what about a cup of tea first?

Simons thought this an excellent idea—as did Bobby himself—and they forthwith put it into operation at a neighbouring tea-shop. Thence they proceeded to Topper Court, one of those great fortresses of habitation that have sprung up in such profusion of recent years. The flat occupied by Mrs Tinsley was on the top floor, and Simons expressed his thankfulness that no electricity cut was preventing the automatic lift from working. Nor did he seem to notice Bobby's offer to race him up the stairs to the top. No better way of keeping in training than running upstairs and down again, Bobby remarked. But Simons was already in the lift, his finger hovering over the appropriate button. So Bobby followed, Simon's finger descended, and the lift ascended.

Fortunately Mrs Tinsley—she wore a wedding ring—was in. She was a small, dark, active-looking woman, restless and quick in her movements and strongly built. Her full lips, her large, flashing eyes, gave the impression of a passionate nature, not too well controlled, and to Bobby, at first sight, there seemed something of a contrast between a certain fluffiness in her attire and a degree of business-like severity in the furnishing of the flat. There was a typewriter on a side table, together with books and papers. At the moment she was plainly very excited and nervous. She showed them the evening paper, and was voluble in her expressions of horror and surprise.

"I can't believe it," she said more than once. "I suppose it's true? I saw him this morning, and he was just as usual. It doesn't seem possible. I—I—I—"

She was doing her best to control herself, but Bobby began to be afraid that she was going to break down. He tried to say something sympathetic, but she did not listen. She went out of the room abruptly, and then came back, looking more self-possessed.

"I am sorry," she said. "It has been such a great shock."

Bobby murmured sympathy, said he was sure they could depend on her help, and went on to ask a few questions. She was a widow, she said. Her husband had been a scientific worker, and as he had not left her very well provided for, she did a little work in the way of copying difficult scientific articles or translating from the French or German. That was how she had first met Mr Findlay. Yes, she had called to see him that morning, and he had admitted her himself. She had seen no one else there, and as far as she knew no one else had seen her.

"It is such a wilderness of a place," she said. "Dozens of rooms and miles of passages. You could camp out there for weeks and weeks without any one knowing."

Answering more questions, she declared that her visit to Mr Findlay had not been connected with any work she was doing for him. He had not asked her to do anything for him for some time. Her visit had been of a private nature. She did not intend to say what it was. Others were involved. No, she was in no way an intimate friend of Mr Findlay's. They were just friends, that was all. Nor was she in any way intimate with Mrs Findlay. In fact, she had only met Sibby Findlay on very few occasions, and the fewer such occasions were, the better she was pleased. In her opinion Sibby Findlay was not so much a Woman, as a Nightmare, a Vampire. Most people tried to avoid her, only of course they didn't dare show it. She had a way of looking at you—ugh. Yes, she was more than sorry for Ivor. Any one would be sorry for any man who was Sibby's husband, and she, Mrs Tinsley, couldn't imagine why he had ever married her. She was perfectly sure he hadn't wanted, but men somehow often seemed so helpless. They got themselves into a hole and didn't know how to get out again. Bobby wondered if he were being a bit unfair in thinking that this remark concealed a well-founded belief of Mrs Tinsley's that for her part she could always get out of any hole she ever got into. He was also inclined to think that possibly she had had certain successful experiences in that way. She was telling him now what a charming man Ivor Findlay was and how much everybody liked him. Oh, no, no one could possibly call him a flirt—just pleasant and agreeable. Inconceivable he should have been murdered. If it had been Sibby now—Mrs Tinsley left the sentence unfinished, but gave the impression that in that case she would have felt very little distress.

Bobby judged the time had now come to make his questions a little more direct. He said:

"There is a Count Ariosto, a man of British nationality but Italian descent and still using an Italian title. He is a friend of Mrs Findlay's. Is he also a friend of yours?"

Mrs Tinsley hesitated, and Bobby felt she was considering rather carefully how to reply.

"Not a friend exactly," she said at last. "We meet occasionally. We have mutual acquaintances. That's all."

"I must ask you to be careful in your answers," Bobby said, for this reply had not impressed him as being entirely frank. "It does appear as if you must have been almost the last, probably the very last person, apart from the murderer, to see Mr Findlay alive."

"It's so dreadful," exclaimed Mrs Tinsley. "So impossible. I can't realize it even yet."

"We have information," Bobby continued, "suggesting that you were at any rate at one time in possession of a key to the side door at Dagonby House. Did you use a key to let yourself in by this morning?"

"No, certainly not. I told you. Ivor let me in himself."

"He was expecting you then?"

"He rang up. He wanted to see me. It was private business. I said I would come at once."

"It was important then?"

"Oh, no, not at all. Something private. I said so. Who told you such a wicked, wicked story?"

"The suggestion is," Bobby went on, "that you were seen to hand a key to Count Ariosto and heard to ask him to give it back to Mr Findlay?"

"It's all nonsense," Mrs Tinsley protested, looking more angry than ever, "and I don't think you've any right to listen to such horrid lies. Besides," she added triumphantly, "suppose I did give it him, I couldn't have used it this morning, could I?"

Obviously not, Bobby agreed. "But equally obviously any one with a key can easily get duplicates made. I understand you to say you never had any such key?"

"Never, never," Mrs Tinsley insisted. But now the anger she had shown before was beginning to change into uneasiness, even into some appearance of fear. "I—why are you asking me all these questions?" she demanded.

"A murder has been committed," Bobby answered gravely, "and every scrap of information we can get may be of importance. At present we are very much in the dark. As I said before, you appear to be most likely the last person to have seen Mr Findlay alive, and that makes you an important witness. You don't wish to tell us why you visited him this morning—"

"No, and I won't either," she interrupted him, angry again now. "It's my affair, and nothing to do with him being murdered or anything else."

"Of course, you are quite within your rights in refusing to answer questions if you don't wish to," Bobby told her. "But it's not very wise. However, I won't press you about that just now. I would very strongly suggest though that you would do well to see your lawyers."

"I haven't got any," she interrupted again.

"It's a serious matter for a witness to refuse to answer in court," Bobby explained. "Judges and juries get a bad impression. I think you would do well to obtain legal advice. In the meantime, are you willing to tell us anything you know about Mr and Mrs Findlay? You said you couldn't understand why they married. And some one else suggested that it was her doing. The expression used to us was that she blackmailed him into it."

As once before, this word 'blackmailed' had an immediate and remarkable effect. She stared, started up in her chair, and then sat back again, tried to speak but did not. Yet the impression she gave was not of fear, but of utter surprise, bewilderment, and doubt, and yet also it was as if the suggestion were at the same time overwhelmingly revealing. When she spoke it was almost to herself, almost as if she had forgotten the presence of the two men.

"But she couldn't, could she?" she said at last. "Not Ivor—poor Ivor. She's capable of it, of anything—Sibby I mean. But it doesn't make sense, does it? If he had murdered her, and I wonder he never did, you could understand. Sibby's a beast. She boasts, I've heard her, she boasts she wants to be wicked. Beyond good and evil, she says."

CHAPTER XIII
"NO HOLDS BARRED"

As they were leaving Topper Court after what had seemed, to him at least, just another inconclusive and baffling interview, Simons said, rather gloomily, almost reproachfully:

"Well, Mr Owen, do you still think it better not to say anything about those 'phone threats? They did suggest murder, and murder's here all right. Not the same person, but there must be a connection, in a way."

"Oh, yes, sure to be," Bobby agreed. "I was hoping some one would say something to give us a line to follow up. They haven't. Not so far, that is."

"Well, if we don't say anything about it . . ." Simons protested discontentedly. "In a way, if we don't, how are we ever to find out?"

Bobby looked at him with the blandly innocent air he sometimes put on when it suited him.

"Oh, we'll ask 'em," he explained. "Nothing like asking when you want to know. They always tell."

After that he and Simons parted. Simons had to see to all the routine work that had been going on, and that now more than required his attention. Bobby, for his part, felt it was time he returned to his own office, where there were, he knew, pressing matters waiting for him. As soon as these were either disposed of or postponed, he went on to the very exclusive and expensive and up-to-date restaurant, managed, directed, and very largely owned—nominally, that is, the real owner was the Great Southern Bank—by Mr Noel Lake.

There, when he entered, he was welcomed with grave courtesy that became rather less so when he explained that he wished neither to dine nor to sup, for by now it was late and that indeterminate hour when a meal can be either. He had, he told the slightly scandalized waiter, just had some bread and cheese and pickled onions, and it was on business that he wished to see Mr Noel Lake. A suggestion by the waiter that Mr Lake only saw people on business during business hours, Bobby put firmly aside. His business, he said, was private and important—and pressing.

An air of authority he could assume when he wished ensured first the summoning of the head waiter and then the prompt delivery of his message. Waiting for a reply, Bobby picked up a menu card. It was beautifully produced, and it was composed in the very best French, not indeed of Stratford atte Bowe, but of the kitchen. He found it interesting, as he observed to the still more scandalized head waiter, to notice how far a five-shilling limit could stretch and stretch, till elastic in comparison was rigid as a bar of steel. Then he pocketed the menu in the face of obvious disapproval, and he knew well that this would be regarded as an attempt to prove familiarity with an establishment whose threshold the head waiter was proudly sure Bobby would never in the ordinary way venture to cross. Which incidentally was true enough, since neither his income tax, his expenses sheet, nor his personal inclinations would have made any such visit seem very attractive.

A reply came back that Mr Lake would be happy to see Mr Owen, and Bobby was accordingly conducted to a comfortable, efficient-looking office. Its occupant was a tall, strongly built young man with a thin, dark face and prominent, well-marked features. He wore thick glasses, and the left cheek showed a scar running from below the ear to just under the eye. Apparently he had guessed the nature of Bobby's errand, for he began by saying he had half expected a visit from the police. It was in all the evening papers for one thing, and Miss

Grange had been to tell him what had happened. A terrible, a wholly inexplicable affair, Noel said. Not that Ivor Findlay had ever been what you would call a friend of his, he explained. He had always thought Ivor Findlay a bit of a swine, even though that was hardly the thing to say about a dead man, and one who had just died so mysteriously and so tragically.

Bobby asked a few unimportant questions, explaining that he was trying to get a picture of the background. If he could succeed in obtaining such a picture, accurate, fair, complete, then it would be a great help towards fitting into it the murder that had just taken place. Noel, who was showing some nervousness, and who as he talked kept arranging and re-arranging in an aimless sort of way the different objects on his desk, said he supposed 'fitting into it' meant discovering who was guilty. Bobby agreed, and Noel said he didn't know what he could do to help. He only wished he could. It was all pretty awful, and then there was that odd business of the telephone messages Miss Grange had told him about. He supposed, he said, sitting back in his chair and thrusting his hands deep into his trouser pockets, that almost any one who had any acquaintance with Ivor Findlay came under suspicion.

Bobby explained that it was merely a matter of routine, and Noel didn't look as if he thought this suggestion very comforting. Routine or not, suspicion remained suspicion. Bobby, for his part, was finding it difficult to form an opinion of the other's personality and character, and wished he had been able to interview him at home, in more personal surroundings, instead of in this soberly and efficiently equipped office.

One or two clear impressions he did receive. Nervous, sensitive, and imaginative, Bobby thought him. Probably cautious in preparation, but apt to be rash and hasty in execution. The thick glasses hid his eyes, most expressive of features, and that he possessed business acumen and organizing ability was proved by the commercial success he had achieved. Dexterously, Bobby turned the conversation to Noel's own past, and learned that Noel had served all through the war in the R.A.F.

"Rotten luck I had, too," he said gloomily. "Of course, I'm alive," he conceded as a kind of after-thought, "and most of the others aren't. But I never once got a chance to be in at a really good show."

"Isn't that scar of yours a service memento?" Bobby asked.

"Not from the Hun," Noel explained. "From a pal. An egg of his went off out of line and a splinter nearly gave me mine. So they took me to hospital while he went off to about the best show our lot ever put up. Got him a D.F.C. and promotion, lucky beggar. It's why I have to wear these glasses. One eye got damaged. Put me finally non-operational. It had been like that before. I was always getting grounded for one thing or another, and when I did get a chance our own flak shot me down."

Bobby said it had certainly been rotten luck all round. He was inclined to think all this meant that Noel's self-esteem had been badly hurt. Perhaps he had even been subjected to a certain amount of teasing about the way he was always missing when things were at their hottest. Some of the teasing might even have not been too good natured. To a young and ardent man it might well be galling that he had served so long in the R.A.F., and yet had nothing to show for it, not even a record of fighting service. Injured vanity? And was that something Bobby ought to remember? Could Noel have felt some morbid urge to assert himself? He was going on talking:

"It's how," he explained, "I came to take on this sort of show. I was so often non-operational, I kept being made mess officer. If I couldn't fight with the chaps, anyhow I could see they were well fed." There was again that note of bitterness and disappointment in his voice as he said this. He went on: "The chaps seemed to think they weren't done too badly. Gave me the idea of starting this show."

"You weren't in the restaurant business before?"

"No, the Bar was dad's idea—the other sort of bar," Noel answered. "K.C. and all that was what I was to be headed for. But I didn't feel like going back to it. Too many exams for one thing. You don't have to pass exams to feed people. They've got to eat though, and some of 'em like to eat well."

Bobby agreed.

"And even to drink well," he suggested, and Noel admitted that it was generally on liquor—naturally so—that such an enterprise as his floated to success.

He added that he was supposed to have a flair for choosing wine, though he didn't know what that meant, except knowing a good thing when he came across it. Bobby felt sympathetic. He also was supposed to have a flair, and he also didn't quite know what that meant—except perhaps knowing a bad thing when he came across it. Judging that after these preliminaries the time had now come to get to closer quarters, he said:

"We have information that there had been a serious quarrel between you and Mr Findlay? Is that the case?"

"We had a blazing row the other day, if that's what you mean," Noel admitted. "Who told you? Lord Newdagonby most likely."

"What was it about?"

"Oh, we just had a row, that's all."

"Mr Lake," Bobby said, "in a very grave and serious matter like this, it would be better to be entirely frank, even in the smallest detail. The suggestion made is that you strongly resented Mr Findlay's behaviour to Miss Grange?"

"Well, suppose I did. What's it matter? There's no need to bring Miss Grange's name into it." He added rather sulkily: "She told me it was no business of mine."

"There's every need not to try to keep any one's name back, not in a case of murder," Bobby told him, a little sternly on his side. He went on: "You spoke of the 'phone threats or warnings whichever they were. No one else has mentioned them. Did you send them?"

"No, I didn't," Noel answered angrily. "Has that old devil been saying it was me?"

"You mean Lord Newdagonby? Why should you think so?"

"It would be just like him," Noel answered. "Besides he did sort of try to hint it might be me. As it happens, the first time I was in Scotland fixing up a contract for a supply of salmon.

And it's Ivor Findlay, isn't it? not Sibby, and it was Sibby the 'phone talked about."

"That's a puzzling feature," Bobby agreed. "But murder was threatened, and murder's happened. It seems as if there must be some connection. Possibly the murderer had what he was planning so much on his mind he had to mention it even if he didn't give the right name. Or it may have been a kind of general warning. If we knew, it would be a help. Do you know if Mr and Mrs Findlay were on good terms?"

"Oh, they got along like most people. I do think it was more her idea than his. Not that he was likely to object to a wife with her money. He was always hard up."

"The word 'blackmail' has been used," Bobby said. "It has been suggested that she blackmailed him into marriage."

This time the reaction was first a look of astonishment and then a laugh.

"Rot," Noel said. "How could she? Besides, it was a jolly good match for him. Lord Newdagonby has heaps of influence and all the money you want. The only thing human about the old boy is that he would do anything for Sibby."

"Anything?" Bobby asked.

"No limit, no holds barred," Noel averred. "Not if it's her. She's all that keeps him in touch with ordinary life—except his family pride. I suppose that's a human trait, too."

"I gather," Bobby remarked, "that you aren't on very friendly terms with him either."

"Just as well he isn't the one that's been murdered, or I suppose you would be after me at once," Noel said. "Anyhow, he began it. He made it jolly plain he doesn't like me. Instinctive. Opposite of love at first sight. He knows I mean to marry Miss Grange if I can, and he means I shan't, not if he can put a stopper on it."

"Has he made any open objection, or do you mean he just seems to dislike the idea?"

"Well, he seems to think I'm a sort of head waiter. Of course, every one in the hotel or restaurant line ought to start like that, and as a matter of fact I did a few weeks as a waiter while we were trying to get on our feet. He knows that, and seems to think I would soon have Kitty—Miss Grange I mean—on the same job."

"Oh, well," Bobby remarked, for Noel, tired apparently of fiddling with the various papers and so on on his desk, had risen from his chair and was moving restlessly about the room, "at any rate you don't suffer from the waiter's occupational disease of flat feet."

"Wasn't on the job long enough," Noel answered as he seated himself again. "Look. Tell me. Is it true Findlay was killed by a stab in the back with a kitchen knife?"

CHAPTER XIV
"PROPER RING-A-RING OF ROSES"

THE QUESTION startled Bobby. He was not sure whether it was not intended to convey a hint or a suggestion of one kind or another. He regarded Noel with close attention, but could discern nothing except the uneasy restlessness that had been so obvious before. He said slowly:

"There are so many of them."

"Kitchen knives, you mean?" Noel asked. "We've dozens of them here for that matter," and again Bobby wondered if this time, too, the spoken words carried some hidden meaning—or defiance. Noel went on: "It's what Miss Grange said. She was very upset. You had been asking her a lot of questions."

"She answered very clearly," Bobby said.

Noel was beginning again to fiddle with the various objects on his desk, and there was a long pause before he said:

"She nearly broke down altogether, telling me. It's all pretty awful. I expect she managed to keep a grip on herself with you. I wasn't sure if she had got it right about it's being a kitchen knife." He changed the subject abruptly. "Look," he said. "I don't know what rot you've got hold of about Sibby Findlay blackmailing people. Piffle. And don't get all worked up about her saying she wants to be wicked. If you are wicked, you don't have to try to be."

"I think that's true," Bobby agreed. "But it's true, too, that it's easier to start than to stop. If you raise the devil, you may find when you've got him that he's out of control."

"Mrs Findlay's not like that," Noel said. "She's just awfully puzzled about things and herself, too, and she wants to find out. That's all."

"She did impress me as a bit of a puzzle herself," admitted Bobby. "I think some people find her rather frightening."

"That's only because of the way she has of staring at you," Noel explained. "It doesn't mean a thing. Kitty says so. She's not the sort you want to make a pal of at first sight. A bit on the heavy side. I suppose most people live on the surface, and it makes them feel uneasy and worried if there's some one else trying to get to the bottom of things. Caught it from her father probably. He's by way of being a bit of a swell as a philosopher, you know. Written a commentary or introduction or something to Hegel, I think it is. And there's some new theory he's going strong on. It's about existence being what really matters."

"Ivor Findlay's existence has been very thoroughly ended," Bobby said gravely. "Did you know a kitchen knife was lying about at Dagonby House? It's vanished now, but it was being used to open letters. Did Miss Grange tell you that?"

"It's what was worrying her," Noel admitted. "She thought she oughtn't to have said anything about it."

"It's as well she did," Bobby answered. "Or we might have thought she was concealing the fact for her own reasons. If every one would be frank with us, they would save us a lot of trouble and themselves a great deal of distress. Do you know a Mrs Tinsley?"

"Well, I've met her. She's pally with the Findlays. Ivor has been carrying on a red-hot flirtation with her—he always was with some one or another."

"But you don't think that sort of thing ever caused any serious disagreement between him and his wife?"

"I'm sure it didn't. For one thing Sibby did the same in her own cold, aloof, what's it all mean sort of way—bullying rather than flirting, though it came to much the same thing. She's been taking possession of a chap called Charley Acton recently. You may have heard of him. He's an inventor. Clever bloke. Says he's invented an everlasting razor blade. If he has, it ought to bring in pots of money."

"Was there any resentment on Mr Findlay's side? People don't always like being treated the way they themselves treat others."

"Oh, they got on all right. I told you. For one thing I don't believe either of them cared enough to get jealous. Besides, she had the whip hand. The money's hers. It was very sudden—their marriage I mean. They never seemed to take much notice of each other, not a bit interested, you would have thought. And then there was a notice in the paper to say they had been to Caxton Hall and got married. No one could make it out. Some people even thought it was a leg pull at first."

"Makes one wonder rather what Lord Newdagonby thought," Bobby remarked.

"Oh, it would be all right with him if it was what she wanted," Noel answered.

"Didn't Mr Findlay earn a good income himself, quite enough to make him independent?" Bobby asked next. "I understood he had a considerable reputation as a scientist."

"Oh, yes, quite a swell. He was working on something to do with atomic theory I believe. Some small private line of his own. About neutralizing the after effects of radio-activity, he told me once. Science was about the one thing he took seriously. A sort of religion with him. He would sooner have died than compromised with scientific truth. But in every other way, money, women, anything, he was as irresponsible as any West End playboy."

"Makes an investigation very complicated," Bobby complained, "when everyone concerned seems so very complicated in themselves."

"Oh, well, not every one," Noel protested. "I'm not compli-cated for one."

Bobby was not so sure about that. But he let the remark pass unanswered. He got up to go.

"We shall probably have to see you again," he said. "At present I'm only trying to get the background clear—or as clear as possible. What you've told me is likely to be very help-ful." Noel looked both startled and surprised, and not as if this remark were very welcome. Bobby went on: "There's one thing perhaps I ought to mention. The knife used to kill Ivor Findlay had a piece of paper pushed between the blade and the handle, apparently to make them more secure. That bit of paper looks very much as if it had been torn from the corner of one of your menus. It will have to be sent for expert examination."

"One of our menus," Noel repeated and blinked, evidently trying, and unwilling, to take in the implications of this. "Well, but—" he began and paused. "I don't know any thing about that," he said, rather loudly.

"Obviously," Bobby went on, "a menu is a sort of open doc-ument. Any one dining here could get hold of one or tear a corner off, if he wanted to. I've taken the liberty myself for that matter of pocketing one. No one objected. But it does suggest, doesn't it? some sort of connection somewhere."

"If I wanted to do in any one," Noel remarked gloomily, "I shouldn't be such a fool as to leave anything like that behind."

"It happens," Bobby told him. "There was one case in Aus-tralia when a murderer left his name and address behind him, near the dead body. Murderers aren't often so obliging, but they always leave their signature in one way or another. They can't help it. They've been there, and it's bound to be like that, because no one can be anywhere or do anything without mak-ing their mark. Action and reaction. Nature's dialectic, I sup-pose. The Yes and No principle. The difficulty is to recognize the mark you're looking for and then to relate it to the sort of proof a jury wants."

With that Bobby departed, leaving a very agitated and dis-turbed young man behind him. By now the hour was late, and in spite of the hasty snack of bread and cheese he had allowed himself—the pickled onions had been an imaginative addition for the benefit of a rather too important-looking head waiter—Bobby was hungry as well as tired. He hoped Olive would have something waiting for him. It was a hope proved well founded. Olive had managed—she alone knows how and she never told—to get hold of some sausages, and so 'sausage and mash', that dreadfully vulgar but not unsatisfying dish, was waiting and ready and on the table before he had even time to wash his hands.

There was one interruption at the end of his meal. Inspector Simons 'phoned through to ask if the visit to Noel Lake's restaurant had proved fruitful.

"Well, he did say one thing," Bobby answered, "that may mean quite a lot. No, I'm not telling you. I want you to work on your own lines. I'll send you a full account of our talk though, and if anything in it strikes you the same way, then I shall begin to take notice. Or if you dig up anything in the way of confirmation. But it's too much in the air at present and very likely it's entirely irrelevant, merely a wild goose I've started."

Simons did not much like this notion of being set to search the record of the talk with Noel to find in it whatever it was had struck Bobby as so significant. Besides, it might really be something Noel had not said, for he knew Bobby had a theory that what was not said, or said untruthfully, was often more revealing than the fullest and frankest statement. So his voice sounded a little annoyed as he asked:

"Did Lake try to pass the buck to any one else, same as the rest of them?"

"Well," Bobby admitted, "he did make rather pointed remarks about Lord Newdagonby. Said he would stick at nothing when his daughter was concerned. I'm not sure how much he meant."

"Back where we started in a way," Simons complained. "Proper ring-a-ring of roses."

Bobby laughed, agreed it was a little like that, and rang off, and Olive, who had heard all this and who, moreover, had been given by Bobby, as he disposed of his 'sausage and mash,' a full account of the talk with Noel remarked, as she cleared the table, that Bobby might just as well have told Simons what it was had struck him. It was clear enough, wasn't it?

Bobby said, oh, yes, it was clear enough, but the point was—how important was it? That was what he wanted to know. Did it strike other people as significant, or was he laying too much emphasis on what might be a mere detail. And totally irrelevant.

Olive said she didn't know, and then she nodded towards the door and pronounced the one word:

"Bed."

But Bobby looked at her with sad reproach.

"My poor child," he said, "don't you know yet that when an investigation of this sort is on the poor, overworked, underpaid, generally ill-used policeman has simply got to forget that any such object as you mentioned even exists? My job for most of the rest of the night is to go over my notes and try to pick out what matters and what doesn't. Which," he added ruefully, "is going to be quite a job with so many cross-currents, and likely to take a lot of hard thinking."

CHAPTER XV
"TOO BAD TO BE TRUE"

OLIVE POINTED OUT with more than a touch of eloquence how greatly Bobby would benefit from a good night's rest and how much clearer his mind would be in the morning. Bobby admitted this, but pointed out with much more than a touch of melancholy resignation that even if he did go to bed he would simply spend wakeful hours tossing restlessly from side to side, never even once closing an eye for so much as a split second. It was indeed Bobby's firm conviction that almost any little thing was liable to make him spend a sleepless night. Olive, for her part, says that she has never once known him keep awake much longer than it took him to get his head on the pillow. But that is neither here nor there, for as Shakespeare has pointed out, things are not as they are, but as we think they are. A profound untruth.

So that was that, as the classicists say, and Bobby settled down to consideration of his notes while Olive went off to make coffee, which, somewhat viciously, she made so strong Hercules himself would probably have retired before it, as from a palpably unequal contest.

"There you are," she said, bringing it to him, "if you won't sleep in your bed, you may as well stay awake out of it. But except for what Mr Lake said, and that mayn't mean anything, I don't see that you've got much to go on. Though I'm sure of one thing."

"What's that?" Bobby asked.

"Mrs Findlay's too bad to be true."

Bobby thought this over as he dallied cautiously with his coffee. Then he said:

"That's very much what I think Noel Lake meant. But not too bad to be false perhaps."

"Is that meant for an epigram?" Olive asked suspiciously.

"Now, now," Bobby protested, "you've no need to say things like that, even if I won't go to bed. Let's consider what we know for certain. The clear and admitted facts, that is, as apart from trying to guess their meaning—I mean, of course, subjecting them to a profound analysis of their logical content."

"My," said Olive, much impressed. "But it means the same thing, doesn't it?"

"It doesn't sound as if it did," Bobby pointed out. "Fact the First: Warnings of a contemplated murder were received but directed to the wrong address. Quite a lot to think over there. Never mind at present. Fact the Second: Peepholes in the party wall of Ivor Findlay's work-room, made at a height which shows they were intended for the use of a smallish person. Another fact is that the only two smallish people concerned are Mrs Jacks, the housekeeper cook, and Miss Grange."

"Didn't Mrs Jacks say she heard typing going on after the time when Mr Findlay must have been attacked?"

"Yes," agreed Bobby, "but we only have Mrs Jacks's word for that, and I'm trying to get hold of bedrock fact. The peepholes are actual fact. The typing is only evidence. Evidence can be rebutted, but facts remain."

"Aren't there any finger-prints on the machine?"

"No, probably gloves were worn. They always are. Next fact. On Findlay's desk there are finger-prints, and Mrs Findlay refuses to let hers be taken for identification. Also gave her flat an extra thorough cleaning this morning. The dabs were probably hers because of being outsize and she is a big woman with big hands, while all the other women in the case are rather small. Another fact is that she seems rather remarkably interested in Lord Byron."

"Well, but," protested Olive, "what's that got to do with it?"

"I don't know," Bobby countered, "I've no idea yet what anything has to do with anything else. I'm collecting facts. About Kitty Grange the facts are that she wants to sell a fur coat, and Mr Findlay got her a good offer. She knows the exact amount—a hundred and one guineas—though she says she refused to ask Findlay, and apparently it was only Findlay who knew. About Charley Acton the only established facts are that he says, truly or not, that he is very happily married, that he has been dancing attendance on Mrs Findlay, though it is Count Ariosto the gossip has been about, and that with him the money motive first appears on the scene."

"Why? How?" Olive protested. "Mr Acton doesn't stand to gain anything by Mr Findlay's death."

"On the face of it, it's a loss," Bobby answered. "Acton says he'll probably have to get a report on the practicability of his invention from some one else. He said he didn't think Findlay's letter expressing approval would do by itself, even if it is enthusiastic. Means delay and another fee. Not very important, but some extra trouble and expense."

"Well," Olive commented, "all that doesn't have much to do with Mr Acton's razor blade. Or getting the capital he wants."

"When there's money anywhere about," declared Bobby in his most oracular tones, "you can't be sure of anything—except that money's what makes things go."

"Yes, but—" began Olive, but Bobby checked her.

"Stick to facts," he said. "Facts first, and then logical deduction." Pretending not to hear Olive's murmured, "You mean guessing," he continued: "It is a fact that this invention of an everlasting razor and the possible extension of the principle to all edged tools may turn out of international importance. It would affect every country and every factory in the world. Naturally it has to stand the test of daily use, but it does seem to have got beyond the laboratory stage."

"Suppose," Olive suggested, "it suddenly becomes fashionable again for men to wear beards? Men do follow fashion so blindly, don't they?" She regarded her clean-shaven husband with a somewhat critical eye. "I think I like a nice moustache on a man," she added, thoughtfully. "Why don't you try?"

"Because," said Bobby firmly, "it's not fashionable. Don't keep up this diversionary action, or you'll have Moscow after you. Now we come to our little Anglo-Italian. Count Ariosto."

"Do you really think he is a Count?"

"Oh, he may be. Don't you remember that waiter in Nice who claimed to be a Russian Prince? It seemed to be true. Anyhow, it doesn't matter—irrelevant whether Ariosto is a Count or anything else. The facts about him are that he is flat-footed, that he plays bridge a good deal—often with Mrs Findlay—and seems to do rather well at it. Also he admits to having had a key of the Dagonby House garden door in his hands at one time."

"You don't mean," Olive asked, "that all that comes in somewhere—flat-footed, bridge with Mrs Findlay, possession of key! I don't see how or where."

"I don't either," Bobby said, "but then I'm not trying—only picking out facts. As for Lord Newdagonby, the only certain things about him are that he thinks a lot of his daughter—an unattractive person I should have said, but that's clearly not his idea. It is a fact, too, that he was greatly disturbed by the 'phone messages that seem to have started all this business and that he took them seriously—so seriously that, another fact, he played a silly trick over those pearl beads so as to bring me into it without having to make a formal complaint. Most likely he thought that with his position and influence he could get me to look into it on the quiet. Stupid, but then I take him to be one of those abnormally clever men who are abysmally stupid in other ways. Consoling for the rest of us who aren't abnormally clever."

"But with a flair?" suggested Olive.

"Oh, that's all rot," growled Bobby, always slightly uneasy when reference was made to this mysterious quality he knew nothing about but was supposed to possess. "Another fact in connection with him is that there does seem to have been a kitchen knife, of the sort used by the murderer, knocking about his study, and that it isn't clear what has become of it."

"But you can't think Lord Newdagonby is the murderer?" Olive protested.

"I never think any one is the murderer till I know," Bobby retorted. "But I do think murder would mean little to him as against his daughter's happiness. But that's wandering from fact to theory. Well, come to Noel Lake. About him the facts are that he had a row with Ivor Findlay over Findlay's behaviour to Miss Grange, and that the murder weapon carried a bit of paper almost certainly torn from one of the Isle du Lac restaurant menus. That has still to be proved by the experts, but I think we may be sure of it for what it is worth."

"Not very much," Olive said. "Any one can tear corners off menus."

"There is also one general fact to remember," Bobby continued. "Any reference to blackmail, any mention of the word, seems to have an oddly upsetting effect on some of these people, as if it held some hidden significance of some sort or another."

"Blackmail is always a possible motive, isn't it?" Olive observed thoughtfully.

"Finally," Bobby went on, "there's Mrs Tinsley, who strikes me as a rather deceptive little person. She gave me the idea that she was anything but the fluffy type she was trying to appear. Her flat hadn't any sort of frivolous society air. There are some women who try to combine very solid intelligence with sex appeal."

"It's awfully mean of them if they do," said Olive indignantly. "You ought to be Honest."

Bobby nodded approvingly and said he thought so, too. Then he continued:

"She seems to be the last person to have seen Noel Findlay alive. She admits it, but says it was private business and she doesn't intend to tell us what it was. If the chap on the beat hadn't noticed the number of her car, we might never even have heard of her. Ought to be worth a commendation. I must remember that."

"Isn't it Mrs Tinsley he was said to be flirting with?" Olive asked.

"Yes, but there again, it's only evidence—hearsay evidence. No direct proof. Finally—"

"But there isn't any one else, is there?" Olive interrupted, surprised. "You said 'finally' before."

"There's Ivor Findlay," Bobby answered.

"But it's he who was murdered," protested Olive.

"That's the fact about him—the important fact. Another fact is that one cage had two live guinea pigs in it, and the other cage was empty."

"You can't possibly mean that that has anything to do with it?"

"I told you before," Bobby said severely, "I'm only recording facts for the moment. All the relevant facts as far as I know them. Though I don't know if they are all relevant to Ivor Findlay's murder. But I think it's fairly clear we've got the names of all directly concerned and equally clear that one of them must be the murderer—or murderess."

CHAPTER XVI
"IT'S ALL AWFULLY DIFFICULT"

After all Bobby was able to secure an hour or two of sleep and yet have a more or less satisfactory plan of campaign ready to show his colleagues.

"Something to work on," he told Olive in the morning, and added reproachfully: "There's no red ink in the house."

"What do you want red ink for?" asked Olive, hurrying to get breakfast ready before there arrived the daily woman who took so little pains to hide her conviction that Olive existed only in order to get in other people's way—the people who really had work to do.

"Good gracious," exclaimed Bobby, pausing with razor upheld—he was in the act of shaving—"don't you know yet that red ink is essential to every self-respecting report."

"Well, there's some on your writing-table," Olive told him.

"Oh, is there? I never thought of looking there," said Bobby, deflated, and Olive remarked that it was just like him, and how long would he be? Because breakfast was ready and waiting.

Bobby said he was ready, too, but he didn't know if he could spare time to eat anything, there was so much to be done, so much to be set in motion.

Olive said very firmly that she had never heard such nonsense in her life, and Bobby was on the whole inclined to agree.

Accordingly, he settled himself at the table, and though there very busy, nevertheless found time to go over his notes again.

"The beginning of it," he told either himself or Olive, it wasn't quite clear which, "seems to have been this odd business of 'phone calls talking about murder but naming the wrong person. How far are they relevant? If they were taken seriously, was the husband's murder a precaution to save the wife's life? Were they part of a prepared plan of some sort or merely used by the murderer as a kind of incidental cover? Nothing to show who was responsible, but all the same I'm going to work on its being one of this little group of people.

It hardly seems likely when they are all so mixed up with one another that there can be some one else who has never been mentioned."

"Well, anyhow," Olive pointed out, "Miss Grange can't have made the calls, because she took one, didn't she? And wasn't Mrs Jacks there at the time? So it wasn't her either."

But Bobby shook his head.

"Can't take that for granted," he said. "Miss Grange may have been giving herself an alibi. No independent proof there was in fact any such call at that time. And what Mrs Jacks says is that she had gone out to do some shopping and had just come back that minute for something she had forgotten. So it is possible her absence had been counted on and the idea had been to induce suspicion, not to dispel it."

"Well, I don't see how you are ever going to find out who it was," Olive remarked, starting to clear the table because she thought it was now time for Bobby to get off—there was plenty to do in the flat, goodness knew.

"If you want to know anything," Bobby remarked as he began to gather his things together, "the best way is to ask those who do know."

"Expecting them to tell you?" Olive asked, not without sarcastic intent.

"They'll tell all right," Bobby assured her. "They always do, especially when they try not to. The difficulty is to recognize it, and then to condition it to judge and jury level. A pernickety lot," he added, not without reproach.

"Tried it yet?" Olive asked.

"Not been much time so far," Bobby pointed out. "I asked Noel Lake. He said it wasn't him, and he did produce an alibi. Said he was in Scotland at the time. Not that it does to take too much notice of alibis. Perfectly true that there's nothing like an alibi, and equally true that an alibi is often nothing like the truth."

"Even if you do get some one to admit they thought Mrs Findlay was in danger of being murdered and wanted to warn her," asked Olive, "how does that help when it wasn't her but her husband who was killed?"

"One possibility," Bobby said, "is that she made the calls herself if she had murder in her own mind. A way perhaps of working herself up to it, of justifying what she was thinking of doing by pretending to herself that it was what he was meaning to do to her. She may even have thought she had reason to suspect he really was intending to."

"That's getting awfully difficult," protested Olive.

"It's all awfully difficult," Bobby agreed, "and Mrs Findlay very much so in herself. More than difficult to know what to make of her with her declared intention to find herself in sin as she had failed to do in religion. But not in crime, because crime's only vulgar. But would she think murder was among the vulgar crimes, or would she call it tragedy?"

"I think she might," Olive agreed in her turn. "She might see herself as a kind of Deborah or Judith in private life."

"I was thinking more of another Old Testament character—Eve."

"Eve didn't kill any one," Olive pointed out.

"But she ate of the fruit of the tree of good and evil," Bobby said. "Led to killing. Lots of it. Another thing about Mrs Findlay is that when the word blackmail crops up, as it has done once or twice, it's always in connection with her. Blackmail might come under her definition of sin that isn't merely vulgar crime. Still, why should she bother about using blackmail to get a husband? With her money and position she could have bought one practically anywhere, any day."

"What a horrid thing to say," protested Olive indignantly.

"Murder's a horrid business," Bobby pointed out, "and it's murder we're talking about. What the Findlay woman says is that she wants to find herself, and I'm wondering if she's succeeded and if so what it is she's found."

"I don't see what any one can do about that," Olive remarked.

"Watch and collect facts, both old and new," Bobby answered. "One of the first things will be to find out all we can about Mrs Jacks and her peepholes and about Count Ariosto. He seemed startled when the word blackmail cropped up as if it had some sort of significance for him. Also I think he both much dislikes Mrs Findlay and is mortally afraid of her. Is it conceivable she's been blackmailing him? Then, too, Miss Grange will have to be asked how she knew the exact price offered for her fur coat if she hadn't seen or spoken to Findlay that morning. That may mean that if she's lying about it, she, not Mrs Tinsley, was the last person to see him—apart, of course, from the murderer whoever that was. Which may mean also that one or both of them may have told less than they know."

"There doesn't seem anything to connect it up," Olive remarked. "It would be a lot simpler if it had been Mrs Findlay who got killed."

"So it would, only it wasn't," Bobby retorted. "And it's what we have to think of. All of it must fit in somewhere—guinea pigs, winnings at bridge, everything. I ought to get Professor Haynes's report on the guinea pigs soon. By the way, he has let us have a copy of his report on Acton's invention of the everlasting razor blade. Quite enthusiastic, especially about the prospect of applying it to all edged tools, if the present resulting brittleness can be got over."

"Doesn't that affect the razor blades?"

"Oh, yes. Only there's no great strain on a blade when you're using it. You may have to be a bit careful in drying it and so on. Then there's Mrs Tinsley, who was probably the last to see Findlay, but won't say what her business was."

"She may have all sorts of reasons she doesn't want to talk about," Olive said.

"She may, but there may have been one that was urgent and that may have been murder."

"Had she any motive?"

"None known, but between man and woman there is always one possible motive. Till we know more about her, she has to be rated fairly high in the list of suspects."

With that Bobby departed to set in train the various lines of inquiry he had sketched out, and this task was hardly completed and various plain-clothes men given their instructions when he was informed that Professor Haynes had called. He proved, when introduced into Bobby's room, to be a tubby little man, rather smartly dressed, looking indeed more like a prosperous business-man who was accustomed to do himself well than the conventional professor of common imagination. But Bobby did not know that Professor Haynes was a famous gourmet in the correct sense of that much misunderstood word, and that his opinion on the merits of a wine was regarded with deep respect. It was said that on one occasion he had narrowly escaped death from apoplexy when an American visitor had informed him that on account of the difference in price, French wines could not compete with those from California.

In answer to Bobby's questions he repeated that he had the highest opinion of Acton's invention. Immense possibilities. When the company was floated, he intended to get in 'on the ground floor'.

"Acton," he explained, "has promised to let me have an initialled application form. Very good of him considering what I wrote a few months ago in an issue of 'Matter, Man and Mind'. I described him as a charlatan, I'm sorry to say, and I still think his scheme for an artificial radio-active satellite to revolve round Mars and make it habitable is mere fantasy—stuff for a boy's story, Jules Verne stuff. I must say he seems to bear no grudge, and in fact he told me it was precisely because of my attack on him that he wanted my report—to make it plain there was no prejudice in his favour on my side."

"Yes, I see," Bobby said. "Very interesting. Have you come to any decision about those guinea pigs? I mean, those apparently missing from the cage in Findlay's room."

"A dreadful affair," the Professor said. "Stabbed in the back, wasn't he? Have you any idea who did it?"

"We haven't made a great deal of progress," Bobby admitted. "A great many lines to follow up, and all of them contradicting each other."

"Look out for the woman," the professor advised. "Where there's a woman, there's trouble. The poor fellow's reputation in that way was no secret."

"So I understand," Bobby answered. "About the guinea pigs."

"Got them on your mind?" The professor smiled. "Very mysterious. It's really what I came to see you about. You want to know the cause of death? But you don't know if they really were dead. You haven't found bodies?"

"No, there's nothing but an empty cage," Bobby admitted.

"Well, you're asking rather a lot, aren't you?" suggested the professor, still smiling. "I'm to discover a possible cause of death of two guinea pigs which perhaps aren't dead at all? Or even were never there at all. I don't see quite why you think they might have been."

"An empty cage," Bobby repeated. "I've a"—he only just stopped himself in time from saying 'flair'—"I've a feeling," he said instead.

"Probably you don't know," the professor went on, "that Findlay was carrying out research into the after-effects of radio-activity. In my humble opinion he was working on entirely wrong lines. Not that he was at all explicit. Very secretive, very secretive in all his work. His own private iron curtain so to speak. He had an article in 'Matter, Man, and Mind' last month that did suggest some interesting possibilities, but that was all. Far too vague to form any real opinion, but clearly he was starting from a totally unproved hypothesis. Occasionally very important results can follow from what's really no more than a lucky guess."

"Radio-activity can be pretty lethal, can't it?"

"It can—and is," agreed the professor grimly. "In ways we don't fully understand. If poor Findlay had subjected his guinea pigs to some form of ray or injection, they would very likely have died, and he may have wished to get rid of the bodies in his mania for secrecy. Not unlikely. You've told me all the facts?"

"All that I know."

"Well, Mr Owen, I won't deny I think the deduction you've drawn from those facts rather doubtful, to say the least. But I'll certainly try it out if you wish. Only you know it'll be fairly expensive. I charge for my time."

"I know," Bobby said glumly, "and if I'm all wrong I shall get it in the neck. They'll want a long report justifying the expenditure, and they won't like it when they get it."

"Oh, well, that's your affair," said the professor heartlessly. "I should like to see Findlay's notes. It might help me to make out what he was driving at and what experiments he may have made. Could you let me have then?"

"I understand there are none or very few," Bobby answered. "And what there are are written in some kind of private shorthand or cypher. In any case, they would have to be regarded as the private property of Mrs Findlay, except in so far as we could claim that they might throw some light on the murder. We should have to prove it, too, because I doubt whether we should find Mrs Findlay very co-operative."

That ended the interview, and after the professor had departed Bobby remained sitting there for long enough, thinking over what he had been told, and trying to decide whether or no it had any relevance to the concrete problem he had to solve of finding sufficient evidence to justify an arrest.

"And if," he told himself gloomily, "there's anything in these blackmailing hints, there may soon be another problem for us to deal with."

CHAPTER XVII
"IT MUST BE TAKEN SERIOUSLY"

A day or two passed in the usual routine of such an investigation. C.I.D. men were kept busy here and there, searching for any small indication or hint that might lead towards the truth, interviewing various people, all of whom had either nothing or far too much to say. All this, as Bobby told Olive, with little apparent result.

"We've got a few facts," he said, "but they don't seem to lead anywhere much. Rather a dead end at present. We've made some inquiries about Mrs Jacks. She was married in a small village near Aylesbury. The husband is dead, and there was one daughter. Then we know Findlay was a frequent visitor to Mrs Tinsley's flat. The porter says he was there three or four times a week. But that doesn't take us much farther forward, and we could have guessed as much anyhow. Except perhaps that it does seem as if his connection with her was rather more serious than with most of his other lady friends. No new development otherwise."

"I suppose," Olive said, looking a little superior, "you never thought of asking Mrs Brett, did you?"

"Mrs Brett?" repeated Bobby, puzzled, for that was the name of the daily woman of the passing moment. "What's she got to do with it?"

"You," explained Olive.

"Me?" Bobby repeated. "What on earth are you getting at?"

"She works here, comes here every day," Olive pointed out. "So she sees you every day, and so of course, she knows all about it. All her friends regard her as getting it 'straight from the horse's mouth'. The horse," Olive added, with a kind smile, "being you. And that's better than being another sort of smaller animal with a shorter name."

"She's not turning amateur detective and using my name, is she?" Bobby asked, slightly alarmed.

"Very likely she tells all her friends she is your chief assistant," Olive answered. "And one of them has another friend who knows another who works for some one who knows the Actons, and what it comes to is that Mrs Findlay and Mr Acton are going to get married, though they're not saying anything yet."

Bobby was not often taken aback, but this time he was very much so.

"If that's true, I wonder if it is," he said slowly. Olive expressed no opinion. Bobby said: "It may be only gossip."

"Haven't you always said in your lectures no one should ever despise gossip?"

"What a man says in his lectures isn't evidence," Bobby retorted, but he had still a very worried air. "Most likely it's all nonsense," he decided. "But it'll have to be looked into."

"Could it—" Olive asked hesitatingly, "could it be a motive?"

"For Findlay's murder?" Bobby said. "But which of them? It seems like deliberately asking to be suspected. Acton was certainly dancing attendance on her in rather a marked way, but he also took care to tell me he was very happily married."

"If he is married already," Olive said uneasily, "he can't, can he? I mean, not marry Mrs Findlay."

"Not while his wife is still alive," Bobby said.

"Only he could, if anything happened to her," Olive remarked, almost to herself.

"He would be free then," Bobby said, "just as Mrs Findlay is free now something has happened to her husband. You know, Olive, I don't like this. I don't like it at all. It does suggest Mrs Acton may be meant to follow Ivor Findlay. Only it's incredible. Too open, too barefaced. Yet sometimes people do incredible things and get away with it just because they are incredible. And then I'm not sure but that you couldn't call Mrs Findlay incredible."

"Do you think Mr Acton can be in love with her? You said he was dancing attendance on her?"

"As a personal opinion," Bobby declared, "and though there's no accounting for tastes, I can't imagine any one being in love with her. I suppose she may show a different side to her father, who does seem fond of her. But she gives me the idea of being a cold-blooded bully, the sort who would make the ideal Fascist or Communist—'Think as I do or take what's coming to you.' That sort of thing."

"Well, she can't seem like that to Mr Acton," Olive said. "I'm sure there's something in Mrs Brett's story."

"What the daily help doesn't know, isn't knowledge," suggested Bobby. He went on: "There's been an odd hint of blackmail once or twice in this business. Is it cropping up again?"

"You can't possibly think she could blackmail two men, one after the other, into marrying her?" Olive asked incredulously, and Bobby agreed it didn't seem likely, but that didn't go for much in such an entirely unlikely world as this, and he thought he would try to find time to pay a visit to Abels End, the village where the Actons lived. It might be possible to learn something there.

"It's on the way to the place near Aylesbury where Mrs Jacks was married," Bobby remarked. "I think I would like to have a go myself at seeing if there isn't a chance of picking up something there the local people may have overlooked. You can never give any one else a complete view, background and all, and often it's the background that matters. Something that happened years ago working itself out to-day. It's like that sometimes. I could get off to-morrow perhaps or next day."

But next day there was a message from Lord Newdagonby requesting an early call, rather in the manner of a managing director requiring the prompt presence of a somewhat unsatisfactory junior clerk. Bobby, however, since he had more important things to think about, ignored the tone of the message, and answered that he would come immediately. Hanging up, he said to Simons, with whom he had been discussing the case and recent developments or rather lack of them:

"Sounds to me as if his lordship was getting a bit rattled. If I can manage to rattle him a bit more, there may be a chance to get somewhere."

He departed accordingly, and in the Dagonby House library found Lord Newdagonby prowling up and down, looking with his long, thin, bent form, his small piercing eyes, his enormous nose, more than ever like some hovering vulture. Kitty Grange had brought Bobby into the room, and Lord Newdagonby wasted no time in preliminaries, but snapped out:

"It's begun again, and it's got to be stopped." He paused to glare at Bobby. "Unbearable. I've rung up the Home Office—pack of idiots."

"Oh, I wouldn't say that, really I wouldn't," Bobby protested mildly, and a trifle smugly, for once or twice certain Home

Office officials had seemed inclined to suggest much the same of the whole of the police force. So now he felt he was ladling out coals of fire in defending them. "What's begun again?" he asked.

"I told you, didn't I?" the other snapped. "Those 'phone messages. I've had one myself—first thing this morning. And Kitty had two yesterday—Miss Grange, I mean."

"What were they about?" Bobby asked.

"Good Heavens, man, what do you suppose?" demanded Lord Newdagonby even more angrily than before.

"I never suppose when facts are available," Bobby retorted, and, somewhat hastily, Kitty intervened.

"They were just like the others," she said. "They said it was to warn us Mrs Findlay was going to be murdered. It"—she was a little pale now—"it's upsetting, I mean after . . . after . . ."

She left the sentence unfinished. That she was indeed 'upset' was sufficiently plain. So was Lord Newdagonby for that matter. But while Kitty was nervous and excited, Lord Newdagonby was angry and—Bobby felt sure—frightened. He threw himself into a chair, glared at Bobby afresh, and demanded:

"What have you done so far? My son-in-law murdered in my own house and nothing done, nothing at all."

"No effort is being spared to bring to justice those responsible," Bobby answered in his most official tone, and when Lord Newdagonby twisted his features into that sneer for which nature seemed specially to have designed them, he added still more formally: "Certain clues are being followed up."

"What are they?"

"That, of course, cannot be explained at present," Bobby answered. The sneer became still more pronounced. "I could mention one perhaps. Guinea pigs—possibly dead, certainly vanished."

"Guinea-pigs," repeated Lord Newdagonby in what would have been an intimidating roar had his small rather soft, low-pitched voice been capable of producing any such effect. "What in blazes have guinea pigs—dead, alive or missing—got to do with it?"

"Now that," said Bobby, beaming on the angry peer, "is just exactly what I want to know if only somebody would tell me."

"Bah," said his lordship, comprehensively.

"Exactly," said Bobby, resisting an impulse to point out that it was not sheep but guinea pigs that had been mentioned. He drew up a chair to the writing-table, produced note-book and pencil, and said: "May I have details of these new threats or warnings?"

In answer to his questions, Kitty was unable to give the exact time beyond the fact that one call had been in the morning of the previous day, and one early in the evening. She had been too 'upset', to use her own expression, to think of noting the exact time or the precise wording. Nor had she recognized the voice, though she did think it perhaps resembled that she had heard on the previous occasions. So did the wording used, which was to the effect that Mrs Findlay was in immediate danger of being murdered. The message received by Lord Newdagonby that morning had been slightly different, and he was certain it had been a woman speaking.

"Undoubtedly a woman," he repeated. "Hysterical. Mere abuse chiefly, and then there was a sort of sob or gasp and the receiver banged down. The exact words were: 'Tell that bitch of yours she'll get the same she did to him and not so long to wait either'."

"A direct accusation of murder," Bobby said gravely. "It must be taken seriously."

CHAPTER XVIII
"WELL, SIR, WAS IT YOU?"

AT THIS, Lord Newdagonby and Kitty exchanged uneasy glances. They evidently found the remark as disturbing as unexpected. Bobby asked a few more questions. It appeared that the only other persons in the house at the times of the receipt of each of the three warnings had been Mrs Jacks and the daily help. Not that that was of much importance, one way or the other. Mrs Jacks, for instance, could easily have slipped out to the nearest public 'phone box and been back again before Kitty had, according to her own story, recovered from being 'upset', to use her general expression for describing her feelings at the renewal of these mysterious and ominous warnings. Moreover, queer tricks can be played with extensions. Lord Newdagonby remained positive that the voice he had heard had been a woman's, disguised, he thought, but certainly a woman's. Kitty was not sure. It had been an odd, high voice, probably disguised, but whether man's or woman's she could not say. Lord Newdagonby took the opportunity of intimating very plainly that he had a poor opinion of any detective or police organization incapable of doing anything so simple as tracing a telephone call. Bobby said he had noticed that most people had a poor opinion of most other people. He had even observed a tendency in that direction in himself, and he looked rather hard at Lord Newdagonby as he said this. He added mildly that the automatic system put certain difficulties in the way, but if Lord Newdagonby had any suggestions to offer, he, Bobby, in particular, and the police all over the world in general, would be exceedingly grateful.

Lord Newdagonby said very angrily that it wasn't his business, and Bobby said, that of course there was one method and a very good method too. You could ask.

"Ask who? Ask what?" Lord Newdagonby demanded.

"Ask all concerned if they had done the 'phoning?"

"I suppose you expect them to tell?" said Lord Newdagonby with his very best, high-powered sneer.

"Oh, everyone always tells," Bobby assured him. "Always. The difficulty is to know it when they do."

"Well, you had better try," snapped the other, more contemptuous than ever.

"Well, sir, was it you?"

"Was I what?"

"Was it you 'phoned?"

Lord Newdagonby had been sitting half-doubled up in his chair. Now he drew himself up. His body was so long and lean, this took him quite a long time. He said in a tone again meant to be thunderous, but still only small and now even squeaky with indignation:

"Am I to understand you are asking that seriously?"

"Certainly. Police are always serious, very serious in a case like this."

"Then I refuse to answer."

"Thank you," said Bobby amiably. "That in itself is an answer." He turned to Kitty: "Was it you made these calls?"

"Of course not," she answered, puzzled. "How could I when I took them?"

Bobby refrained from pointing out that for that, or even for the calls themselves, there was no evidence in the first two cases save her own word. Instead he said that in view of what had happened he would arrange to post a plain-clothes man in the house, if that would be acceptable. An ungracious assent to this suggestion was made, and Bobby also promised to take such other steps as might seem likely to be useful.

"We will try as far as possible to keep some sort of watch on all the women whose names have been mentioned," he said. "We shall have to do it very carefully, and it can't be very efficient."

"I don't suppose for a moment it will be," Lord Newdagonby snapped. "But why not?"

"Because if we made it too complete it would only defeat itself," Bobby answered. "It's not only a question of who is actually making these threats, but of who is meant. Last time, Mrs Findlay's name was given, but it was Mr Findlay who died. Now it's Mrs Findlay again apparently, but again some one else may be meant."

Lord Newdagonby looked thoughtful. He evidently found this suggestion also somewhat unwelcome. Kitty had become rather pale. Plainly she liked it no better. Bobby rose to go. Kitty came to see him to the front door. She said as they went:

"It's all most awfully upsetting. I can't think of anything else."

"Information has reached us," Bobby said, "that Mrs Findlay and Mr Acton intend to get married soon."

"Who told you that?" Kitty asked quickly.

"It's what we call 'information received'," Bobby explained. "We never give names, you know."

"It's such nonsense," Kitty declared angrily. But she seemed a little excited. "Sibby's always saying things she doesn't really mean. It's just talk."

"Is talk ever just talk?" asked Bobby. "Talk is a way of acting, isn't it? And sometimes what you say has its own kind of compelling force. Every policeman knows that. Make a threat and feel bound to carry it out. Has Mrs Findlay told you she might possibly marry Mr Acton?"

"How can she? He's married already."

"So was she, but not now," Bobby replied, and Kitty stared at him in pale horror. "Yes, I know," he said, answering now not her spoken words but that pale horror she showed so plainly. "But everything must be considered, especially when mysterious messages are received making direct accusations, even though we can't be sure who is meant. A woman, of course, because of the expression used, but which woman?"

"But what other woman could it mean?" Kitty asked. Bobby did not answer. She went on: "I don't think you ought to pay any attention. Of course, it's awfully upsetting, but I expect it's only some one being spiteful. People don't understand Sibby. It's what she's doing herself. Trying to understand. She's not bad or wicked the way she pretends. It's just that—trying to understand."

"Trying to understand what?"

"Things—herself. Really at bottom, she wants to be good."

"Yes," said Bobby doubtfully, in fact very doubtfully.

"Well, she does," Kitty insisted. "Most people never trouble about it. They just potter along. I suppose I do. But Sibby always has, always. She went into a sisterhood once. She didn't like it. She said it was only being one of a flock of sheep. So she came out to find for herself her own way."

"Her own way where?"

"To understand, she says she wants to know—to know what she is and what everything is, and so she must try everything."

"Another Eve to eat of the fruit of the knowledge of good and evil. Suppose she has found it easier to learn about the last?"

"You mean you do think it was her?"

"My dear young lady," Bobby said, "in these cases I always have to spend half my time explaining that every one is suspect till cleared. When every one else is cleared, then the one left is guilty. Not that we can always produce legal proof. That's different."

"Do you suspect me?" Kitty asked.

"I said every one," Bobby answered; and he watched her closely, for as yet he had had no explanation of how it was Kitty had known the exact amount of the offer for her fur coat made to a man she denied having seen or spoken to that morning.

But he felt that the time had not yet come to question her about that. She was saying now:

"There's Lord Newdagonby? Do you suspect him?"

"The same thing applies. Do you?"

"Do I what?"

"Suspect that perhaps he himself may be the murderer?"

"Of course I don't!" she cried with angry resentment. "You've no right to suggest such a thing."

"Why not? Why shouldn't you suspect him?"

"Why should I? Why should you or anyone? It's silly. Why should he murder Ivor?"

"I think he is very fond of his daughter. Her life was threatened. He may have thought he knew where the threat came from, he may have believed it was a true warning the 'phone gave. And so have taken his own way to end it."

"I think you're being horrible, I think it's horrible to say such things," she protested, and now she was trembling a little.

"Something very horrible has happened," Bobby answered gravely. "Isn't that what you ought to say—and remember?"

"What did you mean just now," she asked, "when you said that about not knowing who the 'phone message meant?"

"Well, there was no name, was there?"

"You think perhaps it was me was meant?" she asked in a low voice.

"There's no reason to think so," Bobby answered. "Every possible precaution will be taken."

He went away then, a good deal disturbed by this new development. At the Yard he wrote out a report to be added to the growing dossier of the case. To Inspector Simons, coming to consult him on the following up of some of the different lines of the investigation, he said:

"We've got to take this 'phone business seriously. Very possibly it's mere malice or some of those semi-imbeciles who are always turning up when any sensational case gets into the papers. But I don't at all like this story of Mrs Findlay and Acton intending to get married."

"Sounds crazy to me," grumbled Simons. "Asking for it, in a way. Telling every one she had a motive. But then she sounds crazy anyhow. What's she mean? Understand herself? What for? I don't reckon she knows. What's next?"

"Routine," Bobby answered. "Keep on watching and trying to dig up what we can. I've an idea this thing started years ago. To-morrow I think I'll take a trip to Abels End, where the Actons live. Acton went out of his way to claim to be happily married, and I should like to know if that's the general impression. It's a small village, and they ought to know—they generally do. Not much they don't know about each other in these small places."

"You can't always tell," Simons said wisely. "Darby and Joan outside, and cat and dog indoors."

"I'll put my trust in village gossip," Bobby answered. "And I'll try to find the time to go on to where Mrs Jacks lived after her marriage before they came to London. There are those peepholes to remember, though of course they may have nothing to do with her—or the murder. Clear, too, she could be doing this queer 'phoning business, though again there's nothing to show. I can't help feeling she's in it somehow."

ABELS END is a small and picturesque village in what, before the days of cars, motor buses, cycles, was a lonely and not easily accessible district. Now motor buses roar through it every hour on their way between two neighbouring towns, the nearer of which is on the main line to London. Less than two hours comfortable travel from cottage door to Piccadilly Circus. But this has in no way affected the lovely view across the village green with the old Elizabethan cottages and in the distance the ancient church. A drawing of it had once appeared in a London Sunday paper—to the immeasurable pride of the villagers, even though most of them had had that view before their eyes all their lives and never given it a second glance. The drawing had been reproduced on a post card and was much in evidence at the two or three small village shops.

So when a day or two later, as soon as his other work permitted, Bobby arrived in the village he had an excuse to start a chat in the small general shop and post office where these postcards were most prominently displayed. He bought one or two, chatted about them and the beauties of the village, and presently learned that it was Mr Acton, 'an inventor gentleman', who lived in the house on the hill above the church. He also learned that the Actons were well liked and respected in the village and always ready to take part and help in any of the village activities. Unfortunately, as they were Roman Catholics, they could not share in those more strictly associated with the church.

"Disappointing for Vicar," explained the post-mistress, "and him so hard put to it to keep the congregation up and Sunday school and all seeing Mrs Acton going off so regular to the Roman Catholics every Sunday, and weekdays as well very often."

Bobby agreed that this was hard luck on the Vicar, especially when Mr Acton was so well known through his inventions. He remarked that he expected visitors to the village often asked about him. The post-mistress said that was indeed so. Only the other day there had been a lady asking quite a lot about him and Mrs Acton, too.

"Very curious like," said the post-mistress, eyeing Bobby now a little doubtfully, as if she thought he were showing the same quality in an unusual degree.

In all this there had been no hint or suggestion, though Bobby had left the way open once or twice, that Mr and Mrs Acton were anything but a model married couple. So Bobby changed the subject to more general topics, such as the weather, and then strolled off to the village public-house, the Abels End Arms, for a glass of beer and a chat. There he was told much the same thing, learning once again that the Actons were Roman Catholics, and that Mrs Acton regularly, and Mr Acton frequently, attended their own church in the neighbouring town.

"Seems wrong to me," pronounced the landlady, who served him. "What I say is people ought to be more broad-minded like, taking good money out of the village is what it comes to."

Bobby remarked it was a pity more people couldn't take a broad-minded view and what a really pretty village this was. He had never seen one more charming and picturesque. He thought he would take a stroll round and secure a few snapshots. By the way, a lady he knew had told him what a lovely little place this was. He wondered if she had been recently. He gave a brief description of Mrs Findlay, but the landlady shook her head. No one like that had been recently so far as she knew. Bobby produced two small photographs he had secured, one of Kitty Grange and one of Mrs Tinsley. The landlady recognized Mrs Tinsley's photograph at once.

"That's her," she said. "Asked a lot of questions when she came in for a bite of lunch. Said she would like to settle down in a quiet place like this, but as I told her, there isn't nowhere to let for miles. Snapped up immediate if one comes empty."

Bobby said it was like that almost everywhere. Leaving his car in the Abels End Arms yard, he walked across the village green to the church and thence on and up the hill towards the

Acton dwelling—Abels End Cottage he noticed it was called. The path he followed led past the house, on by a ruinous, deserted cottage, and then over the hill.

From what had once been this cottage garden, now a desolation of weeds and straggling grass, there was a fine view over the village and the country beyond. Bobby sat down on an old tree-stump that had apparently at one time been within the cottage garden, now only to be distinguished from the hillside by a greater luxuriance of wild and unchecked growth. It was a fine, warm, sunny day, but Bobby was in no mood to enjoy either the sunshine or the view.

What, he asked himself uneasily, was the meaning of this abrupt re-entry of Mrs Tinsley on the scene? Why had she come here making inquiries about the Actons and more especially about Mrs Acton? Was there any connection between this recent visit and the visit she had paid to Findlay before his death on some errand or for some purpose she had refused to explain? Disturbing, too, disturbing in the extreme to know that the Actons were practising members of the Roman Catholic church. For that seemed to rule out any chance of a divorce to make possible marriage between Acton and Mrs Findlay, if it were true that such a thing was in contemplation.

Only through divorce or death can a second marriage become possible. Death had freed Mrs Findlay, and was it going to be death once more that would free Charles Acton?

It was such dark, unhappy thoughts that possessed him as he sat there in the warm sunshine, conscious of ominous possibilities and responsibilities he saw small hope of meeting with success. For police action can be taken only on accomplished fact, not on doubt or on suspicion, however well founded these may seem. Presently he saw a woman come out of Abels End Cottage. Two small children were with her. A common enough sight—common-place indeed. A mother with two little, laughing children by her side, sometimes leaving her to run after some treasure they had noticed, and then running back to take her hand or show for her admiration what they had found. The sentimentalist, but fortunately there are few in these days, might call it the loveliest sight on earth, and all the lovelier for being as yet not too rare.

But to Bobby as he watched the little party, mother and children, slowly making its way down the hill-side to the village, it seemed they went from the light and sunshine on the hill to the brooding shadows lower down where the light no longer lay and into which soon they vanished from his sight.

He turned his thoughts to Mrs Findlay, that amateur of evil, that seeker after knowledge by a road that might lead, Bobby felt, to a knowledge of little worth, to a knowledge not of truth but of falsehood.

He roused himself from such troubling thoughts, and looking round he wondered idly why this cottage had been allowed to fall into such ruin. The landlady of the Abels End Arms had declared that there was no vacant habitation for miles around, and yet here was what apparently had been a perfectly good cottage no one had troubled to keep in repair. Even now it would certainly cost no great sum to make it habitable again. Even if no one in the village required accommodation, there is a steady demand for week-end cottages. Especially for those in such a pleasant situation. Lack of labour possibly, Bobby thought. Even the garden could soon be brought back into cultivation, and Bobby noticed that there was a well.

He went across to look at it. Once there had been a high stone surround, but this, like the cottage, was now in ruin, some of the stones of which it had been made lying about near by. It rather looked, Bobby thought, as if there had been wilful damage. Mischievous children perhaps, though the stones looked heavy for children to displace. Bobby noticed too that the well, fairly deep, had no covering. It seemed to have run dry. Dangerous, he told himself. If children did come here to play, a bad accident might easily result.

He went back to the village, collected his car, and drove a mile or so along the London Road till he came to a railway cutting. There, as had been arranged with the local superintendent, punctual to the minute, waited for him the constable stationed at Abels End. Bobby invited him to a seat in the car and drove on slowly, asking a few questions on the way. The answers confirmed much of what he had already learnt. The Actons were well liked in the village. There was not the least hint that their married life was not perfectly happy. They were Roman Catholics, and Mrs Acton was zealous in her support of her church. Mr Acton was less zealous perhaps and a little apt to stay at home on Sundays, but still he attended fairly regularly, and after all he did live outside, well outside the three-mile limit which is sometimes supposed to excuse occasional absence.

Bobby asked if visitors to the village often inquired about Mr Acton and his inventions. The constable said fairly frequently, more especially since there had been so much talk in the papers about his suggestions for manufacturing an artificial, radioactive satellite or planet to warm Mars and make it habitable. Yes, there had been a lady in the village a day or two ago, asking quite a lot about the Actons. Bobby described Mrs Findlay and showed his photographs of Kitty Grange and Mrs Tinsley. Again it was Mrs Tinsley who was picked out. The constable had noticed that she went off up the hill towards the Actons' house, but he did not think she called. She might just have gone to look at the old tumble-down cottage up there. She had said something about the village being a lovely place to settle down in.

"Oh, yes," Bobby said, "that reminds me. I took a walk that way myself just now. There's an open well. It's dry but it's quite deep and no covering at all. A little dangerous, don't you think? It looked as if some one had been meddling with the stone parapet round it, too. If children got playing near, one of them might easily fall in."

"That's old Mr Moss's doing," explained the constable. "I've been on at him about it. Only found out the other day. He says it wasn't him took the well cover, but most like that's a lie. Good sound bit of wood such as isn't so easy to get these days. I had a look round his place, but I couldn't identify it. Most like sawn up and used for repairs soon as took. But he had to own up he had been carting some of the stones from the well-head. I told him I was reporting to Mr Acton, and he could be summonsed for wilful damage and such. But Mr Acton said not to bother, if he put the stones back where he got them, in position again. Moss promised faithful, and I'll see he does, though there won't be an excuse he won't think up. A good weight, too, some of them. Wanted them for a new pigsty seemingly."

"I suppose he never troubled his head about the danger to other people," Bobby remarked. "Any one might fall down there in the dark or even simply through carelessness and not looking. Does the cottage belong to Mr Acton? I was wondering why it had been allowed to go to ruin."

"Well, it was like this," the constable explained. "When Mr Acton built his house he had a well sunk, and it tapped the old cottage well. Went dry as a bone. There was talk of the law and damages, only one of the two old people who lived there died, and the other went to live with a daughter. So Mr Acton settled the law talk by buying the cottage. But now he can't let it, along of there being no water. Runs short himself, too, when the weather's a bit dry. So it's just going to rack and ruin."

Bobby remarked that it was a pity with housing so short everywhere. He added that he was much obliged for the very clear answers he had been given. A little disturbing, he had found them, he said. He did not explain why, though the constable was plainly surprised at the observation. Bobby went on to say that if there were any more visitors who seemed unusually interested in the village and its inhabitants, he would like a report made. He would ask the local superintendent if that could be arranged. He would like photos taken, if possible. Of course, the visitor must have no idea it was being done for police purposes. Probably, if that got into the papers, there would be a question in Parliament.

The constable turned pale at this, and Bobby's own voice had sunk to a cautious whisper as he made the suggestion. For a question in Parliament is the present-day equivalent of the ancient thunderbolt from high Olympus. The constable, recovering slightly, said he didn't think his superintendent would much like taking such a risk. Bobby said, no, of course not, but it could be done quite easily and no risk at all. Did the constable know, no doubt it was an extreme demand, but did he, by any chance, know an intelligent boy who could be trusted, and who understood photography?

The constable said, a little doubtfully, that he had a nipper of his own who wasn't any worse than others and liked playing about with his camera.

"Good," said Bobby. "Tell him when he sees a visitor to take a snap quite openly and then offer a card promising to supply any copies required for half a crown or so. Quite likely he'll get an order or two. He might even work up a little business of his own like that. In any case whether he does or not, get him to develop all his snaps and send copies to me. I'll 'phone your people and get their consent."

The constable, much impressed, said it took brains to think up a scheme so simple, easy, safe, and effective. Nor did Bobby, who had learned by experience never to deflate admiration by explanation, tell him that in London streets men were doing just that, and that already it had in one or two cases proved useful to the authorities. There was an international crook of the 'con man' type, who had hitherto always most successfully avoided having his photograph taken, but of whom two or three excellent snaps were now on file at Scotland Yard.

CHAPTER XX
"WAS IT A BOY?"

THE VILLAGE to which Bobby now drove on, the one where Mrs Jacks's marriage had taken place, was of a type very different from Abels End. In the course of years it had changed from its original rustic and self-contained community to what is sometimes called a 'dormitory'—that is, a place where a high proportion of the inhabitants earn their living and spend their working life in a neighbouring town.

Here, then, there was no such continuity of communal memory as can often be found in the true village. Nor were there any postcards of local beauty spots to serve as a start for a friendly chat. Even at police headquarters, generally a veritable mine of local information, the name Jacks was totally unknown. It was only as the most forlorn of forlorn hopes, and because he felt he must do something, however hopeless, however vague a gesture, that Bobby decided to look up the record of Mrs Jacks's marriage in the parish registry.

He had no idea what he could find there to help, but almost the first thing he noticed was that one of the witnesses was a Ferdinand Findlay. A mere coincidence, perhaps, for Findlay is not a very uncommon name, but Bobby never trusted coincidence. Behind coincidence he used to say was almost always cause, and over this coincidence, if such it were, he thought a good deal as he drove home.

"Just as well to look up things yourself when it's at all possible," he told Olive. "Any one who hadn't known the background would very likely never have noticed the names of the witnesses. Or have thought it worth mentioning if they had."

"I don't see how it's going to help," Olive said. "I suppose you've got some idea in your head, but it all seems pretty dim and remote. Like those guinea pigs that weren't there you're always worrying about."

"I'm not," protested Bobby. "I only like things explained. The guinea pigs aren't there, so where are they and why aren't they? That's all. And if there is any connection between witness Findlay some thirty years ago and murdered Findlay the other day—well, I want to know what it is."

Accordingly, the next day found him alighting at the small Monmouthshire station nearest to New Dagonby Hall. On the Dagonby estate surrounding it—still of undiminished size, for the owners of the estate had always been successful merchants and traders as well as landlords—one of the farms was that which had been occupied ever since mediaeval times by a Findlay. First Bobby went to the cottage that served as the village police station. By arrangement, the sergeant in charge of the district was there waiting for him. Naturally the murder had caused much interest and general talk in the district, both because it had taken place in the London home of the great man of the neighbourhood and because the Ferdinand Findlay occupying the ancestral farm was a cousin of the victim.

"Not that we ever saw Mr Ivor down here," the sergeant told Bobby. "Not since his old father's death. Nor did people want. He hadn't a good name in these parts. Mr Ferdinand told him straight he wouldn't be welcome there."

"Mr Ferdinand took over the farm, I suppose," Bobby asked. "Was there any ill feeling over that?"

"Oh, no, Mr Ivor was glad enough to be quit of it by all accounts," the sergeant answered. "Had his own job in London and didn't want to give it up. So that they settled it between them Mr Ferdinand was to carry on. They've never had anything to do with each other since though."

Bobby asked how old Mr Ferdinand was, and learned he was comparatively young. So clearly he was not the Findlay who had acted as witness at Mrs Jacks's marriage. From further questions Bobby learned that there had been two brothers, Ivor, the father of the murdered man, and Ferdinand, presumably the marriage witness. Ivor, the elder of the two, had stayed on the farm, succeeding his father as tenant. Ferdinand had been apprenticed to a Birmingham firm. Both were dead, and each had left one son—the murdered Ivor and the Ferdinand who had taken over the farm on his uncle's death.

"Farming's in the Findlay blood," said the sergeant, "but not in Mr Ivor's seemingly."

Discreetly he hinted that Mr Ivor had, however, taken after his father in one respect.

"The old man was always after the women," the sergeant explained when Bobby asked about this. "Thought more of skirt chasing than the land. They do say he would have been sold up only for marrying a by-blow of his lordship's. But maybe that's only talk and gossip, and I wouldn't mention it to anyone, only to you, sir, being official as you might say."

"I want you to tell me everything, everything," Bobby said. "You never know what may not help."

"Gossip," repeated the sergeant. "Before my time. May be nothing in it."

"There's often something to start gossip," Bobby said. "Not always but often. Do you know if there was in this case?"

"Well, the girl had been in service at Dagonby Hall," the sergeant answered. "And a baby arrived only two or three months after the wedding. That's in the registers here."

"A baby?" Bobby repeated. "Was it a boy? Ivor?"

"That's right. A deal of talk there was, too. But the child died in a year or so, and people forgot. The Mr Ivor that's been murdered up in London was born the same week the other died."

Bobby sat considering this for some minutes in silence. He felt obscurely excited, vaguely aware of meanings and implications he at the moment could not fully grasp. He saw the sergeant looking at him curiously. He said:

"At any rate, there's no doubt about this Ivor being really his father's son?"

"Oh, no," the sergeant agreed. "Old Mr Ivor was very sweet on his wife, by-blow of his lordship's or not, and she kept him up to the mark, too, as long as she lived. Some said she had the whip hand in the money line, along of what his lordship settled on her to keep her tongue still. But there, it's all long ago, and it's hard to know the rights of it."

"It always is," Bobby agreed, "and things that happen long ago sometimes start to work themselves out to-day. Didn't you say the young Ivor had the reputation down here of being like his father in running after women?"

"He had a bad name for it," answered the sergeant. "People haven't forgot either, not about Mary Jacks they haven't."

"Mary Jacks?" Bobby repeated, startled. "Who was she?"

"Buried in the churchyard," the sergeant explained. "Drowned. Accident, the jury brought it in, but there was many believed she did it herself because of what Ivor Findlay had done and left her. But others said it was as much her to blame as him. And some thought maybe it was him did it— pushed her in to still her tongue. None believed it was accident no more than did the jury that brought it in. Being official as accident Vicar let her be buried in the churchyard, though hesitating."

"There's a Mrs Jacks who is Lord Newdagonby's house-keeper in London," Bobby said. "Keep that to yourself for the present. I don't want any more talk than we can help or anything getting into the papers. Mrs Jacks will most likely have to give evidence at the inquest, but that's been adjourned. Do you know anything about her or her family?"

"They were Birmingham people, friends of the Ferdinand Findlays. That's what brought Mrs Jacks here. She was a widow and came to be housekeeper to old Dr Kaye when he lost his wife. It was Mrs Ferdinand got her the place with him. After what happened to her girl she went away and hasn't been back since so far as I know. Seemingly, she put some of the blame on Mrs Ferdinand for not stopping it, but Mrs Ferdinand said she thought it was honest courting and not just Ivor taking advantage."

Bobby had been listening to all this very intently. He thought the implications were grave. The peepholes seemed to fall into place now. Only what significance to attach to them? But the missing guinea pigs which had been worrying him so much were fading away apparently. Had he, he wondered, been mistaken in attaching possible importance to the one pair being no longer in their cage? He supposed, rather ruefully, that there could quite easily be any number of perfectly simple explanations.

On the other hand, the puzzled, searching, seeking figure of Mrs Findlay seemed emerging into prominence, drawing sensibly nearer to the centre of things. Then, too, there were all those vague hints about 'blackmail'. Had they acquired a new significance? Could Mrs Findlay have learned from Mrs Jacks this old story of a distant tragedy with its hint of a dreadful guilt? Could it have been used by Mrs Findlay to force marriage on a reluctant Ivor? A far-fetched theory, but one that could not be ignored.

"I take it," Bobby said, "there was no question of charging Ivor Findlay with the murder of this girl? Nothing more than talk and gossip, was there?"

"That was all," the sergeant agreed. "Not a hint of anything solid to go on, and him with a good, sound alibi as well."

"Well, I wonder if whoever killed him in his turn will have an alibi, a good, sound alibi?" Bobby remarked. "Not that we've got anything like as far as asking anybody for one," he added.

He got up and went to the window. Opposite, on an old hoarding, was a tattered advertisement of a film—'The Bad Lord Byron'.

"Ever seen it?" he asked the sergeant, and the sergeant, a little surprised at so abrupt and irrelevant a question, said he didn't go very often to the pictures, hadn't got the habit of it, like the young folk. Hadn't the time either, not with always being on duty and the garden and one thing and another that kept you on the go all the time. Not like town, where you went home at night and shut the door and nobody bothered you.

Bobby said that was one way of looking at it, and he would write to the sergeant's superintendent to say how grateful he was for, and how helpful he had found, the very complete information the sergeant had gathered together.

"I hardly know how you did it at such short notice," he said to the highly gratified sergeant.

"Well, you see, sir," the sergeant explained. "In a little place like this folk remember. Nothing like poor Mary Jacks's death ever known here before. And not so many leaving the district either. There's some I went to see as were on the jury at the inquest and remember it like it was yesterday."

CHAPTER XXI
"HOW ABOUT TAILING HER?"

As Bobby was returning to town by rail, not by car, he had plenty of time, sitting in the corner of his carriage, to try to integrate into the pattern of the Findlay murder all this new information he had now been given.

He had not much success. Nor did he find it easy to decide what steps should next be taken. It did seem as if the hitherto divergent and uncertain lines followed by the investigation were drawing closer together, centring on Mrs Jacks and the bitter cause, now disclosed, she had for enmity against the dead man. That, too, seemed to bring the peep holes Bobby had found in the party wall at Dagonby House into closer relationship with what had happened. Yet it is a long way from spying on a man to murdering him. Nor had there yet appeared anything to show why on this particular day and hour so dreadful a crisis had been reached.

Then, too, those strange and ominous threats made over the 'phone had to be considered seriously, since previously such threats had been the precursor to murder and might, Bobby felt, well prove to be so again. Either this time of Mrs Findlay herself or possibly once more of some one else.

But that in some way or another, as principal or in the background, consciously or unconsciously, actively or passively, Mrs Findlay was deeply concerned, Bobby felt well assured. Nor had he yet succeeded in expunging from his mind his conviction that the disappearance of the two guinea pigs concealed a vital clue if only he could manage to discover it. Or bring to the test a theory floating vaguely at the back of his mind.

There he had to leave it for the time. He arranged to see Simons next morning to tell him what he had learned and to talk it over, and in his correspondence, when he arrived at the Yard, he found the first fruits of his visit to Abels End. The constable's young son had taken two snapshots, one of them of a stranger, a man, the other of a woman in whom Bobby recognized at once Mrs Tinsley.

"Her second visit there," he said to Inspector Simons when that officer presently arrived. "What do you think she can be up to?"

The Inspector said he had no idea, so far nothing to show she had any interest in or any connection with the Actons, husband or wife.

"How about tailing her?" he asked.

"I think that may come, but not yet," Bobby said. "We might ask her first."

"Ask her what she was up to?" Simons said doubtfully. "Well, she won't tell, will she?"

"Oh, everybody always tells," Bobby assured him again, and Simons shook his head more doubtfully still.

"Lies mostly," he opined.

"All the more interesting," explained Bobby. "Lies are so much more colourful, and where there's colour there must be light somewhere, mustn't there?"

Simons pondered this optical theory, but plainly did not think much of it. So Bobby proceeded to tell what he had learned the previous day on his visit to Monmouthshire. To this Simons listened with great interest, equally excited and puzzled.

"Don't know what to make of it," he said. "Seems to point all ways at once, don't it?"

"More like chaos than a pattern emerging," Bobby agreed. "I don't like these renewed threats though. I don't like them at all."

"You don't think it could be Mrs Findlay herself been doing it, do you?" Simons asked. "Or Mrs Tinsley? She didn't seem to like Mrs Findlay very much."

"She didn't," Bobby agreed again. "Anyhow if we go to see her now we can ask her that, too. Take a 'bus, shall we? We don't want to attract any more attention than we can help."

A 'bus accordingly took them to the corner of the street where were the flats in which Mrs Tinsley lived. When they knocked Mrs Tinsley herself appeared and showed no sign of being pleased to see them.

"I suppose you had better come in," she said grudgingly. "I do think you might do something though to keep reporters away. They're pestering the life out of me."

"Sorry," answered Bobby with real sympathy. "But keeping reporters away is beyond human power. The price we pay for a free press. The best plan is to ask them in, give them a cup of tea, and talk hard and long about the weather. It annoys them very much, and it generally works in the long run."

This—very good—advice did not seem to be much appreciated. Mrs Tinsley muttered something uncomplimentary under her breath, though whether about newspaper men or about himself, Bobby was not sure, and led the way into the lounge, to use the word that in the full tide of evolution has replaced the almost primaeval parlour, the more recent drawing-room and is probably destined to be replaced in its turn by 'bar'.

"You know," Bobby began, "how before Mr Findlay's murder, threats against Mrs Findlay were received by 'phone. That's started again."

"You don't mean some one's been ringing up to say she's to be next?" Mrs Tinsley asked. She stared at Bobby as if wondering whether he were serious, and again she looked small and formidable. "Don't believe it," she said at last. "At least, not unless she's doing it herself."

"Have you any reason to think that?" Bobby asked.

"Probably she's trying to pull wool over your eyes," Mrs Tinsley snapped. "Not too difficult either," she added, still staring at him.

"I daresay you're right there, regrettably right," Bobby said. Simons emitted an angry grunt. He always thought defiant witnesses were guilty witnesses. Bobby went on, speaking very smoothly: "But it may be just a little more difficult to keep it there."

Mrs Tinsley's stare wavered a little, as if she were not now feeling quite so confident. With what seemed like a sudden change of tactics, she said:

"Haven't you guessed yet who did it?"

"This isn't a guessing competition," Bobby told her.

"It was her," Mrs Tinsley said. "Tired of him, got him and then didn't want him any more."

"What makes you say so?" Bobby asked. "It's a serious accusation to make."

"She's trying to put you off, that's all," Mrs Tinsley repeated, without attempting to reply to his question. "She's bad, bad, bad all through."

"What you say to us is privileged," Bobby told her. "But if you said that to any one else, it would be slander and actionable. It is a curious coincidence that the same accusation was made in these 'phone calls. Or is it coincidence?"

"What do you mean?"

"I mean that I must ask you whether it was you who 'phoned and who made the accusation against Mrs Findlay you have just repeated?"

"No, it wasn't," she answered with vigour. "And there's no coincidence about it. It's plain enough. Of course she did it. Who else?"

"That's what we are trying to find out," Bobby said. "Have you changed your mind yet about telling us why you went to see Mr Findlay shortly before his death?"

"It was something private, nothing to do with any one else."

"You understand you are sure to be called at the inquest?"

"What about it? There's nothing I can say. I've told them so. I suppose what it all means is you think it was me? Well, it wasn't. Why should I? He was my friend. I expect you know that. I expect you mean to bring it up at the inquest. I don't care if you do." She was on her feet now, speaking with a kind of controlled intensity of anger. "I expect the porter told you. He would, the spying, snooping swine. I don't care. I'm not ashamed. It's all right."

"Was he ceasing to be your friend?"

"No, he wasn't. That's a lie. Mrs Findlay told you that, did she? She would. I know what you think. There were other women. There weren't. Not to count. It was only me. He never wanted to marry her. He had to. He told me so. Oh, she's a wicked woman, wicked."

"If she wanted so much to marry him, why should she kill him?" Bobby asked.

"She's wicked," Mrs Tinsley repeated, more calmly now. "She says so herself. She says she wants to be. She says she wants to know, to find out. That's why."

Bobby let this pass without comment. He said instead:

"I was hoping you would change your mind about letting us know why you went to see Mr Findlay that morning. It does mean you were probably the last person . . ."

"Yes, I know," she interrupted him. "So you think that proves I killed him, don't you?"

"I haven't said so," Bobby answered quietly. "There's no real evidence as yet, no substantial grounds for suspecting any one more than any one else. What I was going to say was to ask if you were willing to tell us why you went to Abels End yesterday and at least once before."

"I don't know what you mean," she exclaimed angrily and hastily. "I never was, never."

Bobby produced the snapshot taken by the Abels End policeman's son.

"I think this is you," he said, showing it. "It was taken there yesterday."

"Well, suppose it was?" she asked sullenly. "What's it got to do with you? I haven't got to ask your permission when I go anywhere, have I? Did you put that boy up to it? He said he was trying to work up a business. He offered to let me have copies." She was staring at him again, flushed and angry, and now afraid as well. "You've no right," she said. "He was doing it for you, was he? A dirty trick."

"Was it?" Bobby asked. "I am afraid we find it convenient to be able at times to check what people tell us. Do you care to say why you went there?"

"It's Sibby Findlay," she answered slowly. "There's something between her and Charley Acton. I think perhaps he knows it was her and she thinks he may tell."

"What makes you say that?" Bobby asked.

"It's what I think," she answered. "There's something. They've always hated each other. But then she hates every one nearly. There's a story going about that she means to marry him."

"Because she hates him?"

"Well, why not? Sometimes you can't bear being away from any one you really hate. It's all the same."

"Does Acton hate her?" Bobby asked.

"He's afraid of her," Mrs Tinsley answered. "She makes him run after her like a little dog."

"Count Ariosto, too," Bobby observed.

"Oh, him," Mrs Tinsley answered contemptuously. "He's only some one she likes to bully."

"Acton is married already," Bobby reminded her. "So how can she expect to marry him?"

"There are ways," she answered moodily.

CHAPTER XXII
"I DREAM OF GUINEA PIGS"

INSPECTOR SIMONS lost no time after they had left the flat in expressing to Bobby his opinion of what they had just heard. They were still going down in the lift in fact when he declared with some emphasis:

"Crazy, plumb crazy. The whole outfit. In a way," he added, more slowly. "There's method. I ask you—wants to marry him because she hates him."

"Well, it's a reason," Bobby remarked. "Better than marrying for no reason at all like some people. It's been said they aren't so very different—hate and love."

"Wants to know what it's like to be wicked," Simons went on, ignoring this last remark, which he thought merely silly. "Well, if it was her did him in, that's wicked all right. So she knows already."

"If," Bobby reminded him. They were walking away from the flats now, both of them as bothered and worried as any one could wish. "A lot in an 'if'. I don't believe she either hates or loves—not at present. Too much occupied with her soul."

"With her what?" demanded Simons, open-mouthed.

"I'm not sure I shouldn't describe her as a 'malade imaginaire' of the soul—a sort of spiritual hypochondriac, and of course any doctor would tell you that if you think you're ill when you aren't, then you are very ill indeed. It may be something like that with her."

"Well, where's all that going to take us?" grumbled Simons.

"I've no idea," Bobby admitted. "Not the least. Except to the fact that we're up against it pretty badly. I dream of guinea pigs."

Simons gave him a quick glance, inclined to think for the moment that perhaps Bobby was trying to be funny—unless of course he had been indulging in too many early morning cocktails.

"Guinea pigs?" he repeated doubtfully.

"Oh, sorry," Bobby said. "I'm really rather worried. Mrs. Findlay is a bit of a problem. But I'm not sure she would count murder as quite what she means by wickedness. I've heard her call crime merely vulgar."

"Isn't it wicked, too?" demanded Simons.

Bobby agreed. Simons said he thought he ought to be getting into touch with some of his men. There weren't enough of them, he complained, to follow up so many different lines of inquiry. He departed therefore, and Bobby strolled on slowly, his mind full of many thoughts, till presently he reached New Dagonby House. There, when he knocked, Mrs Jacks came to the door. Before he could speak, she told him Lord Newdagonby was out.

"Well, it's really you I've come to see," he explained. "Do you think you could spare me five minutes?"

"Is it about what's happened?" she asked mistrustfully. "I've told you everything I can—all those questions and questions over and over again."

"Are you sure you've told us all?" Bobby asked in return. "You know the inquest has been adjourned? The coroner's officer has seen you, hasn't he? When it's held, you may be asked still more questions. It might be a good idea if you made a preliminary statement to me if you care to do so. I was making some inquiries yesterday on the Dagonby estate in Monmouthshire. There was an inquest held there once. A long time ago. But I do not think you are likely to have forgotten."

She was very pale now, and her breath was coming in quick, uneasy gulps. She put out her hand to the wall as if for support. Without speaking, she turned and began to walk away. He followed her. She opened the door of a small plainly furnished room and went in. She sat down, a little as if she could no longer stand. She said:

"How do you know? Who told you?" When Bobby did not answer, she went on: "It was my girl. He murdered her, and it's only right he's been murdered too. I wanted to, but I never dared. I was afraid. I got some poison once, but I threw it away. I was afraid," she repeated. With a sudden outburst of passion she exclaimed: "He murdered my girl, even if he didn't push her in that night. He swore he didn't, but what's that worth? It was him made her do it, and now God has made it come to him."

"There are holes in the party wall upstairs," Bobby remarked.

"You've found them?" she asked. "I used to watch. Sometimes I thought I would wait till he was asleep, but I knew I wouldn't ever dare. I got to know things."

"What things? What for?" Bobby asked.

"That Mrs Tinsley," she said vaguely. "I thought some day I might get hold of something I could use."

"Did you?"

"What was the good? Every one knew. She knew all right—his wife, I mean. She took no notice if you hinted. She only stared at you and waited—and then you went away. You never know with her, only she makes you afraid."

"Why?"

"I don't know. She does, that's all. I thought at first she had done it, but I don't now."

"Do you still say you heard typing after the time the doctor says the attack took place?"

"It's why I don't think it was her," Mrs Jacks answered. "She's not used to it. She's slow. And this was some one doing it quick, the way Miss Grange does, without ever stopping."

"You are sure you didn't see or hear anything else that could help?"

She shook her head and repeated that she had told everything she could. Over and over again, she added. So it was no use asking her any more. But Bobby was not convinced. He felt it was very possible she might be keeping something back. She herself was by no means cleared of suspicion, and Bobby was much inclined to think she would be more willing to help rather than to accuse any one she believed guilty. Almost certainly she would do anything she could to assist whoever it was had killed a man she admitted she herself had wished to kill.

"You said you have seen Mrs Tinsley—" he began, but she interrupted quickly.

"It wasn't her," she said. "I heard him call after her as she was going."

"Your evidence seems to clear every one else," Bobby said with a slight emphasis on the last three words.

She evidently noticed it, but she said nothing for a moment or two, and when she looked up at him she had suddenly the air of one who was tired to the extreme of exhaustion.

"I didn't do it," she said slowly, "but I don't care if you think I did and get me hanged for it. I wanted to all right, but I didn't, and I don't know who did. That little Italian perhaps. It was a knife it was done with."

"He isn't an Italian, you know," Bobby remarked. "British by birth apparently. And it isn't only Italians use knives. Besides, why should he?"

"It might be her made him," Mrs Jacks suggested. "She can make people do what she says. She's like that. She tells you and stares and waits for you to do it. And you do."

"Not murder, surely?" Bobby said. He went on: "I expect we shall have to see you again. I'm rather hoping you may be able to remember more next time. Things come back to you, don't they? You were in Mr Findlay's room that morning, you told us. Tidying and putting things straight. There were guinea pigs in two cages, you remember. Was that usual? I mean, did Mr Findlay often use living animals in his work for experimenting on?"

"I don't remember he ever did before. Why?"

"Did you notice anything about those guinea pigs that morning?"

"Two were dead. I noticed because two in one cage were quite lively and running about, and the other two in the other cage were so quiet, I looked. I thought at first they were asleep, but they weren't, they were dead. He must have been doing experiments on them."

"What became of them?"

"Do you mean the guinea pigs?"

"Yes, the dead ones, their bodies. The cage was empty when I saw it. There was fresh food and water though. Did you take them away?"

"No, I never touched his things, only what was in the waste-paper basket, and that wasn't much. He had a sort of electric stove he used to burn things in. He didn't like anybody to see anything of his."

"I looked in the electric furnace," Bobby said. "I don't think it had been used that morning. If it had, it had been most carefully cleaned. Some one must have taken the guinea-pig bodies away."

Mrs Jacks shook her head and repeated that she knew nothing about that, nothing. If the bodies of the animals had been taken away, she had no idea by whom or why, and she plainly didn't think that it mattered in the least.

"I think that's all I can ask you at present," Bobby said. "Oh, yes, there's one thing. A question I'm asking every one. You know fresh 'phone calls have been made, threatening Mrs Findlay again? Have they come from you?"

"From me?" she repeated. "How could they? Of course not. I was here almost always at the time. More like it was her. You never know what she's thinking when she looks at you with that hidden stare of hers, asking and asking."

"Hard to tell what any one is thinking, hidden stare or smiling face," Bobby remarked.

"You mean Miss Grange? She's got a smiling face, but it couldn't be her very well, could it? Not unless—"

"Unless—?"

"Nothing. Unless it was, that's all."

"You know she thought she had been insulted by him?"

"She slapped his face for him," Mrs Jacks said. "Hard, too. She meant it. She was in a tear. If there had been a knife handy she might have used it then, and I wouldn't have blamed her. But she didn't go near him that morning. She said she would never have anything to do with him again or speak to him or anything, and she meant it, every word of it."

But Bobby remembered that it had never yet been explained how it was that Kitty Grange had known the exact price offered for her fur coat she wished to sell. It was a point he had left untouched at the time, but now it would be as well, he decided, to question her about it.

He asked if Lord Newdagonby had said when he would be back, and Mrs Jacks said she expected him for lunch. So Bobby said he would wait, but had no need to, for as Mrs Jacks opened the door of the room where they had been talking, the front door of the house opened too, and they heard Lord Newdagonby speaking to a companion.

"There's his lordship," Mrs Jacks said. "I'll tell him you're here." She went away, and in a few moments came back. "He's in his room," she said, and added: "Mrs Findlay's with him."

CHAPTER XXIII
"PEOPLE WILL BE AMUSED"

"MR OWEN," announced Mrs Jacks and closed the door behind him.

Lord Newdagonby, thin and upright, was seated in his usual chair, between the fire and his writing-table. Mrs Findlay was wandering round the room, apparently giving all her attention to those remarkable examples of modern, or advanced, or abstract, or what you will, art with which the walls were adorned. She bestowed on Bobby her usual coldly questioning stare, and then, as if to imply that she found him and his errand equally devoid of interest, resumed her inspection of the paintings, one or two of which seemed to be new additions. Bobby found a wild desire rising in his mind to put her across his knee and apply a slipper where it was likely to do the most good. He rebuked himself sternly for indulging in such Utopian and unofficial thoughts. Lord Newdagonby said severely: "I do hope you have at last some progress to report. It is high time. All this notoriety is most unpleasant, most unwelcome. I feel Mrs Findlay and myself have reason to complain."

"Just possibly," Bobby remarked, "your son-in-law also felt he had some reason to complain as he lay dying upstairs."

Lord Newdagonby scowled. He had a peculiarly vicious scowl. He felt this remark to be in the worst possible taste. Mrs Findlay paused in her interested inspection of the very latest new art on the walls and turned to bestow on Bobby another of those cold, questioning stares of hers.

"Have you anything to tell us?" she demanded.

"I was rather hoping," Bobby explained, "you might have something to tell me." He spoke to Lord Newdagonby: "Can you inform me of any purpose for which Mr Findlay would be likely to require guinea pigs?"

"Guinea pigs?" repeated Lord Newdagonby. "What guinea pigs? What do you mean?"

"There were two in a cage in his room," Bobby said. "Perhaps you did not notice? I think they are still there. Mrs Jacks was asked to look after them for the time. Apparently there had been two others, but they had died and the bodies removed. I don't know by whom or why."

"Did you expect them to be carefully preserved?" inquired Lord Newdagonby. "Every fool"—he quite plainly included Bobby in this category—"knows guinea pigs are used for experimental purposes. May I suggest that you should turn your attention to more serious matters?"

"Death is a serious matter," Bobby answered quietly, "and death visited that room twice. Once it came to a man, once to two guinea pigs. Do you think there might possibly be a connection?"

"Nonsense—a purely frivolous suggestion," snapped the other, but Mrs Findlay had now lost all interest in the new art.

She came across the room and sat down near her father, facing Bobby.

"You say there were two dead guinea pigs up there?" she asked. "How do you know if you didn't see them? You say they had been removed?"

"It seems a reasonable deduction from the evidence," Bobby answered. "You were in Mr Findlay's room that morning, I think."

"You've said so, I haven't," she interrupted him.

"So I was wondering if you could tell me anything about them," he went on, taking no notice of this.

"Really," protested Lord Newdagonby, "this all seems entirely beside the point. Frivolous in the extreme, a waste of time."

"Oh, I assure you," Bobby said. "I do indeed. I can't help asking myself what killed them and why the bodies of the poor little beasts have disappeared. It does rather look as if some one wanted to get rid of them."

"The first thing surely any one would want," Lord Newdagonby interposed.

His daughter turned to look at him, and when she spoke her tone was less cold, less aloof, more human in a way than Bobby had ever heard it before. Indeed, he almost thought there was a touch of amused affection in it as she said:

"Dad, aren't you being rather obtuse?"

"Obtuse? Me?" repeated Lord Newdagonby in a very surprised tone indeed, and he blinked as if not sure he could possibly have heard correctly.

"Definitely," Mrs Findlay said, and to Bobby, she said:

"Well, go on."

"Unfortunately," he answered, "that's just what I can't at present. For the moment it's full stop. I was hoping you might be able to help."

"Why?"

"I imagine there must be things you know," he answered. "Things that for one reason or another I have not yet heard about. And I take it you are anxious to know who murdered your husband?"

"Oh, but I know already," Mrs Findlay answered in her most casual tone.

"Eh? what?" exclaimed Lord Newdagonby, sitting even more upright than before. "Don't fool, Sibby. This is serious."

"I never fool," she answered, and Bobby felt that that at least was true.

"Will you explain who you mean?" he asked. "And your reasons?"

"Certainly not," she answered. "I've no proof, I might be wrong. Shall we say a woman's intuition?"

She was mocking him now, that was evident.

"A woman's intuition is often most valuable," he remarked. "But I admit facts are more useful in court. I learned some yesterday, for instance, when I went to interview relatives of your husband's—the cousins who took over the family farm when old Mr Findlay died."

"That appears to me to have been most unnecessary," Lord Newdagonby said with more heat than he had hitherto shown.

"I suppose you mean you've raked up that old story about Mrs Jacks's daughter committing suicide?" commented Mrs Findlay.

"Exactly," Bobby agreed. "Your intuition again?" he asked, and now there was a touch of mockery in his own voice. He went on: "Anyhow you knew about it?"

"Of course. My husband told me. Mrs Jacks hadn't even changed her name. He recognized her at once."

"Did she know?"

"Know we knew?" Mrs Findlay made a faintly contemptuous gesture. "It was never mentioned, if that's what you mean, neither by her nor by us. After all, it was an old story, over and done with."

"There are so few things that are ever over and done with," Bobby told her.

"If the object of this mud raking of yours," Lord Newdagonby said, still with considerable heat, but also with a slightly relieved air, "is to suggest that Mrs Jacks is guilty, I must say I consider the idea absurd. Mrs Jacks is not at all that sort of person. I should advise you to turn your attention to Mr Lake, the young man who appears to own an extremely expensive restaurant."

"We're not forgetting him," Bobby answered. "I heard other things in the course of what you describe as mud raking—and I agree it would be much nicer if there were no mud to rake in. A pity there so often is and that mud so often hides well, what mud may be useful to hide. I was told of an old scandal. It seems there was a general belief that old Mr Findlay was not the father of the first child—a boy—born almost immediately after his marriage with a girl who had formerly been in your lordship's service."

There was a sudden silence, broken by a high, abrupt laugh from Mrs Findlay.

"Well, now, dad," she asked, "what have you to say to that?"

"Please ring for Mrs Jacks to show this person out," said Lord Newdagonby, whose voice, however, was less calm than he could have wished. "I do not propose to take any notice of his impertinence."

"Not impertinent, I think, in one sense of the word at least," Bobby told him. "It may turn out to be very pertinent indeed." He got to his feet. "I am perfectly willing to withdraw if you wish it," he said, and though he did not know it, his voice had taken on a grim and menacing note as he continued: "I suggest, though, that it would be wiser to discuss this in private. Rather than in court at the inquest. You will certainly be questioned about it, you know."

The door opened and Mrs Jacks appeared. It did not seem she had been far away, and she looked very anxiously from one to the other. Mrs Findlay said hastily:

"It's all right, Mrs Jacks. Don't trouble."

Mrs Jacks stood for a moment in the doorway, silent and very still; and for the moment, so strangely she looked, she might have seemed one of the dreadful sisters, exultant that their long pursuit was at last drawing to its destined end. Then in the quietest, most ordinary of tones, she said:

"Very good, madam."

The door closed, and again there was silence; for that moment, so still, so quiet, had made its impact on all three of them. Lord Newdagonby spoke first. He said in an angry, injured tone:

"Nothing to do with us. What's the matter with the woman?"

"She hates us for it all the same," Mrs Findlay said. "Because you helped him and I married him."

"Absurd," pronounced Lord Newdagonby. "Mere unreasoning emotion." He turned to Bobby, and his voice was still very hurt and indignant. He said: "I do think common decency should have suggested to you that this was not a suitable subject to discuss before my daughter, before any woman. Common decency," he repeated. "Of course I knew of the stupid, scandalous, utterly unfounded gossip you've managed to get hold of. I contemplated taking legal proceedings. I was advised not to. Undignified. Likely to cause more talk. I was told it would soon die out and be forgotten. I accepted the advice. I deeply resent this old, foolish, long-discredited tale being raked up. Especially in my daughter's presence. I shall take steps to make my resentment felt."

"Oh, come off it, dad," said Mrs Findlay.

Lord Newdagonby, quite taken aback, gasped and stared. Bobby said:

"I think Mrs Findlay means she knew all about it and always has."

"It was plain enough," Mrs Findlay said. "Ivor wasn't getting all that done for him simply because he was a nice, promising boy. Not likely. I wondered why. It didn't take me long to find out. Nobody wanted to say it outright, but they looked down their noses, and now and then I got hints. It wasn't difficult to put two and two together."

"Did you never wonder," Bobby asked a very disconcerted-looking Lord Newdagonby, "why your daughter wanted this marriage so much?"

"It was her own choice," Lord Newdagonby muttered.

"Not his, do you mean?" Bobby asked. "Did it never strike you that Mrs Findlay was also showing a rather unusual amount of interest in Lord Byron?"

"What on earth has Byron to do with it?" demanded Lord Newdagonby, his bewilderment now utter and complete.

"The bad Lord Byron," said Bobby. "There was a film with that title. I haven't seen it. I wonder if it shows Manfred magnificently meditating on a mountain-top, posturing in defiance of God and man—both rather uninterested, I imagine. I wonder if Mrs Findlay ever saw herself like that in her search to go beyond both good and evil."

"Trying to be funny, are you?" snarled Mrs Findlay. "Or just to be rude?"

"What on earth—" repeated Lord Newdagonby, but his bewilderment was too complete to allow him to get any farther.

"Anyhow, if I wanted to marry Ivor, I wouldn't want to murder him, too, would I?" Mrs Findlay asked. "If that's what you're trying to hint."

"Yes, but—Byron," interposed Lord Newdagonby. "Why Byron?"

"If you remember," Bobby said, "there was a good deal of talk about him and a half-sister of his. I suggest Mrs Findlay imagined she was marrying her half-brother and was going to emulate Manfred on his mountain-top and even perhaps be known in the future—in a film—as 'The Bad Mrs Findlay'." He paused and permitted himself a chuckle. "The point is," he explained, "that the possible half-brother died when a baby, and no one has ever suggested that Ivor Findlay wasn't his father's son and therefore no blood relation to the Dagonby family. I'm afraid Mrs Findlay got it all mixed up—two and two making not four, but sixes and sevens. It all sounds rather silly, doesn't it? But then you know it's difficult to be bad without being silly as well," he paused again and looked at Mrs Findlay, and he spoke rather viciously, for he felt she deserved what she was going to get and more: "I don't know if all this will come out at the inquest, but if it does—well, people will be amused."

Mrs Findlay got up and walked out of the room.

CHAPTER XXIV
"DEATH MAY COME AGAIN"

FOR A MOMENT or two after this sudden and abrupt departure that was so like a flight, neither Lord Newdagonby nor Bobby spoke: the former lost in a kind of pale bewilderment, the latter hoping that just possibly this bewilderment might find relief in offering some sort of comment or explanation that might be of value.

Then Lord Newdagonby spoke, and now with a certain dignity.

"Was it necessary to say all this?" he asked. Without waiting for a reply, he went on: "I had no idea . . . I never . . . it never occurred to me that she had even heard of all that old business. It never entered my mind that she could know anything about it. Before she was born." He paused and looked at Bobby: "Do you mean," he asked, "that she deliberately planned to marry Ivor because she thought he was her half-brother?"

"Yes," Bobby answered. "She wondered why you were so interested in him. She got hold of odds and ends of the old story and put them together—wrong. Why in fact were you willing to help him if you knew—I suppose you knew?—he was no son of yours?"

"Of course I knew," Lord Newdagonby answered with something of his old manner of impatience. "He blackmailed me. He had letters I wrote to his mother. I did not wish them published. They could have been misunderstood."

"Did he give you back these letters you speak of?"

"Yes, I burnt them. He made good use of the money I gave him. I got interested in him and continued my help. I didn't blame him for using his opportunities. A clever lad."

"He made no further attempts to blackmail you?"

"Certainly not. He had letters of mine, and I bought them. That's all. The transaction was a simple one, and we never referred to it again. I am sure, he had no more idea than I had of Sibby's most unfortunate misconception." He saw how Bobby was looking at him, and he seemed suddenly to understand. "Good God!" he cried. "You aren't going to suggest now that I murdered Ivor because of a bit of blackmail years ago?"

"It is a possibility that might come to be put forward," Bobby answered gravely. "At present there seems nothing to show that the blackmailing hadn't continued. Nothing to show it had been, of course, but—"

Before he could complete his sentence the door was thrown open and Kitty Grange came almost running in. She halted abruptly when she saw Bobby, and stood looking uneasily, with fear indeed, from one to the other of the two men. She said, speaking to Bobby:

"What have you been saying to Sibby? Why is she so upset?" When he did not answer immediately, she turned to Lord Newdagonby: "Is he trying to make out it was Sibby?"

It was Bobby who answered this, however. He said:

"I am not trying to make out it was any one. What we are trying to do is to rule out the any one and find the some one."

"Why was Sibby so frightened?" Kitty demanded. "Because she was—she was awfully upset. I never saw any one look like that." She turned again to Lord Newdagonby: "What has he been saying?" she asked.

"Mr Owen," Lord Newdagonby answered, "appears to have got hold of some old, forgotten story of something that happened when I was a mere boy. He thinks it shows that if it was not Sibby, then it was me."

"A suggestion of a possible motive, that's all," Bobby said. "Identity of time and place of course. As for others also."

"It's only silly to suspect Sibby," Kitty said as she had said before.

"I hope it's even sillier to suspect me," Lord Newdagonby said; and Kitty gave him a sudden look that Bobby, watching them both, saw and remembered.

"What made you think Mrs Findlay was frightened or upset?" he asked Kitty.

"It's how she looked," Kitty answered. "It was awful. You must have said something awful. What did he?" she asked, appealing again to Lord Newdagonby.

"I don't think we can go into that," Bobby interposed. "It is more or less confidential. It may have to be mentioned, but that's not necessary yet. It's not quite clear how it links up. You can ask Mrs Findlay about it if you want to. It concerns her."

"But she's gone away, she said she wouldn't be back for a day or two," Kitty answered.

"Gone away? Where?" Lord Newdagonby exclaimed.

"I don't know, she rushed out just as I got here," Kitty told them. "She looked most awfully upset. I ran after her. There was a taxi passing. She stopped it and she was getting in. I asked her what was the matter, and she said she was going away and wouldn't be back for a day or two, and the taxi drove off. Is it that silly story about her marrying Charley Acton?"

"That wasn't mentioned," Bobby said. "I intended to, but she went off in such a hurry there was no chance. Did you hear what address she gave the taxi-man?" When Kitty shook her head, Bobby continued: "I hope she will let you know soon where she is. Or come back. We have to remember the renewed threats over the 'phone. Death followed those earlier ones, though not hers, and death may come again—and still not hers. Or it may be hers this time."

"She didn't take anything with her, she can't have, hadn't time," Lord Newdagonby said, but rather with an air of trying to reassure himself. "She can't mean to be away long."

"She could buy what she wanted," Kitty said, also with evident uneasiness. "She always has plenty of money with her— I've seen her take a great thick packet of notes out of her bag."

"We shall have to try to trace her," Bobby said, "unless we hear very quickly."

Lord Newdagonby did not seem to like this remark, but, though he moved uneasily in his chair, he said nothing. Kitty seemed lost in her own thoughts, thoughts clearly by no means reassuring. Bobby got to his feet and said that must be all for the present. He asked, however, that if Mrs Findlay returned, or any communication from her was received, he should be informed at once. He reminded them again of the renewed threats made against her life. They suggested ugly possibilities. He added some conventional remark to the effect that the situation needed careful watching. Neither of the other two made any comment on these observations. Bobby moved towards the door. Kitty followed him. In the corridor outside she said with a sudden intensity of manner:

"Unless you find out soon who it is, we shall all go mad." With a little gasp, she added: "Everyone's suspecting everyone else."

"Mrs Findlay told me she knew, but she wouldn't say anything more," Bobby said. "Have you any idea who it was she meant?"

"No, I haven't," she answered. She went on, excitedly, almost hysterically: "She said that to me too. I asked her. She said Count Ariosto. I don't think she meant it. It was only to put me off. I asked her why, and she said, well, he was an Italian, and it was a knife used. I don't suppose she does know. It's only that she suspects someone. We all do. That's what's so awful. There's nothing to show, is there?"

"There are pointers," Bobby told her. "We are working on them. We have to clear them up, one by one. One of them is that you knew the exact amount of the offer made for the fur coat you wanted to sell. That was the morning of the murder. The offer was made to Mr Findlay in a letter. No one else knew of it apparently. Yet you knew the precise figure, though you told us you had not seen him or spoken to him."

"I hadn't," she exclaimed quickly. "It was the house 'phone. We have one, you know. It's such a wilderness of a place, and then Lord Newdagonby loves fiddling about with gadgets and things. I heard it ring, and I went to answer it. I just said 'Hullo', and it was Ivor. I knew his voice of course, and he knew mine. He said: 'One hundred and one guineas firm offer for that fur coat of yours. Come up and see me about it.' I didn't answer. I hung up and went away. I would rather have kept it than let him sell it for me. That's all. You can't call saying 'Hullo' on the 'phone when you don't know who it is, talking to him, can you?"

"Well, hardly," Bobby agreed, and he thought to himself that the story, true or not, had to be accepted.

No corroboration, of course. Only her own word for it. Plausible enough though, even probable. But also an explanation that could very well have been thought up to account for a knowledge that a guilty mind could easily have seen was extremely compromising. Evidently she guessed what was in his mind, for she said sharply:

"I expect you think I've made that up?"

"One has to think of everything," Bobby answered. "You said yourself a moment ago that every one was suspecting every one else, and I think you still suspect Lord Newdagonby."

"Oh, I don't!" she cried. "I told you so. Why do you say that again?"

"I saw you look at him just now," Bobby answered.

"I didn't," she protested. "I never did. I mean not like that. You've no right to say I did. It's not fair. If I did, it's only because . . ."

"Because what—"

"He said once he thought it must be Noel—Mr Lake. I was afraid he might be going to say so again, and I didn't want. But I expect you've thought about him, too."

"Well, of course," Bobby agreed. "What did you say when Lord Newdagonby suggested it was Mr Lake?"

"I expect I lost my temper," she admitted. "It was so silly. I told him it was much more likely to be him. Every one knew how he hated Sibby marrying Ivor."

"What did he say to that?"

"I think it upset him rather, and then he got angry and he said most likely I knew it was Noel Lake and I was trying to cover up. So I got angry, too, and I said I would go and live somewhere else, and he said good thing, too. But Sibby said we were both fools, and so I never did, and uncle never said anything more either. I didn't really want to go while all this is happening."

"It might be better not," Bobby agreed gravely. "I don't want to have two people to look for. And it's no good giving the papers any sort of a handle—out of airy nothings they can build the most remarkable edifice. Are handles ever airy nothings? Never mind. I must be going."

"Tell me first. What did you say to Sibby to upset her so?"

"I'm afraid I can't tell you that. Policemen want to be told things. Not to tell them to others."

"Nobody understands Sibby," Kitty persisted, as she had before. "She's just got lost somehow. She's all wrong on top, but she's all right deep down inside her."

"I wish I could feel as sure of that as you seem to be," Bobby answered, and now his voice was grim and hard again, and Kitty had both hands pressed over her heart as she said somewhat flutteringly:

"You make me afraid, when you look like that. Like death," she said.

"Death has been here once," he reminded her.

"Well, it wasn't Sibby," she persisted stubbornly. "It's only that she's just all awfully puzzled inside herself. She thinks about things too much and too long ever really to do anything about it. If she ever wanted to kill any one she would think about it and think about it and never do it. It's that silly gossip about her going to marry Charley Acton you've been asking her about, isn't it? Enough to upset her or anyone else if you did."

"It's upset me anyhow," Bobby said, "that and these new threats some one has been making by 'phone." They were standing in the entrance hall now. Bobby put out his hand to open the front door. "There's no substantial evidence against any one yet," he said. "Do you know, I'm inclined to think Lord

Newdagonby is troubled because he is half afraid it may really have been his daughter?"

"I'm quite sure he isn't," Kitty answered at once. "What he's worried about is being afraid you may be going to try to make out it was her, when it never was. Isn't Sir Wilkin Wiggins the lawyer who always gets people off when they're being tried for murder? Noel says so."

"He doesn't get them off," Bobby explained. "It's only that he shows the jury their innocence like that of the unborn babe."

"Oh," said Kitty doubtfully, as if not quite sure where the difference lay. "Well, he's been to dinner. Uncle got some awfully swell place to do it all—butlers and waiters and everything. It must have cost ever so much. He got some frightfully special wine back from the country, where he sent it to be safe during the war, because there's none of it left anywhere else. I had a glass," Kitty added. "You can't think how horrid it was."

"Natural to take precautions," Bobby observed. "I hope they will prove unnecessary. Do you know a Mrs Tinsley?"

"Mrs Tinsley? Yes. No. I mean I've met her once or twice, but that's all. I don't like her much, and she hates me."

"Does she? Why?"

"Oh, she hates any female who has anything to do with Ivor. And of course you never knew with Ivor. Not that he ever really meant anything very much, only it was so disgusting. She wanted to marry Ivor herself. I think she still hoped she might some day. She told every one that marrying Sibby must be like marrying a perpetual cross-examination, and she was sure Ivor would never stand it long."

"Do you suspect her?"

"Mrs Tinsley? She wasn't here. How could it be her? Besides, it was Sibby she hated, not Ivor. I did think sometimes it might be her making those 'phone calls, but it didn't sound a bit like her. Noel Lake says Count Ariosto has been saying it was her—about the 'phone calls. And he says perhaps that's why it was done, because some one was afraid Ivor was being egged on to kill Sibby and he had to be killed first to save her. I told Noel he ought to tell you, but he said it was no good repeating what was only gossip. Besides Count Ariosto had been drinking. I think that makes it worse."

"So do I," agreed Bobby. "How did Mr Lake hear?"

"It was one of his staff told him," Kitty answered.

"How did he know?" Bobby asked, and did not look much impressed.

"There's a club for hotel staff somewhere, only it's for the very important ones, not ordinary staff. Head waiters at the big hotels and head chefs and porters and so on. Some of them make an awful lot of money, you know, and they elect a few proprietors as honorary members. It's supposed to be a great compliment. Noel's one. There's one hotel in Scotland where the staff heads expect to earn a thousand pounds each just in the season. And sometimes they get Stock Exchange hints from visitors when they've had too much to drink. Noel goes to the club sometimes just to keep in touch, and it's where he got his head waiter. Noel says he's worth his weight in gold and ought to be running the Ritz, only he's such a fool in everything except remembering you if you've ever been there before, and what you had for dinner, and what a clever choice it was, and that's why he remembers you. Men simply lap it up. Noel says most men would rather be respected by a head waiter than loved by their wives. But, of course, that's silly."

"Well, they aren't," Bobby observed. "I mean, respected by head waiters—a cynical race. Where does Count Ariosto come in?"

"The club's where he said it all," Kitty explained. "I suppose he must be an honorary member, too. Noel says he has something to do with a small hotel in Mayfair somewhere, I think. Of course, all Mr Lake's staff are awfully interested. They all know Noel was a friend of Sibby's, and I expect they know Noel had a row with Ivor, and everything else as well. Noel says it's terrifying what waiters know."

"Not as much as barmaids," declared Bobby, jealous for a profession from whose members he had before now received much interesting and useful information. "Anyhow, I'll have a talk with our Count and warn him against saying things like that. I wonder if the Coroner's officer has seen him. I must ask. Mrs Jacks has been hinting he might be the man we want. And there does seem to be some ground for thinking Mrs Findlay had some sort of hold on him."

"How could she?" Kitty asked, surprised. "Sibby's only known him quite a short time. There was a sort of fascination about Sibby every one felt, if that's what you mean. But that's not a hold. It's only because people felt somehow she was trying so hard to find out. It frightened them."

"Find out what?"

"The real difference between being good and being bad. Lots of people think there isn't any, except what's convenient. Uncle says all that matters is just 'being' by itself."

"Is that existentialism?" Bobby asked. "Well, that's outside my job—or is it? I don't know."

He went away then, wondering a little if what he had just earnt was going to prove of any value in solving the problem before him.

CHAPTER XXV
"SHEER DEVILRY"

"IN MY VIEW," declared Simons, returning after lunch for a final report to Bobby on the complete failure of what had at first seemed a promising line of investigation, "it's plain as a pikestaff Lord Newdagonby's our man. He hated to see his daughter marry out of her class. He was afraid those 'phone calls meant she was going to be bumped off unless he got in first, and so he did. Motive and opportunity, time and place, all fit in. And the murder weapon provided in advance, ready when needed. Pretty thin story he tells, too, to explain having a kitchen knife handy. To open envelopes. Well, I ask you. I call it a good sound case to take into court."

"So it is," agreed Bobby.

"And now there's Mrs Findlay done a bunk," Simons continued. "In my view, when any suspect does a bunk, it's as good as a confession—better, because you can't go back on a bunk and say it was all because of police bullying and thumbscrews and so on. A bunk's a bunk."

"So it is," agreed Bobby.

"It's all there, plain as a pikestaff," Simons went on. "She married Ivor F., thinking she was giving him a lift up, and then she finds he's still running after other women. More than she can stand, so she puts a knife into him, grabbing the one her dad has lying about, same as jealous women are always liable to do. There's that dab on Mr Findlay's desk and Mrs Jacks's evidence to show it must have been made that morning when Mrs F. says she wasn't there. Enough to hang her twice over."

"So it is," said Bobby and added: "There's Mrs Jacks, though."

"I should say there was," exclaimed Simons. "Put her in the dock, and those peepholes we found in the party wall would settle it with any jury out of hand. At least that's my view. All the opportunity you want for her to get hold of a kitchen knife, and what you've dug up about her daughter—well, there's a motive you can understand."

"So there is," agreed Bobby.

"Of course, there's Miss Grange," Simons went on. "I've had my eye on her from the start. In my view, almost watertight re her. She admits there was a flaming row between her and him. Claims it was only him being rude made her slap his face, but dig down a bit and you might find there was more to it than that. Lord Newdagonby says the envelope-opener kitchen knife got lost, and how about her finding it? And her saying she hadn't seen Mr F. that morning, and anyway wasn't ever going to speak to him again, and yet knowing the exact figure offered for her fur coat. Enough to get a jury thinking they needn't even leave the box."

"So it is," said Bobby once yet again.

"Only in my view," Simons continued, "that bit of paper in the handle of the murder weapon coming straight from one of Mr Lake's menus and knowing what we know about him and Ivor F. rowing over the girl—well, we know what happens likely as not when two fellows are after the same girl. Only a little thing, that bit of paper, but isn't it the sort of little thing that's hung murderers before to-day?"

"So it is," agreed Bobby, still the perfect chorus.

"Bring him in and grill him a bit, and in my view," said Simons, "there would be a good chance of getting a confession."

"Confession's not worth much these days," Bobby pointed out. "At one time you had to have a confession, because without it you wouldn't dare take the risk of hanging an innocent man, and obviously no innocent man would confess. So with a confession in your pocket you could go ahead with a clear conscience—even if it was a red-hot-poker technique got the confession there. Nowadays, the idea is that no one would ever be such a fool as to confess unless bullied into it by the police, and they wouldn't try unless they hadn't any proof. But if there wasn't any proof, then the accused must be innocent. Clear reasoning and shows you how things change, only stay much the same."

"So it is," agreed Simons, unconsciously plagiarizing Bobby. "Of course," he added thoughtfully, "there's that Mrs Tinsley." He paused and went on: "In a way, we've got something there. Last person with the victim, and nothing would ever have been known but for good work by the chap on the beat. Wanted to marry the dead man herself and got turned down at the last moment. The classic jealous-woman drama. 'If I can't have you, she shan't.' Seen it often enough. What I say is, grill her a bit, and ten to one she'll come out with the whole story. They often do. Because of not thinking of it as murder, but only him getting what he deserved, and every one must see that, mustn't they? Good sound case."

"Like all the others," said Bobby, varying his response this time. "There's one thing we've rather forgotten though. You remember Mrs Jacks's evidence about hearing typing going on for some time after, according to the doctor, Findlay had been attacked."

"No corroboration," Simons pointed out. "Invention to give cover for self or some one else. Or imagination."

"You haven't mentioned Mr Acton?"

"Keeping him for the last," explained Simons. "Because in a way it may turn out there's no sex in it at all. Money instead. One of 'em or both of 'em—Acton and Findlay—trying to do the other down over this everlasting razor blade of theirs. Money makes the mare go, and money makes murders, too."

"So it does," agreed Bobby. "There were those guinea pigs," he reminded Simons.

"Guinea pigs?" repeated Simons, puzzled for the moment. Then he remembered and tried to hide a respectful smile. "Yes, sir, of course. The guinea pigs. Mustn't forget them. No. Only I don't quite see where they come in."

"Two alive and two dead," Bobby said.

"Yes, sir. That's right. Only, speaking for myself, guinea pigs, two dead, especially when not able to produce same, isn't what I would want to try to impress a jury with. Of course," he admitted generously, "there might be something to them if we knew what it was."

"That is rather the difficulty," Bobby admitted. "I've had two more of the poor little beasts sent to Professor Haynes."

"Professor?" repeated Simons, trying to remember the name. "Scientific swell," Bobby explained. "Wessex University. Acton wanted two independent reports, and he was getting one from Ivor Findlay and one from Professor Haynes. Haynes had sent Acton his. Quite enthusiastic, apparently. So now I've asked him for a report on the guinea pigs."

"The same guinea pigs?" Simons asked. "I mean the two that were left alive in Findlay's room?"

"Yes, it seemed fairer," Bobby answered.

Simons looked very puzzled; but as Bobby said no more than that Simons should see the report when it arrived, he left the subject of the guinea pigs in abeyance for the time. But all the same he was conscious of an uncomfortable feeling that there was more in it than he knew, and he also knew that Bobby would expect him to think that one out for himself if he could. Nothing would be said unless and until there emerged some definite fact. Bobby never kept a fact back and never pressed his theories on others. It bothered him, and by way of precaution Simons said now:

"I've a notion that in a way Acton may turn out to be our best bet after all. He was on the spot, he could easily have got hold of that kitchen-knife envelope-opener Lord Newdagonby had knocking about, and then there's that poker he grabbed to take along with him up to Findlay's room. I've always had that poker at the back of my mind. Just one of those things you feel ought to fit in somewhere."

"So it is," agreed Bobby as always.

"Only it don't," said Simons. "And no known motive. Might be Acton suspected Findlay was going to patent that thing of theirs on his own. If you remember, there was something said about Acton not taking out a patent, so perhaps Findlay was going to do it for him and leave Acton in the soup."

"It's an idea, a possibility," Bobby agreed. "No evidence though. And then Findlay was like a lot of other people and worked on two entirely different moralities—one for everyday affairs and a pretty shaky one, too. But also one for the scientific side, and quite uncompromising there. You might as well suspect a bishop of bigamy as Findlay of not living up to his professional standards."

But Simons looked very doubtful.

"Wouldn't you say," he ventured, "crooked in one thing, crooked in all?"

"Our job would be simpler if people were like that," Bobby told him. "But they aren't. Rotten bad except in one spot, and there sound as a bell. Or honest as the day except for cheating the income tax or trying to dodge paying a railway fare. We're all a rum lot, a jolly rum lot."

"I'm not going to forget Mr Acton," declared Simons, and Bobby said he wouldn't either, and Simons said what about Count Ariosto. "I've been wondering," he said, "if we oughtn't to pull him in and put him through it. He was pally with Mrs Findlay, though I shouldn't have thought they were each other's sort, not in a way."

"More would I," said Bobby. "No accounting for tastes though."

"There was a bit of gossip about them being so much together," Simons continued. "Always together at cocktail parties and liked to be partners at bridge and so lucky when they were, people were beginning to talk. Doesn't seem to tie up with the murder, but there it is. There were hints at one time about blackmailing going on, if you remember."

"It didn't seem very clear who or why," Bobby remarked. "Didn't seem to tie up with the murder any more than the bridge business."

"No, I know, but if Ariosto was trying to put the screws on Mrs Findlay, it might be a line to follow up."

"That's our trouble," Bobby replied. "Too many lines by far, and all of them diverging as hard as they know how. But I've asked Ariosto to come in for a chat this afternoon, so we'll see what he has to say for himself."

"Think he's really a Count?" Simons asked. "They don't seem to know anything about him at the Italian Consulate."

"They wouldn't," Bobby answered. "British by birth apparently. Claims descent from a famous Italian poet, and if he likes to call himself a Count, there's no way of stopping him that I know of—or any reason to."

Nor was it long in fact before Ariosto appeared. He was very smartly dressed—dressed in fact, if not to kill, yet to impress—and also he was clearly very nervous. Before he had even taken the seat offered, he was protesting that he knew absolutely nothing, nothing at all beyond what he had already stated.

"I wasn't anywhere near at the time," he said. "I was in the park. I told you so, and it's gospel truth."

"Have a cigarette?" asked Bobby, pushing a box over. "You see, in a case like this, every little detail may be important, even when there's no direct connection. I think you know of a club run for hotel staff—high-grade staff that is. You are a member, aren't you?"

"No, I'm not," Ariosto snapped. "Nothing to do with me. I'm not a waiter."

"Sure?" asked Bobby.

"What do you mean?" Ariosto cried, jumping to his feet. "I don't know what you mean."

"Now, now, sit down," Bobby said. "Suffer a bit from flat feet, don't you?" Ariosto sat down abruptly and muttered something. Bobby said: "Well, never mind. I don't think you had very friendly feelings towards Mrs Findlay, had you?"

"What about it? That doesn't prove I murdered her husband, docs it? If it had been her killed now, you might talk. But it wasn't her, it was him."

"Adds to the general mix-up," Bobby said. "But I wish you would tell me the whole story instead of my having to drag it all out of you bit by bit. I have proof you were at that club I spoke of—"

"I never said I wasn't, I said I wasn't a member," Ariosto interrupted. "But what's it matter, what's it got to do with it? I was taken in by a member—head waiter at a smart hotel in Scotland. Swell place. He knew I had an interest in the Bliss, where I'm stopping—always do when I'm in town, and he thought I might get him a job at the Bliss. He's a bit down on his luck at the moment."

"Must be," Bobby agreed, "if a head waiter at a swell hotel in Scotland wants a job at the Bliss. Never mind that. What I want to know is why you made those threats by 'phone about Mrs Findlay's life being threatened?"

"What I felt like," Ariosto answered gloomily; and then in a surprised, very startled, and rather frightened tone: "I didn't. I never did. How did you find out?"

"Well, I've asked all the others concerned," Bobby explained, "and they all said it wasn't them, so you were the only one left. Besides, it was plain you didn't like Mrs Findlay and fairly plain that for some reason you were frightened of her, so were you trying to frighten her in her turn? Why have you started doing it again?"

"I haven't," Ariosto protested vehemently, and this time Bobby was inclined to believe him. "If she leaves me alone, I'll leave her alone. If there's been any more of it, it's not me."

"Where did you meet her first?"

"Never you mind," Ariosto retorted with a kind of feeble, fluttering defiance. "You've no right."

"Only the right of a murder committed and not yet solved," Bobby answered. "What I'm trying to get at is the background of the case, and until we get that clear, we're working in the dark. What I'm suggesting is that you have a job at a fashionable hotel in Scotland, and that your earnings there are enough to keep you the rest of the year. You're busy at your job in Scotland when you tell your friends you're visiting your relatives in Italy."

"You must think I make a lot," Ariosto grumbled. "I don't do so bad," he admitted grudgingly. "I've made some pretty good investments, too."

"Congratulations," said Bobby, "I wish I had. Takes me all my time to pay my income tax. It was there Mrs Findlay saw you?"

Ariosto nodded gloomily.

"Most of 'em never notice a waiter any more than they do the chairs or the carpet. But she did. Spotted me at once when at a cocktail party. Let on to be amused. Said she would help me—the she devil. Said she wanted a partner at bridge and how about it? Said she would teach me to be as good as she was herself, and we would make a good thing of it. So we did. How was I to tell?"

"Tell what?"

"It wasn't a partner she wanted, it was a pal to help her cheat."

"So that was it," Bobby said with wonder in his voice. "But why? She didn't need the money."

"No, but she needed a pal to take the rap if we were spotted. See? that's where I came in, me the mug. She got people playing for big stakes often, more than they could pay when it was girls or young men or young married women."

"But what was her idea, was it blackmail? or what?"

"I think it was sheer devilry, sheer wickedness," Ariosto answered slowly. "I don't know. I think so. I think if ever there was a fiend straight out of hell, it's her. What she liked was to feel she was starting people off, telling lies to their husbands or fathers, getting so they had to do something to get the money. It amused her to watch them going down, down into lies and forging and stealing. Just for the fun." Ariosto paused. He had become very pale, and he was trembling. "You may as well know the truth," he said. "When I 'phoned the way I did, I was working myself up to do it—to put a knife in her, I mean, same as you would in a snake you saw was going to bite."

CHAPTER XXVI
"YES, IT WAS. WASN'T IT?"

THE FIRST THING Bobby did next morning was to ring up Dagonby House to inquire if anything had been heard of Mrs Findlay. It was Kitty Grange who answered. She said there was no news and that Lord Newdagonby was very upset and worried.

"He keeps saying it's all you," Kitty added. "He says he is going to the Home Office to complain, and that if anything happens to her you will be responsible. What did you do? He won't tell me."

"Made her seem ridiculous to herself," Bobby explained. "There she was dramatizing herself as a sort of Queen of Hell, and I made her look a fool in her own eyes—with a plain hint or two that she might soon look the same to every one else."

"Oh," said Kitty, and her voice sounded very shocked indeed. "Oh, I do think that was Cruel of you."

"Yes, it was, wasn't it?" agreed Bobby complacently, as he hung up.

He turned to the letters, reports, minutes, piled on his desk, some of them needing immediate attention. They occupied him for the rest of the day. The next day was a Saturday, and Bobby was able to knock off early. On the Sunday he tried to put all thoughts of his work out of his mind, though he was able to spare a sympathetic thought for Detective Inspector

Simons and the other C.I.D. men, all, Sunday or no Sunday, busily following up the different—and divergent—lines of the investigation. Then on Monday he again rang up Dagonby House, and again learned, this time from Mrs Jacks, that there was still no word from or of Mrs Findlay.

"His Lordship's in a rare taking," Mrs Jacks said. "He's still saying he'll go and see the Home Secretary about it and about you, but he hasn't yet, and I don't think he will, not yet anyhow. I think he's afraid of what might come out."

Bobby asked Mrs Jacks to tell Lord Newdagonby that there was no objection to his consulting the Home Secretary or any one else, but he didn't think it would be much use. Lord Newdagonby could be assured that every possible line of action was being considered, and he could also be assured that he was not the only one growing extremely uneasy.

Shortly afterwards Inspector Simons appeared, with nothing much to report. He suggested that another conference should be held, and Bobby, who for his part had no great love for conferences, which he was inclined to look on as devices for distributing responsibility and lessening the chances of swift action, said the suggestion would go forward in the usual way. But, he said, this was one of those cases consisting for the present almost entirely of dead ends, and a conference over dead ends was not likely to be very useful. Afterwards, however, he had a message from the Assistant Commissioner, suggesting a chat, and to that dignitary Bobby admitted that he was feeling very uncomfortable.

"I gave her vanity, and that's most of her make-up, an awful shock," he said. "It may have disturbed her mentally. She's not normal."

"You mean she's insane?"

"Oh, no, not more than any one else," answered Bobby. "In fact, I think she's too much the opposite. Too sane, I mean— too sane for a largely insane world. She seems to have decided that the only thing that really matters is what's right and what's wrong. Good and evil. Her idea has been to try them both out and see for herself. At least, that's what Miss Grange keeps telling me. So she tried good first and found it a bore. But I think she confused good with alms to the poor and attending church services, and it didn't click. So then she decided to have a go at the other thing, and then I came along and made her look silly to herself. And now I don't feel too comfortable about what the result may have been."

"Do you think she is guilty of the murder?"

"Well, I do think in the mood into which she had worked herself, she might have done anything. I don't know. Ariosto, who seems really quite a decent little man, says she's a fiend, and produces what if I were writing a report I should call strong confirmatory evidence. But Miss Grange sticks to it that at bottom she's all right. A bit confused, that's all. Lost. And that anyhow she would always spend too much time thinking about action ever to take action."

"A sort of Hamlet in real life?" the Assistant Commissioner suggested. "But Hamlet took sufficiently violent action in the end, didn't he?"

"I'm inclined to think though," Bobby went on, ignoring a reflection that for that matter had been much in his own mind of late, "that if she isn't guilty herself, she knows who is. I don't know. I thought of going to Abels End this afternoon to have another look round."

"It might be an idea," agreed the Assistant Commissioner. "That's where the Acton chap hangs out, isn't it? He's not been much in the news lately."

"But ever in my thoughts," Bobby answered, nor was his tone as light as his words.

"Heard anything about those guinea pigs of yours?" asked the Assistant Commissioner. "I mean those you sent to some professor or another."

"There's been a note to say they were both dead. There were two you remember. So he got two more. If they die, he'll make a full report, but he wants to wait till then. Apparently he wants his conclusions confirmed."

"I see," said the Assistant Commissioner, and he looked grave. "Yes, quite so. Well, we must just wait, I suppose. But

I agree with you. The sooner we get on Mrs Findlay's tracks, the better."

"You can depend on our doing our best," Bobby said, and then he went off to get out his car for a drive to Abels End he would have enjoyed more if he had been less uneasy as to the ultimate result on Mrs Findlay's somewhat unusual mentality of what he had told her.

"Must be," he reflected, "rather disturbing to try to be awfully wicked and then find out you've only been an awful fool."

On reaching the village he stopped at the Abels End Arms for a belated lunch, and there, getting into desultory talk with various people, soon learned that of late nothing had occurred to ruffle the placid surface of village life. Afterwards he strolled off to visit the police sergeant now, since these events, sent to the village. He asked about the Actons, and was told that the previous Saturday Mrs Acton and her two children had left rather suddenly for a second holiday at the seaside.

"Seems she didn't much want," the sergeant remarked. "There was words about it and the short notice and all, though in general him and her hit it off a marvel."

"Well, most people have no objection to a second holiday," Bobby remarked, and the sergeant said enviously that he only wished he and his missus had the chance.

Bobby asked one or two more questions, and the sergeant said he had inquired and, as Bobby had already been told, nothing unusual had happened recently in the village. He added that in his opinion, nothing ever did, had, or would happen at Abels End.

"They jog along," he said, and Bobby said that happy was the village where nothing ever happened.

Leaving the sergeant considering somewhat doubtfully this proposition, Bobby went on up the hill towards the Acton residence. Reaching it, he stood looking at it thoughtfully. Was it possible, he asked himself, or was the suggestion too fantastic, that Mrs Findlay had sought refuge there, and was that why Mrs Acton and her children had been bundled off at short notice?

On the general principle that if you want to know, the best thing to do is to ask, he decided to knock and inquire. His summons was answered almost immediately—by Noel Lake. He and Bobby, equally surprised, stared at each other, and then both uttered a loud and simultaneous "Oh." After that, Bobby, the first to recover himself, said:

"I wanted to see Mr Acton. Are you staying here?"

"I thought it was Acton when I heard you knock," Noel said. "He isn't here. I'm waiting for him."

He turned and went back into the house. Bobby followed through the entrance lobby and into a lounge hall, comfortably and pleasantly furnished. Noel said again:

"Acton isn't here. I'm waiting for him."

"Did he say when he would be back?"

"I don't know. I haven't seen him. There doesn't seem to be a soul in the place."

"How did you get in, then?"

"Well," answered Noel with some hesitation, "I kept knocking and no one came, so I went round to the back. I thought there might be some one there, but there wasn't. Not a sign. I tried the back door, and it wasn't locked and I pushed it open and shouted. Nobody answered, and I thought I had better have a look round and see if anything was up."

"A bit like housebreaking, wasn't it?" Bobby asked.

"Well, the door wasn't locked," Noel said.

"Mr Acton may not think that an awfully good explanation," Bobby remarked. "Was there any special reason why you were anxious to see Mr Acton? It's not usual to walk into other people's houses, you know."

"Well, Kitty—Miss Grange—thought there might be a chance that Mrs Findlay was here," Noel explained. "I daresay you know she cleared out in a hurry last week without saying where she was going, and Kitty says they're all awfully worried—especially the old man. Kitty asked me to find out if Mrs Findlay was here. That's all."

"She's not, is she?"

"Not unless she's sound asleep or something. I haven't been all over the house, you know. But I've shouted, and there's no answer. I was going to wait outside for Acton when I heard you knock."

"Did Miss Grange say why she thought Mrs Findlay might be here?"

"It was just an idea of hers. She must be somewhere. I dare say you know there's a story going round that she was going to marry Acton next. He's married already, but I suppose he could get a divorce. Anyhow, that's the talk. You can get a divorce easy enough nowadays."

"Now we are both here," Bobby said, "I think we had better have a look round upstairs."

"Acton may be back any moment," Noel protested. "He would kick up an awful fuss most likely."

"More than most likely," Bobby agreed. "If he does catch us at it, I shall explain that I found you here alone, and I thought it my duty to make sure that nothing had been disturbed or taken."

"Hang it all," Noel exclaimed indignantly, "I'm not a thief."

"But certainly a trespasser," Bobby pointed out. "Found on enclosed premises for a presumed—or at any rate possible—unlawful purpose. Also you must please remember you are not yet cleared of suspicion of complicity in the murder of Ivor Findlay. There's always that bit of a menu found in the murder weapon and coming from your restaurant. I've known stranger things than that if you wanted Ivor Findlay out of the way for any reason, now you find you have to dispose of Charley Acton as well."

"God in Heaven, man, you can't mean that?" Noel fairly shouted.

"Why not?" Bobby asked. "Anyhow, I think we had better look through the house, and I think we had better do it together. Then you see, if there is anything wrong, we shall be joint witnesses. Whether Mr Acton has gone off somewhere or is just out for a stroll, at any rate Mrs Findlay's friends have some reason for feeling anxious."

"You don't mean—you aren't—I mean, you don't mean you think Mrs Findlay . . .?"

He left the sentence unfinished, and Bobby said:

"I never think if I can possibly help it. Except perhaps that it wasn't very prudent of her to come here alone, without telling any one."

CHAPTER XXVII
"SHE'S VERY WELL"

THE RAPID search of the house the two of them now carried out together showed, however, nothing of any interest, no sign of any recent disturbance, nothing in fact in any way suspicious or unusual. In the bathroom Bobby noticed that such masculine toilet accessories as razor, shaving-cream, and so on were still there. So, unless Acton had a duplicate set, or intended to buy fresh, presumably he would be returning that day, since in this clean-shaven era no man can afford to be separated from his razor for more than twenty-four hours.

The search over, they left the house, and Noel said he must be getting back to town. There was business to attend to.

"I like to be on the spot if I can," he explained.

He added that he would ring up Kitty and let her know there was no trace of Mrs Findlay at Abels End, so far as he had been able to discover. Bobby said he would wait for a time in the hope that Acton would return before long. Acton might just possibly know something.

"Well, if he does, I hope you'll tell him you satisfied yourself I didn't do any burglary," grumbled Noel.

"Housebreaking," Bobby corrected gently. "No forcible entry though, so I suppose it wasn't. Or is lifting a back-door latch using force? You can settle that with Mr Acton if you want to. I don't think there's anything for me to take notice of officially. At present anyhow."

Noel didn't seem to like this observation very much. He muttered something inaudible, and then as he was going added, over his shoulder, with deep sarcastic intent:

"Mrs Tinsley's been here, so hadn't you better be thinking of getting after her?"

"Mrs Tinsley?" Bobby repeated. "Why? Have you seen her?"

"Yes. First time I knocked and couldn't get an answer I walked round a bit. I thought perhaps some one would turn up. There's a tumble-down old cottage higher up, and she was there. She went off in a hurry when she saw me coming. It looked as if she didn't want to be recognized."

"Which way did she go?"

"Down the hill, towards the church."

With that, Noel departed. Bobby, slightly disturbed, wondering what Mrs Tinsley could possibly have been doing at the ruined cottage, went to see. There was no more sign of Mrs Tinsley's presence here, however, than there had been of Mrs Findlay's in Abels End cottage. Bobby noticed that one or two of the heavy blocks of stone formerly a part of the parapet round the well had been brought back. Evidently the police warning given to the neighbouring peccant farmer had been effective—in part at least. But Bobby also felt certain that parts of the parapet were much lower than they had been, and indeed showed on a closer look clear signs of very recent disturbance. Apparently what had been returned under police pressure had been compensated for by more being taken. Possibly under the idea that it was only the larger blocks that mattered or could be identified.

He sat down to wait, thinking it as good a place as any, since it overlooked the approach to the Acton residence. It was rather pleasant sitting there. A great part of any detective's life is spent watching and waiting, often in extremely uncomfortable circumstances. He could remember very vividly in his own early days spending all of a cold winter's night with one eye glued to a crack in a hoarding round which all the winds of heaven blew all the rains of earth. And all to no purpose, because some one had forgotten to tell him that the man he was supposed to be waiting for had been arrested earlier the same day. It was a memory made almost pleasant by contrast with his present comfortable, half-recumbent position on this warm, sunny, sheltered bank. Then he sat up abruptly as he saw the figure of a woman coming up the hill on the path leading both to the Acton residence and to this ruined cottage where he waited.

His first idea—and hope—was that it might be Mrs Findlay. But soon he felt certain that was not so. More like Mrs Tinsley, he thought. The figure came on steadily, and Bobby still watched. At Abels End Cottage, it stood for a time and then turned back towards the village, and then once more turned and came on along the path. There was an odd hesitation, a kind of reluctance that seemed to show in this varying progress by one whom Bobby was now able to recognize as in fact Mrs Tinsley. It was almost as if she were being drawn against her will, fighting against a compulsion, a fascination she did not know how to resist.

Bobby wondered if she, too, had been on the watch for Mrs Findlay. Possibly she had been down to the village for tea and was now returning. Or possibly she had decided to give up, and yet some obscure uneasiness had prevented her from doing so, had driven her back to continue her vigil. Some such conflict between two impulses, an impulse of reason to go, an impulse of instinct to remain, might be driving her to continue on watch.

Had she any reason to suppose, for instance, that Mrs Findlay might be seeking refuge with Acton? Any reason, that is, other than the apparently widely spread rumour of a possible impending marriage between them. But why should she be interested? Apparently she hated Mrs Findlay. So perhaps she hoped to be able to find out some discreditable intrigue, involving her? Or, of course, there might be some other and more serious reason? Or even for that matter a less serious reason, mere curiosity!

Mrs Tinsley was nearer by this time, and even now, when she was hardly a hundred yards away, she made an abrupt turn, and for the moment Bobby almost thought she was going to run. But once yet again she resumed her upward climb. A growth of thick bush hid him very effectively from the view of any one approaching by the path, and he waited quietly till she was actually within the old, overgrown garden of the cottage. Then he got to his feet. She gave a loud and startled cry, and she would probably have tried to run had he not been between her and the path. Instead she drew back a little, seeking support against the rather shaky looking cottage wall, as if fearing that otherwise her limbs might fail to support her.

"I'm sorry if I startled you," Bobby said. "I don't think I should lean against that wall though. It doesn't look too safe to me."

She drew away then, slowly, still watching him. She sat down on a tree-stump, an uncomfortable seat, but she didn't seem to notice that. She muttered:

"Why are you here? Why?"

"That's exactly what I was going to ask you," Bobby said. "I'm awfully sorry if I gave you a fright—you looked as if you had seen a ghost."

"I didn't," she snapped. She was beginning now to recover her self-possession. She said: "I shouldn't mind seeing your ghost."

"That doesn't sound very kind," Bobby protested mildly. "Especially as I think we are probably both on the same errand. You are looking for Mrs Findlay, aren't you?"

"Suppose I am? Nothing wrong in that, is there?"

"Oh, no," he agreed. He found a dry log and sat down on it close by. He offered her a cigarette. She refused it with a shake of her head. He remarked: "You don't look very well, if I may say so?"

"You wouldn't either," she retorted angrily, "if the only person you cared for in the world had been murdered—brutally murdered."

"Perhaps not," Bobby agreed. "You still think Mrs Findlay is guilty?"

"It doesn't matter now," she said, and suddenly she looked very tired. "It doesn't matter now," she repeated.

"You see, I think it does," Bobby answered gravely. "I think it matters quite a lot."

"I suppose you came here to find her?" she asked. "Well, you won't, you never will."

"What makes you say so?"

"Because you won't. You thought she had run away with Charley Acton, didn't you? I did, too. I came to find out. Well, she hasn't." She gave a short, harsh, rather disconcerting cackle of laughter. "All wrong," she said.

"Yet you are still waiting here?"

"Why shouldn't I?"

"It rather looks, doesn't it? as if you still thought something might happen. As if you still thought it possible Acton might join her here."

"I'm sure he won't." Again she gave that cackle of hard, strange laughter that sounded as if at any moment it might break into uncontrollable hysteria. "The very last thing he wants or intends."

"Have you any idea where she is?"

"If I had, I wouldn't tell you. It's her business—it's between her and Charley Acton. I'm not interfering."

"Yet I think you are, or why are you here?"

"That's my business," she retorted.

"You realize you yourself are still under suspicion of being concerned in the murder?"

But that she only answered by another of her hard and rather disconcerting laughs.

"Well, I'll be going," she said, rising. "It's getting dark."

"I hope I'm not driving you away," Bobby said. "I had no idea I was likely to find you here."

"I didn't expect you either," she retorted. "You won't see me here any more—at least not if I can help it," she added. She shivered. "How cold it is, how cold. It'll be dark soon. I'll go. You needn't worry any more about Mrs Findlay. You'll never find her. She's very well—very well indeed where she is."

She began to laugh again, and she was still laughing as she moved away.

Bobby remained sitting where she had left him, and there still sounded in his ears an echo of that strange, distant laughter of hers. He could almost have thought she was still laughing, when presently the increasing darkness hid her from his view.

He got up and began to collect dry twigs, the remnants of what once had been the garden fence, and such other bits of wood as he could find. As he did so, he noticed a light was now showing at Abels End Cottage, so he supposed Acton had at last returned. So much the better, very much so, in fact. He went on with his task, and when he had collected enough to make a small bonfire he lighted it and then sat down again to await the result.

It was a little time before at last he heard footsteps approaching and saw the occasional gleam of an electric torch switched on and off as some one picked a doubtful way along the rough, upward path.

He waited till the newcomer was nearer and then he called: "That you, sergeant?"

A sharp answer came:

"Who are you? What's that fire?"

"Mr Acton, isn't it?" Bobby said.

CHAPTER XXVIII
"GUINEA PIGS FOR A CHANGE"

THERE WAS no answer for a moment. Then from out of the evening gloom Acton emerged into the flickering light of the fire. He stood for a moment, and Bobby noticed that his hand was in his coat pocket.

"What's all this," he demanded. "What's that fire? It might spread. It might do a lot of damage. I came to see."

"I'll take care it doesn't spread," Bobby answered.

"You're that Scotland Yard chap, aren't you?" Acton asked. "You were there when poor old Ivor was killed?"

"So I was," Bobby agreed. "We had a talk with you, hadn't we?"

"Nothing I could tell you," Acton said. "You haven't done much towards finding out who it was, have you?"

"It's not the knowing who it was that's the difficulty in these cases," Bobby explained as he had so often before. "It's getting proof. A jury has to be satisfied. Quite right of course. But knowing is one thing. Proof's another."

"Yes, I can see that," Acton said, and there was a perceptible sneer in his voice as he went on: "And is this fire of yours some deep-laid, subtle scheme for getting that proof?"

"Might be," Bobby answered. "The trouble with deep-laid, subtle schemes is that life isn't like that, and generally speaking they don't come off. I'm all for simplicity, the direct approach, ask your questions and get your answers."

Acton seemed rather amused now, and he almost laughed as he said:

"Do you get them—your answers, I mean?"

"Oh, everybody always tells," Bobby answered.

"Makes it easy, doesn't it?"

"Not always in words though—sometimes without knowing," Bobby added.

"And is that fire of yours going to get any one to talk?"

"Well, we are, aren't we?" Bobby pointed out. "Shall we go on? About Mrs Findlay?"

"Mrs Findlay? Why? She rang me up last week. She asked me to meet her here. She never came. That's partly why I wondered about your fire. I thought I had better see. And then of course it might have spread if there had been nobody watching."

"Rather an odd place for her to fix on to meet you, wasn't it?" Bobby asked. "If she was coming, why not call at the house?"

"I should say that was probably because there was some perfectly absurd gossip going on about our being likely to marry. As if we could! I'm married already, and I get on all right with my wife. We are even rather fond of each other. You would think that would put a stopper on such a yarn. But it was going the rounds all the same. I don't know if the idea was that I intended to murder my wife or divorce her, or if a trifle of bigamy was expected. The way people talk. Makes you sick."

"So it does," agreed Bobby. "But sometimes less sick than what they do."

"You mean what was done to poor old Ivor? I know. Rotten. I think some one must have started the story that Mrs Findlay killed Ivor in order to be free to marry some one else. And that started them off guessing who it could be. What made them pick on me, I can't imagine, except that I suppose it had to be some one. My wife heard. Well, you can guess for yourself. She knew it was the most utter rot only—well, you know what women are. It worried her. Sort of feeling all the time that she knew perfectly well it wasn't true, but, all the same, just suppose it was. I got her to go away to the seaside for a time till people got tired."

"Was that a very good idea?" Bobby asked. "Wasn't it rather more likely to make the talk go on?"

"Well, it all seemed so silly," Acton said.

"You say Mrs Findlay made an appointment with you but didn't keep it?" Acton nodded, and Bobby looked over his shoulder. "I thought I heard something," he explained. "Over there, by that old well."

"I didn't hear anything," Acton answered carelessly. He threw the beam of the electric torch he was carrying towards the well mouth. "Nothing there," he said. "Cat or rabbit perhaps."

"Perhaps," agreed Bobby. "Or my imagination. You kept the appointment Mrs Findlay made?"

"Well, yes, couldn't very well help. I thought it was rather decent of her not to come to the house. But she wasn't here, and I haven't heard since. Mrs Tinsley was though."

"Mrs Tinsley? Here?"

"That's what I said."

"Instead of Mrs Findlay? Did she say anything? Explain at all?"

"I don't know that I asked. I was rather taken aback. And she seemed in an excited, odd sort of mood. You would have thought she was going into hysterics, only there was nothing to be hysterical about. She was throwing stones down that old well. What's the matter?"

"I thought I heard that sound again," Bobby said. "Near the well, I mean. As if some one were there."

"There isn't any one," Acton repeated. He went a step or two nearer, threw the light of his torch on the well-head, all around, came back to Bobby. "Nothing there," he said. "Bit nervous, aren't you? Dark and lonely up here, of course."

"I suppose I must be," Bobby agreed. "As you say—dark, lonely, up here. I don't suppose many people come this way. Mrs Tinsley didn't say anything?"

"Oh, yes, she did. Rather. Nothing you could make head or tail of though. All about Ivor and how he had always wanted her and no one else. You know, it's my idea she thinks it was Sibby—Mrs Findlay—killed Ivor."

"Do you?"

"I would rather suspect myself."

"Is there any one you do suspect?"

"Oh, no, not really. I mean I've thought of every one else. I daresay they've thought of me. There's Noel Lake of course. I did rather pick on him at first. There was that business of the bit off the menu card from his place and then they had such a blazing row. Not that Ivor meant anything about Miss Grange—just his way with every girl he came near. Only Noel thought it his duty to take it seriously. Got to show his girl she had a he-man to look after her. That sort of thing."

"Yes, I know," Bobby agreed. "Primitive impulse. We want them to admire us—the peacock showing its tail. Do you still think it might be Mr Lake?"

"Oh, no. Too easy, that scrap of menu, I mean. As soon as you came to think it over, you couldn't help feeling it was more like a crude sort of fake."

"It did look that way," Bobby agreed.

"There's Kitty Grange herself, of course," Acton went on, "but she's not the sort to do a thing like that. And there's the little Italian who calls himself a Count and looks like a waiter. But then all Italians do."

"Do they?" asked Bobby, surprised. "I never noticed that," and he wondered if this meant that Acton knew about Ariosto—told by Mrs Findlay perhaps.

"I don't see though," Acton went on, "that there's much in that. Ariosto wouldn't dare—not the way it happened. Needed some one with guts to do a thing like that. A cool customer. Does his killing in the chap's own room in his own house under his own roof, and then quietly walks away. I should say Ariosto was out. That doesn't leave any one much except old Lord Newdagonby. I wouldn't put it past him. He had no use for Ivor. He thought Sibby had made a big mistake. Possibly she had. But my own idea is that if he wanted to get Ivor out of the way, he wouldn't have done it quite so crudely. Not in character. Much more likely that Ivor would have vanished without trace. Not much that old boy doesn't know. No, vanished without trace would have been the idea for Ivor if papa-in-law had been in it. What about somebody you've never even heard of? Some disappointed inventor who thought Ivor had done him down, or more likely some one whose woman Ivor had been messing about? He told me once he had had threats. Laughed about it. Rather flattered."

"We've considered that," Bobby said. "No evidence. Anyhow, if he didn't vanish without trace, apparently his wife has."

"Mrs Findlay? What do you mean? She hasn't vanished, has she?"

"Didn't you know she left home without saying where she was going? That was three days ago, and they haven't heard from her since."

"Well, that's hardly vanishing without trace, is it?" Acton asked. "Three days isn't such an awful time. May have gone abroad. Nothing to worry about. She'll write or wire when she thinks of it. Or just come back."

Bobby was again looking over his shoulder towards the old well-head. This time he turned on it the light of his own torch.

"I keep thinking . . ." he said and paused. "Oh, well," he said. "Nothing there."

"Still a bit jittery?" Acton asked smilingly.

"Seems like it," Bobby admitted. "You know, what you've told me is very interesting. All the evidence suggests that Mrs Tinsley is the last person known to have seen Mr Findlay before his murder. And now it's beginning to look as if she were also the last person known to have seen Mrs Findlay before her—disappearance."

"Good God!" Acton exclaimed. "You don't. . . you can't mean . . . not—That."

"I'm only stating what appears, from what you've told me, to be the fact," Bobby answered.

Acton got up and went across to the old well. He stood there for a moment. Then he came back.

"I don't believe it," he said loudly.

"Believe what?"

"Oh, nothing—you know all right. Nothing. About Mrs Tinsley. Nice little woman. I've always liked her. So did my wife. Not that we ever saw much of her. She had hurt her hand. I mean, when I saw her the other evening. She had a handkerchief round it. There's some one coming."

"Come to see about the fire, I expect," Bobby said. "It's getting a bit low now. Never mind. It can go out. It's the sergeant from the village, I think. Hullo, sergeant."

"Oh, it's you, sir," the sergeant answered, recognizing Bobby's voice. "It's the fire. I thought I had better have a look. Might have been a tramp. So I came along."

"I hoped you would," Bobby said. "I thought you were pretty sure to see it."

"Well, I can't say as I did rightly see it, sir," admitted the sergeant. "I was indoors listening to the wireless. Got some real music to-night you can listen to and enjoy. Accordion programme. And right in the middle of it comes this lady knocking at the door to say there was a fire on the hill up above Mr Acton's. Well music's music, but duty's duty."

"So it is," agreed Bobby. "Did you know the lady?"

"No, sir, and when she had spoke, off she went, and me in my shirt sleeves and socks—fair whipped off into the dark afore I could do a thing."

"Oh, well, never mind," Bobby said. "It was probably Mrs Tinsley. Well, sergeant, there's a job waiting for us. Get on your super quick as you can, will you? Tell him I'm here, and ask him for tackle and men to help clear out the old dry well here. Mr Acton tells me Mrs Tinsley has been pushing stones down it."

"Down—down the well, sir?" the sergeant asked, quite bewildered, used though he was to the eccentricities and absurdities of all senior officers.

"Yes. I want you to ask your super to make the necessary arrangements. Tell him from me that it's urgent—even very urgent. Oh, by the way, you know a neighbouring farmer had been carting away stones from the well parapet, and he was going to be told to bring them back. Did he?"

"I saw to that all right," the sergeant answered. "Came up special to look."

"Have another look," Bobby said, "and see if you think all he brought are still there."

"Some one else been at them?" the sergeant asked, and did as directed. He came back and said very indignantly: "Half of 'em gone again or thereabouts. What do you think of that? No sooner brought back than took again. I'll get after whoever it is."

"Get on with this job first," Bobby said. "Your super won't be in bed yet. Ring him up and tell him what I've said, and tell him it's urgent."

"Very good, sir," said the sergeant, obedient though puzzled.

He went off, and as they listened to his heavy footsteps dying away in the dark and the distance, Acton said gravely:

"I can see what is in your mind."

"Well, I dare say that wasn't too difficult," Bobby remarked.

"All the same," Acton continued, "I can't help feeling you're wrong, if you don't mind my saying so."

"Not at all," Bobby assured him.

"Not Mrs Tinsley," said Acton firmly. "I can't believe that. No."

"Who then?" Bobby asked and got no answer.

"I'll wait and see if you don't mind," Acton said after a long pause.

"I hoped you would," Bobby said. "It may be rather a long wait. Let's talk about something else, shall we?"

"Something else?" Acton repeated. "Good idea. Take our minds off it while we're waiting. Only what about? Not politics, I hope."

"I wasn't thinking of politics," answered Bobby. "How about guinea pigs, for a change?"

CHAPTER XXIX
"TWO TAKEN AND TWO LEFT"

ACTON DID NOT answer at once. He was lighting a cigarette and finding it difficult to get his automatic lighter to function. By its tiny flame, when at last he got it going, Bobby could see his face clearly. Bobby had the idea indeed that the lighter was being held as it was precisely so as to make that possible. Nor was Acton's voice other than quite untroubled, his hand less than perfectly steady, as presently he said:

"My dear chap!! Guinea pigs! Why guinea pigs? Why not cabbages and kings?"

"I think because just now I find guinea pigs more interesting," Bobby explained. "In the room where Ivor Findlay died there weren't any cabbages or even kings. But there were guinea pigs—not to mention the guinea pigs that weren't there."

"How do you mean?" Acton asked. "All the rest of the guinea pigs in the world weren't there, I take it. Guinea pigs are a sort of general raw material of science, aren't they? I think I do remember two of the little brutes in a cage. What about it?"

"Oh, I'm not interested in them," Bobby answered. "I'm thinking of the special two out of all the rest in the world that had been there but were not any longer."

"That weren't there?" Acton repeated. "Is this an up-to-date version of the dog that didn't bark?"

"History repeats itself, doesn't it?" Bobby remarked.

"Does it?" asked Acton, and managed to give an impression of a slightly bored impatience. "Look, I'm not bothering myself at the moment about the guinea pigs that were or weren't in poor old Ivor's room. I'm not even wondering who killed the poor chap. You see, you've made it pretty plain you've an idea that Mrs Findlay has been thrown down the well here. Well, I don't know if that's really what's in your mind. But it's a pretty grisly thought, and it's what you've got me thinking. Isn't that what you've been thinking too?"

"I never think if I can help it," Bobby told him. "We can leave that till the men and the tackle I've asked for arrive. Then we shall know. So till then, shall we still consider guinea pigs?"

"The guinea pigs that weren't there?" Acton asked again. "If they weren't, what do they matter? Where do they come in? For that matter, how do you know they had been there?"

"An empty cage," Bobby answered. "An empty cage with fresh water and fresh food to show it had recently been occupied. I asked myself why the cage was empty and what had become of its occupants. Two taken and two left. Why?"

"Did you think they might have killed Findlay and then run away?" Acton asked and laughed lightly.

"Indirectly perhaps. Indirectly. Because it did rather seem as if the murderer had had some reason for getting rid of them or rather of their bodies."

"Their bodies?"

"Mrs Jacks, the housekeeper, you remember, told me she had noticed that morning that they were dead. Their death had been followed by Ivor Findlay's. I had to consider whether there could be any connection."

"Isn't that a bit far-fetched?"

"Just as now I have to consider whether there can be any connection between what happened to Mrs Findlay here—if indeed anything did happen, which has not been proved yet—and her husband's death."

"Yes. Well. I can see that's a possibility," Acton agreed. "I don't follow you in your excursions into guinea-pig land. But I do suppose that whoever killed Ivor may have had an equally good or bad reason for getting rid of his wife. Look. I'll ask you a plain question. Do you believe that Mrs Tinsley has thrown Mrs Findlay down this well?"

"I am at least perfectly sure," Bobby answered slowly, "that she knows or at least suspects something. When I questioned her just now she told me once or twice that Mrs Findlay was well—indeed very well. She said it in an odd sort of way, almost hysterical. It did strike me that it was possibly a rather grisly sort of pun. A kind of play on words. I wondered if in a rather over-wrought, hysterical way she was identifying Mrs Findlay with the old, disused well that may perhaps have become her grave."

"What a horrible idea," Acton protested. "Ugh. Is that what made you so jittery just now? What made you keep thinking you heard something?"

"Possibly," Bobby admitted.

"I expect I shall start that, too, now," Acton muttered, and he shivered slightly, almost the first sign of emotion he had given during this strange talk in the darkness by the ruined cottage and the yawning well-head. "Only, you know—I can't quite believe it. Why should she do such a thing? Unless, of course, you think she killed Ivor out of jealousy and disappointment—he did rather let her down, and you know the old saying. The one about 'Hell hath no fury—'."

"It's well known," Bobby agreed. "Some truth in it still. I've had it in mind. From the first it was fairly certain—not absolutely certain, but good enough as a working theory—that the murderer was one of a small group. Our job was to clear each one in turn, one by one, till only one was left. Then, of course, that one has to be the criminal."

"You mean you've done that?" Acton asked. "All except Mrs Tinsley? So you argue she must be guilty? Is that it?"

"Oh, no," Bobby said mildly. "You remember—those guinea pigs! You see they don't fit. What could a woman like Mrs Tinsley have to do with guinea pigs? Didn't jell. And I really couldn't imagine Mrs Tinsley walking off with two dead guinea pigs in her handbag."

"Well, then—who?"

"You, of course," Bobby answered. "Hadn't you guessed? I thought you must have."

Acton threw back his head and laughed and laughed, laughed till the surrounding darkness seemed full of his loud merriment. Bobby sat waiting patiently till it should end. Acton said, his voice still shaking with his mirth.

"Oh, come, now then. My best pal! And can you imagine me walking away with my pockets stuffed with dead guinea pigs?"

"Yes," said Bobby

"Oh, well, now then," Acton said.

He was silent then, as silent as the vast darkness of the night in which they sat. Down below in the village a few lights showed here and there, and on the road other lights shone where cars were passing up and down. Acton rose to his feet and went across to the well-head. He stood there for a moment or two, and Bobby threw the light of his torch after him so that it made a bright pool by Acton's feet. He did not seem to notice. Bobby noticed that his right hand was again in his coat pocket. He began slowly to return, making a slight circuit so that it seemed that whereas before he had been sitting on Bobby's right, now he would be taking up his position on Bobby's left. It was a manœuvre Bobby managed unostentatiously to defeat by a slight shift of his own position.

"Look," Acton said, "I don't know what all this is leading up to. If you've just been amusing yourself trying to work me into a state of jitters, well, you've pretty well succeeded. I could have sworn just now there was some sort of movement over there by the well. I thought I heard—well, never mind. But I could have sworn there was something moving. And a light. A sort of light that came and went and then came again. Go and look for yourself."

"Curious," Bobby observed. "Very curious. But I think all the same I'll wait for the men and tackle I've sent for. If Mrs Findlay has really been down there since she was last heard of—three days, that is—another three quarters of an hour won't make much difference."

"I think at any rate," Acton went on, his voice still perfectly calm and even, "I have a right to ask you to explain yourself more clearly. You've hinted you believe Mrs Findlay has been thrown down the well here, and you seem to suspect Mrs Tinsley, and in some odd way you seem to hint you see some connection between guinea pigs—of all things imaginable—myself, and Ivor Findlay's death. I really quite fail to understand why you suppose I could have any interest in disposing of a man with whom I had intimate and very satisfactory business relations. Very friendly as well. I don't know if you think I have had anything to do with Mrs Tinsley or Mrs Findlay's disappearance—if she has disappeared, that is. Do you?"

"Oh, yes," Bobby answered. "Difficult to work it out, of course. Quite interesting, though."

"Rather callous to talk like that," Acton said rebukingly.

"A callous affair, murder," Bobby remarked. "There's one small point I've noticed. Quite small. Insignificant. Not a thing you could mention in court. When the jury comes back at the close of a murder trial to give their verdict, you can always tell at once what the verdict is. If all the members of the jury look at the prisoner, it's 'Not guilty'. If they are all careful to look away from him, then it's 'Guilty'. In the same way, all the others I've questioned about this affair have always spoken of Ivor Findlay's death as murder. None of them showed any hesitation in using the word. They've called it what it was— murder. You have invariably called it killing or some similar word. Never murder. A word too ugly, a word so ugly you can't admit even to yourself it could apply to what you did. Curious, the power of words, a power almost like magic at times."

"Oh, that's fantastic," Acton interrupted. "As fantastic as your non-existent guinea pigs. As fantastic as all the rest of the vague sort of atmosphere of suspicion you seem to be trying to build up, and about which I think you are likely to hear more. Have you even one single concrete fact—established fact—you can mention?"

"The poker," Bobby said.

"Poker," shouted Acton. "First guinea pigs and then a poker. You must be crazy—or trying to be funny."

"Neither," Bobby answered. "I mean the poker you snatched up that day at Dagonby House when Mrs Findlay came to tell us she couldn't open the door of her husband s work-room and she thought he must be ill because she could hear groans. I asked myself why a poker was needed."

"To force the door with, of course," Acton answered promptly. "Really, what do you suppose? Sibby said it was locked."

"Pokers aren't so very useful for forcing doors," Bobby pointed out. "There are quicker ways. I wondered if it had struck you that supposing Ivor Findlay were alive, as you had thought him dead, and supposing he had strength enough to name his attacker, then a poker might be useful for effecting an escape. A tap on the head might have put out of action a certain officer of police unexpectedly and inconveniently present."

"You do give your imagination full play, don't you?" Acton commented, still to all appearance quite unconcerned.

"The whole secret of detective work," Bobby explained, "is to work yourself into the suspect's skin. Then you may be able to understand both his reasons and his actions. He always has reasons, however bad in logic, in morals. But still reasons."

"And is this web of fancy what you are trying to make out is substantial ground for suspicion?"

"Oh, no, only the background," answered Bobby. "Background is awfully important. And then I remembered that you wouldn't run upstairs to fetch Findlay for luncheon because you said you didn't even know which was the room he used on the attic floor. A labyrinth you said, and you had never been there. Yet when we all went hurrying to see what had happened, you led the way, you got there first."

"Oh, come now," protested Acton, still unflurried. "I didn't mean that absolutely and literally. Just a way of talking. Of course, in an emergency of that sort—well, one does remember somehow. I suppose I felt somehow that if poor old Ivor needed help, then I had to remember, and so I did remember. Well, is that the end of this wild exercise in fantasy you can hardly expect me to take seriously? Or any one."

"One thing more," answered Bobby. "Mrs Jacks says she heard typing going on for half an hour after the time when the attack was probably made. That typing must have been done by the murderer, and that means he must have been a man of extraordinary nerve and self-control—of such self-control as you have shown to-night when first I let you think that I suspected Mrs Tinsley and then allowed you to see that it was in fact yourself."

CHAPTER XXX
". . . THE INEVITABLE MISTAKE"

BOBBY DISCOVERED that now he was alone. Suddenly and silently Acton had slipped away into the darkness. As silently Bobby shifted his own position till he sat with his back against a wall of the derelict, half-ruined cottage. He did not feel at all sure what form Acton's reactions might take. Possibly he had determined on flight. But that Bobby did not think likely. Acton was both resolute and intelligent. He would realize that the case Bobby had so far outlined was one of strong suspicion only, a multitude of small indications, and that flight would simply intensify such suspicions to nearly, if not quite, the point of certitude. Probably Acton had not gone far, was still quite near, brooding in the night what he should do next.

Bobby felt very tired all at once. He had risked his life before this more than once in physical struggle and danger and yet been less conscious of fatigue than he was now after this conflict of words and wit in which he had hoped in one way or another to force his adversary into some false move or self-betrayal. He was not sure now that in this he was going to succeed. Down below in the village more lights were showing, not scattered lights but lights clustering together. Bobby supposed that there was assembling the help—men and tackle—he had asked for. Acton's voice sounded abruptly:

"Where are you?" it asked. "You haven't gone off, have you?"

"I'm still here," Bobby answered. "I was beginning to think you had gone off yourself. I didn't hear anything, but you weren't there."

"I started to go back to the house," Acton said slowly. "I was going to ring up my lawyer. You know, it's pretty serious, what you've said."

"Less serious than what's been done," Bobby answered. "One dead man and a woman, and where is she?"

"I changed my mind," Acton went on, unheeding this interruption. "I thought I had better get things a bit clearer. You've said you suspect me of killing Ivor Findlay. Your chief reason seems to be that I didn't use the word murder in speaking of what happened."

"Oh, no," Bobby protested. "Not my chief reason. A straw—a straw to show the way the wind blows."

"If you want to know," Acton went on, "I didn't call it murder because I'm not at all sure it could be called murder. I suggest that some woman may have gone to see him, some woman he had done the dirty to, and that there was a quarrel, a scrimmage, and that the knife was used in self-defence—accidentally."

"Doesn't the knife suggest premeditation rather than accident?" Bobby asked. "What was a kitchen knife doing in what was a kind of scientific laboratory?"

"Kitty Grange used it downstairs to open Lord Newdagonby's letters," Acton pointed out. "She may have used it, too, for the same purpose with Findlay's letters. I'm not thinking of her though. I'm thinking of Mrs Tinsley."

"We've talked of her already," Bobby said. "Just now, wasn't it?"

"Yes, and then you explained you couldn't bring in your favourite guinea pigs with her, as you seem to think you can with me. Well, why? I'm still not at all clear—fantasy or bluff? Which? My lawyer will want to know."

"It was one of the things I noticed first of all," Bobby told him once again. "It did look as if there had been a scientific experiment that had turned out badly—for the guinea pigs at any rate. It looked, too, as if there had been an attempt to conceal what had happened by removing their bodies. By whom? Why? Findlay could have had no reason to hide the result of his own experiment. He had no need even to mention he had made it. So had some client found the result unwelcome, found it necessary to hide it? You seemed to be the important client of the moment. Was that it? Had a trial of your everlasting razor blade turned out badly? Was it that a cut or scratch from it had killed the guinea pigs? You know you made there the inevitable mistake. Two dead guinea pigs in their cage might mean nothing. But two dead guinea pigs no longer there because their bodies had been carefully removed suggested there might be a strong reason why they had to be taken away."

"Go on," Acton muttered. "Go on, why don't you?"

"Then there was the typing Mrs Jacks told us she heard. Why should a murderer stay typing on the spot for half an hour after committing his crime? Obviously because he had to type something for which he had to use Findlay's own machine. A typewriter used can always be identified you know. Well, then, didn't that mean a document was to be forged? A favourable report instead of the condemnatory one the result of the guinea-pig experiment might have made necessary? That's how I reasoned, though I tried out a good many other theories as well."

"You mean," Acton said, "you made a series of guesses for none of which you can produce any factual base."

"Oh, I wouldn't go so far as to say that," Bobby protested. "A certain amount of confirmation from Mrs Jacks for instance."

"Putting suspicion on some one else to save herself," Acton commented. "Perhaps it was her. She may have had reasons, I remember Sibby saying something like that once. Why not Mrs Jacks if it comes to that?"

"A good line of defence," Bobby agreed. "Always is. To say, why not a third person? Makes a jury doubt, and that's everything. A defending counsel's best card. There are reports from Professor Haynes, too."

"Enthusiastic," Acton broke in. "I have them. Enthusiastic."

"So they were," agreed Bobby. "So he told me. But when I put it to him there was a line Findlay might have followed up he might not have thought of—he undertook to make fresh experiments. With guinea pigs. I haven't got his full report yet, and I don't pretend to understand fully. Certainly not the technical terms he uses. What it seems to come to is a suggestion that nuclear energy has been used in your process, and that in the event of a cut or a scratch such as can always happen when a man is shaving, some tiny, literally infinitesimal influence might enter the blood stream and tend to dry it up. With fatal results to those two guinea pigs and possibly to humans as well. Haynes talked about something he called 'isotopes', whatever they are."

"It was a mere fantasy of Findlay's," Acton said angrily. "Even if there was such a danger which I don't accept for a moment—guinea pigs aren't humans—it could easily have been eliminated. I told Findlay so. I showed him how. He practically admitted as much. But he tried to argue that there had to be practical proof by experiment. He wouldn't even promise to hold back his report. It was all so unnecessary. If any hint, even, had got about, it would have been impossible to raise the capital I wanted. And it was there waiting—waiting, ready. Only a few papers to sign, and a start could have been made. Ample time for me to eliminate the fantastic danger Findlay chose to imagine. Ample time. Naturally, I never called it murder. You were right there. Because it was nothing of the sort. No one in his senses could call it murder. It was a necessity. Can't you see what my invention meant? It meant doubling, trebling, quadrupling production. And that might mean saving civilization. Was one pedantic fool to stand in the way of that? Think what it would mean in every factory in the world. My razor blade was only a beginning. One or two more technical difficulties to get over, and then running expenses everywhere would be halved and efficiency doubled. I didn't intend to let all that be scrapped because of the shortsightedness of an obstinate and prejudiced observer with no vision of the larger issues. Of course I took steps to remove him. I had to. Wouldn't you in my place?"

"I'm sure I don't know," Bobby answered. "Not my business. You will be able to explain all that in Court."

"Oh, no," Acton retorted. "I don't mind talking to you. It was a relief somehow. Quite a relief. And then it looked as if you had it all sewn up. But not to any one else, and if you try to repeat what I've told you—a dirty trick, but I wouldn't put it past you, though you know perfectly well I was speaking in confidence. But if you do, I shall simply deny it all. You've no real evidence, nothing solid to go on. Merely the flimsiest web imaginable of guesswork and theory. No witnesses."

"Is that why Mrs Findlay has disappeared?" Bobby asked. "Because she was a witness? Because she knew?"

"Knew what, what do you mean?"

"My guess," Bobby said slowly, "is that she saw you going away after doing what you did up there that morning in Ivor Findlay's room. Her finger-prints on his desk Mrs Jacks had dusted. Shows she had been there, and I've been a good deal worried about her reason for denying it. I expect after being there and going away presently she remembered something she wanted to say and started to return, and caught a glimpse of you hurrying off. Perhaps something in your manner and attitude, in your hurry, made her suspicious. I don't suppose she imagined for a moment what had really happened. But instead of going to ask her husband, she probably thought it would be cleverer and more amusing to get it out of you—with no idea of what that 'it' was. I think when she did know, then she saw herself in her favourite character of Queen of Hell. She was trying as hard to be wicked as any one ever tried to be good. She wanted to be all things and know all things, to be like the gods knowing both good and evil, and therefore like them above good and evil. So she would marry her husband's murderer and make him desert his wife and children she knew he was fond of. The murderer, like the head of a Nazi extermination camp, can yet remain a good family man. Very odd. But it is so. I expect Mrs Findlay thought she was taking another step to complete triumph over good and bad alike, and if it has now led her instead to the bottom of an old well with a few stones thrown down afterwards to make sure, well, she has only herself to thank."

CHAPTER XXXI
"I RANG HIM UP"

BOTH MEN had been wholly, desperately intent on their apparently drifting, even aimless, talk that yet, as both well knew, held in it, in almost every word exchanged, even in the intonation of each syllable, a possible indication of where lay the dreadful truth one of them was so desperately striving to conceal, the other to disclose. In consequence neither so far had been aware of approaching footsteps.

But now the sound of a slow, deliberate tread forced itself upon their attention, and presently the light of a torch came wavering in advance to herald the arrival of the newcomer.

"Your men and their tackle here at last," Acton said, speaking a little loudly, as if he were very willing to be overheard. "Well, if you are right and Mrs Findlay's body is at the bottom of that old well, then I'm prepared to swear, as I said before, that she had asked me to meet her here, and that when I arrived at the time she said, there was no sign of her. But Mrs Tinsley was here. Mrs Tinsley struck me as being in a state of excitement, almost hysteria, I couldn't for the life of me understand at the time. Of course, you know, every one knows for that matter, that she hated Mrs Findlay for having taken Ivor Findlay from her and that she had got it firmly into her head that Mrs Findlay killed her husband. If you want any evidence, I'm prepared to say all that on oath."

Bobby did not answer. Acton was putting up an extremely plausible story. It might well carry enough conviction to make a jury hesitate, possibly even to make a prosecution inadvisable unless more evidence could be obtained. Once again Bobby had to reflect that it is not the knowing, but the proving, that is always the difficulty. True, his story ignored the guinea pigs, but the argument would be that they were ignored because they were irrelevant.

The approaching footsteps were still nearer now. Bobby switched on his own torch. Acton did the same. In the circle of light they made appeared the village sergeant.

"Won't be long now, sir," he said briskly. "I came on ahead to tell you we've got all we want. Evening, Mr Acton. Bad business all this. I've never known the like, not since I was stationed here."

"Shocking," agreed Acton. "Shocking. I can't help thinking there must be a mistake somewhere. It all seems so incredible."

"Yes, sir, it does, doesn't it?" agreed the sergeant. To Bobby he said: "There's a gent come. Tall thin gent, very tall, very thin. I didn't rightly catch his name, but he says he's Mrs Findlay's father and he's looking for her."

"Oh, yes," Bobby said, disturbed by this news. "Yes. What did you tell him?"

"I said to leave his name and address, and he would be let know as soon as there was reliable information."

"What did he say to that?" asked Bobby, not without interest.

"I had to tell him I didn't want none of that sort of talk," answered the sergeant, not without dignity. "Language such as he was using, I said, could not be tolerated, and I said if same continued I should have to consider taking him in on a charge of disorderly conduct."

"Did you, though?" said Bobby, and this time with a touch of awe. "What did he say?"

"It sort of pulled him up short," the sergeant replied, and this time even with complacence. "Especially as he kind of choked just then and couldn't get a word out seemingly, not to make sense. I left it there, not wanting trouble more than same has to be, and he saw the tackle we had got, and he got quiet like and asked what that was for. One of my men, though he didn't ought, it not being for him to give information to the public, said as it was for getting a deader out of an old dry well where a lady had tumbled in or been pushed. But I told him nothing was known for certain, and I said to wait in my office."

"Did he?" Bobby asked.

"I didn't see no more of him," answered the sergeant. "I saw him go off another way. I thought maybe he might have come on here."

"We haven't seen him," Bobby said.

"Seems like a Mrs Tinman or some such a name, had rung him to say Mrs Findlay was meeting a friend hereabouts," continued the sergeant. "He said he was going to ask his friend about it, so I said, who was it, and he didn't want to tell. I put it to him I spoke official like, and then he said the name was Nemo. But there isn't no one of that name in these parts, and so I told him."

"I don't very much like the sound of all that," Bobby said thoughtfully. "Do you, Mr Acton?"

But once again Acton had slipped away silently into the darkness, and this time he did not return. Nor did he answer, though Bobby called him more than once.

"What's he gone off like that for?" the sergeant asked, puzzled. "Not what you would expect, not from Mr Acton."

Bobby offered no suggestion. He said instead, speaking quickly:

"You know what's to be done. I want the old well cleared out. It's possible some one has been thrown down it and then the parapet stones to make sure—and for concealment. We've got to find out. It may be a false alarm. Be careful how you get to work. Understand? Mr Acton may have gone home. I'm going to see if I can find him, but I shall get back here as soon as I can."

"It might be," the sergeant suggested, "as the tall, thin gentleman is a friend of his, and he wants to join him."

Bobby did not answer, though he was fairly sure that the 'tall, thin gent' was the very last person whom at the moment Acton had any wish to meet. He moved away a little from the well-head near which he had been standing as he wondered what dark secret it might or might not contain. For a moment or two he stood still, looking out into the black night that covered the steep and rough hill-side with its impenetrable cloak of darkness. He could see nothing. He listened, but heard nothing. And yet he knew that in that silence, that stillness, that darkness, were loose two of the most dangerous of all animals, two men obsessed by fear and hate. Down below he could see where lights showed in cottage windows. More lights, moving lights, showed in one spot. There, no doubt, the help he needed, and awaited, was completing its preparations.

He knew roughly the direction in which lay Abels End Cottage, the home of the Actons, and he had a moment of pity for the wife and children who knew so little what fruit of the past had now come to ripeness. It would be quicker, he decided, not to try to follow downwards the path he stood on. It passed the house at a distance of two or three hundred yards, and only joined much lower down the other and smoother path, almost a road since wheeled traffic could use it, that led directly to Abels End Cottage. Time would be saved, and his impression was that time might be important, if he struck across the hill-side—it was on the whole not much rougher going there than on the path itself—and so straight on, or as straight as the darkness permitted, to the house.

For whether, as Bobby suspected, Acton had now been driven to contemplate flight, either from the fear of imminent arrest or from fear of the threat that seemed implied in Lord

Newdagonby's arrival, seeking his daughter, or whether he had merely yielded to an instinctive feeling that in his own house he would be safer, it was there he was, Bobby thought, most likely to be found.

With such speed as the rough nature of the ground permitted, Bobby picked his way across the hill-side. He hoped a light would soon appear in an Abels End Cottage window to serve as a guide, but that did not happen. Nor did he use his torch much, partly because he did not wish to give warning of his position, partly because it had been used so much he was afraid the battery might soon give out. His sense of direction was sufficiently good, however, to keep him right, and when he was so near he could distinguish the house, a deeper, darker shadow, looming up against the black sky, he became aware of a sound near by, as of some one cautiously moving. He switched on his torch and threw the light from it in that direction. To his surprise it was the figure of a woman that the ray showed. She stood still, but with her back to him, and he had the idea that she was only hesitating in which direction to run. He called out:

"Who is it? Is it Mrs Findlay?"

"Oh, it's you," she exclaimed as if relieved. "I was afraid at first it was him."

"Who?" Bobby asked, and, drawing nearer, saw it was Mrs Tinsley he was speaking to. "Who?" he repeated.

"Lord Newdagonby," she answered.

"Have you seen him?"

"Yes. Just now. He has been in the house. He got in at the back somehow. He is looking for Mr Acton."

"Why?"

"I don't know. How should I know? I think perhaps he is going to kill him—at least he may unless Sibby's safe. She isn't."

"Have you seen Acton?"

"I think so. I'm not sure. It was some one ran by. When he saw me move he cried out and ran off. I think he knows."

"Knows what?"

"Knows what Lord Newdagonby means. Perhaps he'll be first though. I think perhaps they are looking for each other. If you want to stop them, you had better find them."

"Yes, I had, hadn't I?" Bobby agreed, looking out again into that vast curtain of black night that veiled in utter darkness all the bleak and bare and steep hill-side. He asked sharply: "How do you come to be mixed up in all this?"

"I didn't mean," she said in a low voice. "I never thought it would be like this. I never thought Lord Newdagonby—" She left the sentence unfinished. Then she said: "He never seemed human."

"He is the father of an only daughter," Bobby said. "It may be all that is left in him of human feeling, and it may be all the stronger for that. The one weak spot in his armour of indifference. Well, why are you here? What have you been doing?"

"I rang him up," she admitted.

"What did you tell him? Something you saw at the ruined cottage where that well is? Why did you tell me Mrs Findlay was well—very well?"

"It was only what I thought might have happened—I didn't know."

"Had you been watching her, following her?"

"No, of course not. Only I knew Sibby Findlay had gone away in a hurry after you had been to see them, and I wondered if she was coming here to see Charley Acton."

"How did you know Mrs Findlay had left like that?"

"Mrs Jacks told me. She rang up. I asked her to promise to let me know if anything happened. She always thought it was Lord Newdagonby killed Ivor. I didn't. I knew it must be Sibby, only I wanted to be sure, and now I'm not."

"Why did Mrs Jacks suspect Lord Newdagonby?"

"Because he so hated Sibby's marrying him and then the way Ivor always showed it wasn't her he cared about, it was always me, and he hated that still more—I mean to say, that any one should be put before his Sibby. You see he always thought he was God Almighty and could do just what he liked. Because if there isn't any God, why shouldn't he be God? I heard him say that."

"Been reading Dostoievsky," Bobby commented. "Goes to the head sometimes. Never mind. What was it you actually saw at the ruined cottage?"

"I didn't see anything at all," she answered sullenly.

"How did you come to be there? I think you had better for your own sake tell me all about it."

"I told you I didn't see anything," she repeated. "I don't see what you want to bully me for. When Mrs Jacks rang me to say Sibby had gone off in a hurry, I thought very likely she would be wanting to tell Charley Acton. I left my car at a farm where I stayed once for a night, and I went up to the old cottage to watch if I could see her come. I did see her, but she didn't go to his house as I thought she would. She came straight on where I was. I slipped away before she saw me, only I waited behind some bushes, and then I saw Charley Acton come. She must have been waiting for him. But I couldn't see what happened, because they went behind the cottage where the well is. I saw Mr Acton go away, but I didn't see her go, and I couldn't make it out, why she was staying so long. So I went to look and she wasn't there, and there was no sign of her. But I saw a lot of the parapet wall had been pushed over, and I was frightened and I went away. Only I didn't know what to do, and then you came and I didn't dare tell you. I thought you might think it was me. I rang up Lord Newdagonby instead. I didn't mean him to know who it was, but he guessed because of my voice, he said he knew it. He said I as good as killed her. Because I had made it too late to help her if the fall hadn't killed her. Only it must have with all those big stones on top. He asked me where Mr Acton lived, and I told him, and he said he was going to find him and kill him if he had done anything to Sibby, and then he would come back and kill me, too. Because of not telling him sooner. I think he has lost his head altogether, gone quite mad, so he doesn't know what he is doing, because of Sibby and not knowing."

CHAPTER XXXII
"WHERE IS SIBBY? WHERE?"

MEANWHILE, WHILE those two talked together in their hurried, anxious whispers, Lord Newdagonby and Acton were dealing with their own affairs, for in the dark, on the rough and steep hill-side, they had met unwittingly and faced each other, and Lord Newdagonby, now neither peer nor millionaire, nor philosopher, but only a father, had cried out very loudly, his voice high pitched and angry.

"Where is Sibby? Where?"

And Acton answered warily:

"I don't know. Sibby? I don't know. Why ask me?"

Then Lord Newdagonby:

"She came to talk to you."

"To talk to me? Nonsense. What for? Why should she?"

"She came here, she's been seen. She had a return ticket. I've found that out. The return half hasn't been used."

Acton shook his head.

"I know nothing about all that," he insisted. "Why should she? I mean, want to talk to me?"

"I think she must have wanted to ask you why you killed Ivor."

"You're out of your mind," Acton retorted. "Or else she is. Go home and get a good sleep. She'll be there very likely before you. Good night."

But the other had him by the arm and would not let him go.

"You know, if you've killed her to keep her quiet, I'll kill you myself," he said, a little as if he were saying: "See you at lunch to-morrow."

It was at this moment, while Acton tried to free himself from the fierce grip upon his arm, that they were interrupted by the flash of Bobby's torch as he first caught sight of Mrs Tinsley, and for the moment dreamed that he had found Sibby Findlay safe and well. Acton said:

"There's that meddling Scotland Yard ass. He's still messing about. Go along and tell him and hear him laugh. It's the

Tinsley woman he's after—last to see Ivor, last to see Sibby, last to see them both. It's her he wants to talk to."

"So do I," came the answer, almost whispered, sounding ten times more menacing thus. "But you first. Tell me what you have done with Sibby. Tell me before I strangle the truth out of you."

"I tell you I know nothing about her," Acton repeated, shouting his reply to the other's whisper. "Let me go, you old fool."

By a sudden violent effort he freed himself from the grip on his arm, and at once, before he could take advantage of his freedom, found himself entangled in long, thin arms, like the tentacles of an octopus, so complete and so closely did they seem to envelop him.

He made a fierce effort to free himself, wasting breath and energy the while on a series of angry expletives and epithets. They struggled, swaying to and fro, then tripped and fell. Bobby heard the sound of the scuffle as they rolled on the ground, tearing blindly at each other. He came running, throwing the fading light of his torch before him. Dimly he could see the outline of the two struggling forms twined together on the ground. Impossible at first to distinguish one from the other. But Acton was comparatively young, his bodily vigour not yet sapped by the years. Lord Newdagonby was much the older man; and if his strength was doubled, trebled, by the sort of passionate, excited energy that Mrs Tinsley had called 'losing his head', so was Acton's doubled, trebled, quadrupled for that matter, by the stimulus of a dreadful fear. For he knew that the slow step of justice followed him, and that across his path lay the shadow of the rope. By an enormous effort, an effort far beyond his normal powers, he got to his feet, though Lord Newdagonby still clung to him, still hung upon his neck. With such another effort he wrenched himself somehow free from that old man's entangling grip and flung him away, as a man might throw aside some troubling cape or cloak.

Then he set himself to run with all the speed he could command; and miraculously, bruised and hurt as he was, Lord Newdagonby, too, was on his feet at once and following,

following, pursuing, like some fantastic, upright spider with his long straggling legs and flaying arms, a grotesque and yet somehow formidable figure. Behind came Bobby, running like the others, wondering what was happening, having some advantage from the light his fading torch still gave to warn him how and where to place his feet. The advantage was small, however, for those two he followed ran like men possessed, unchecked, uninhibited, careless of the stones, the tangled grass, the rough, uneven ground so liable to trip a runner.

Such light recklessness and disdain of risk served Acton well, however. It was as if his scorn of every kind of obstacle did in fact, in some queer way, tame them, make them harmless, as if his speed gave them no time to spring their traps and snares. Less lucky was Lord Newdagonby, still pursuing, for though his long strides and the desperate urge that drove him brought him so near that he could stretch out his arm to snatch at Acton s coat, yet at that very moment he put his foot in some hollow or caught it in some tussock of grass, and so went headlong, turning indeed almost a complete somersault, and Acton spared the time to pause and aim at the prostrate man a vicious kick.

Lord Newdagonby cried out with the pain. Acton laughed with pleasure and relief, and set himself to run again, for he knew how great was still his need. Bobby, close behind, knelt by the groaning man on the ground.

"Hurt?" he asked, though he could see immediately that one doubled-up leg was certainly broken. "I'll get help."

"Get him first—it's Acton, he's done something to Sibby. He won't say, make him tell," Lord Newdagonby groaned. "It's my leg. Get Acton. I think perhaps he's murdered Sibby."

Bobby was of the same opinion, but he did not say so, Lord Newdagonby's need for immediate relief and help was indeed obvious, while of Acton's chance of ultimate escape Bobby had a poor opinion. Moreover, any such attempt at escape would provide just the background needed to drive home to a jury the force of Bobby's careful and detailed reasoning.

By this time that cluster of lights Bobby had seen gathering below had left the village and was half-way up the hillside. Leaving his torch burning, so that the glimmer of light it still gave should serve as a guide to the exact position of the injured man, Bobby hurried to intercept the new arrivals. There would certainly be a doctor with them, and so skilled help would be at once available.

"An accident," Bobby explained; and saw that the needed help was dispatched. In his shirt sleeves, for he had used his coat to provide another covering and a little extra warmth for the injured Lord Newdagonby, and so give some further protection against the danger of the pneumonia so apt to follow such an injury to elderly people, Bobby went on up the hill with the rest of the party to the ruined cottage and the old well, whose secret—or no secret—was now to be made plain.

A derrick was being quickly got into position. One of the younger men let himself down into the well and adjusted in the lowered sling the topmost of the stones piled up there. The stone came to the surface and was tilted to the ground. Bobby was stepping forward to look at it more closely when he heard scuffling movements going on quite near and raised voices. He turned to see what was happening. The Abels End sergeant was coming towards him, emerging into the circle of light the lamps of the rescuing party made around the well. He had a woman with him, and was holding her by the arm.

"Lady," he announced, releasing her now he thought he had brought her near enough to Bobby to be free of responsibility for her safe keeping, "as was watching what we was doing, curious like. I could tell there was some one, so I slipped round, and she tried to get away, so I brought her in."

"Why, Mrs Tinsley," Bobby exclaimed, recognizing her, "have you been here all the time? What for?"

"Why shouldn't I?" she retorted. "If she's there . . . I had to know . . . I knew you would do something . . . I waited to see."

"We shall soon know," Bobby said. Then he said: "We must find out next how it happened."

"I told you, didn't I?" she asked. "I told you I saw Mr Acton meet her, and then I saw him go away, and I never saw her again. That was Saturday, three days ago."

"His story is the same," Bobby told her. "He says he saw you and her together, and then after that he saw you alone but not her."

Another heavy stone came to the surface. It weighed probably about twenty pounds. It was deposited gently on the ground close to where Mrs Tinsley and Bobby were standing. She was saying excitedly:

"He's lying, lying to save himself. I don't believe he saw us at all." She pointed to the heavy stone that had just been raised. "You don't think I could even lift a great thing like that?" she asked.

"It wouldn't need lifting," Bobby replied dispassionately. "It would only want pushing over. Please don't think I'm making any accusations," he added. "There's not enough evidence yet even to think of charging any one. Even if Mrs Findlay is really there—her body rather."

"No one could live long," Mrs Tinsley said. She pointed again to the stone at their feet. "Not with things like that tumbling on you. Could they?"

"No," Bobby agreed. "No not if there was any one there for them to fall on, but we don't know that yet for certain."

She gave him a quick glance.

"I think you're sure and so am I," she said.

There was a sound of scrambling. A pale and startled face appeared, rising from the well as from a grave. It said:

"There's a whispering plain as plain: 'Leave me alone, leave me be,' it says and says. If she's dead down there, she's speaking still."

CHAPTER XXXIII
"LET ME BE"

THE WORDS, so loudly uttered in a kind of muffled scream, acted like a spell of immobility. All around heard them, all around stood and stared, as if abruptly paralysed. The Abels End sergeant was the first to speak and move. He expressed the sane, common-sense attitude. He said simply:

"Oh, come off it, Joe."

Mrs Tinsley expressed another, and even more sane, common-sense point of view. She said:

"If she's there and talking, she's alive."

Joe, scrambling hurriedly out of the well, said, speaking to the sergeant:

"All right, skipper, you go down and see for yourself." To Mrs Tinsley, he said: "Alive? and her down there three days with that heap of stones on top of her?"

He had scrambled from the well-mouth to firm ground now. Bobby moved forward. He took hold of the rope and swung himself down till at the bottom of the well he stood uneasily on the stones roughly piled there as they had fallen when dislodged from their position in the old parapet.

"Mrs Findlay?" he called. "Mrs Findlay. Can you hear me?"

A faint whispered answer came:

"Let me be."

"Mrs Findlay," he called again, but this time there was no reply. He shouted to those on the surface that he was sending up more of the heaped-up stones till he had got away enough to see what had really happened, for the doctor and a stretcher to be in readiness, and for a lantern to be lowered. Then he set to work, feverishly and yet with care; since, if one of these heavy stones slipped as it was being hauled up, it would crash on him. Now by the light of the lantern lowered at his request he could see how this apparent miracle of survival had been brought about. To one side at the bottom of the well was a kind of hollow or cavity where at one time the spring feeding it had seeped through. Apparently when the well had first been dug this spring had been missed, but then reached by digging a few feet sideways. A rough attempt had been made to line the resulting cavity with brick so as to prevent it from collapsing. Into this small cavity or kind of cave, Mrs Findlay had managed to crawl, though indeed it seemed hardly big enough to hold a child, much less a full-grown woman. Here, then, she had lain, safe from the stones rained down as the parapet above was hastily demolished, as Acton hoped by their means both to consummate his crime and to conceal it. Yet by the eternal irony of events, his own action in diverting the spring that fed this well for his own use had provided the means whereby his victim had now escaped the last effect of his directed malice.

Bobby, working with all the fierce energy at his command, soon had enough of the stones cleared away, either hoisted to the surface or piled on one side, to free the entrance to Mrs Findlay's refuge. Yet even so it was not easy to liberate her, so narrow and confined was the space into which she had managed to squeeze herself. Nor did she give any help, she seemed unconscious of what was happening, Bobby feared indeed that the whispers just heard had been but a last flicker of life before it became extinct. But presently he had her free, and then she seemed to revive again—with the pain she felt once circulation began to return to her cramped and stiffened limbs. She opened her eyes and closed them again, dazzled even by the faint light of the lowered lantern. She said faintly:

"I thought that you might come."

As he was trying to get her into a convenient position for bringing her to the surface, she said:

"I think I was dead. I thought I was. Why have you brought me back?"

And a third time she said:

"It was better so. Are you alive?"

"Oh, yes, I'm alive all right," Bobby answered. "So are you. Put your arm round my neck and hang on. That's right. Lift a little. So. Now, hold tight."

He had one foot in the sling by which the stones had been lifted. With one hand he held the rope, with the other he supported Mrs Findlay in position across his shoulder. He shouted to those above that he was ready, and they began to haul. Mrs Findlay muttered in his ear:

"If you had let me be, I should still be dead."

He had no breath to answer. They were at the surface now, and hands were thrust out to help. The doctor was waiting, and a stretcher. The doctor took charge. He made a quick, hurried examination.

"Rest and warmth," he said. "Then she should be all right. How long has she been down there?"

"Three days I think," Bobby answered.

"Under all those stones?" the doctor asked. "She's no right to be alive, or to have a whole bone in her body for that matter."

"Oh, I wasn't," Mrs Findlay said, loudly and unexpectedly. "Alive, I mean. Not till he came and brought me back."

"Yes, yes, of course, quite so," the doctor said soothingly. "Just lie still and keep covered." To Bobby he said aside: "Delirious. Quite natural. Any one would be after this."

"I should think so," Bobby agreed.

The doctor, the stretcher with its bearers and its burden, began the journey down the hill. To the sergeant, Bobby said:

"It's too late to do much to-night. Tell your superintendent I'll be along in the morning for a conference. We must pick up Acton as soon as we can. He won't have had time to get far, and he's well known. It oughtn't to be difficult."

"Yes, sir," the sergeant said. "Very good, sir. I'll let the super know. All the same, I can't believe it, not of Mr Acton, I can't."

"It might have been difficult to prove, difficult to bring it home to him," Bobby said thoughtfully, "if she had really been dead when we found her. And it seemed impossible she could be alive. Now we shall have her statement."

"Make it all plain and straightforward," agreed the sergeant. "Open and shut as you might say. Sort of a miracle though. You can hardly believe it, and she didn't herself. Kept saying she had been dead before we found her—brought her back, she said. Must have seemed like that, buried and all in that hole twenty feet down.”

“Anyhow, she is alive now, and the doctor seemed to think she was likely to stay so, unless pneumonia sets in,” Bobby said. “So she'll be able to tell us exactly what happened—and why Acton thought it necessary to try to murder her. That is, when she is strong enough,” he added, remembering her strange, drawn, earth-stained face, like a mask of death.

CHAPTER XXXIV
“ . . . NO MAN PURSUETH”

IT WAS in fact some days before Bobby was informed that the hospital authorities had given permission for a visit to be paid to Mrs Findlay. It was her own stipulation, though one warmly approved by her doctor, that Bobby was to come alone and that there was to be no question of a formal interrogation. Even her father, an inmate of the same hospital, and not in much better shape than herself, had only seen her once or twice, and then only for a very few minutes at a time.

Bobby had a talk with the local police authorities. It was agreed that anything Mrs Findlay was able or willing to say would be important, even though formal, official use could not be made of it until it was in writing, witnessed, and signed.

“Once,” said the chief constable of the county to whom Bobby was talking, “once we have her full story in proper form, we can go ahead,” and with this Bobby fully agreed.

Up to the present, however, the search for Acton had been without result, and though his name had appeared in the official “Police Gazette”—a periodical no member of the public is ever permitted to see and that every policeman will tell you is his most precious aid, so much so that without it efficient police work would be impossible—and though paragraphs had appeared in the press, all that was in the form of a polite request to Mr Acton, ‘believed to be on holiday’, to let his present address be known, as it was thought he might be able to give the police useful information.

The only result so far had been that Mrs Acton, in her seaside retreat, bewildered and unhappy, had been obliged to change her lodgings and even then to appeal for police protection to clear from her doorway numberless pressmen all anxious to extract from her the information she had made it abundantly plain she did not possess.

To the hospital therefore Bobby came alone, and was surprised to find Mrs Findlay much stronger and looking very much better than he had expected. When he said as much, possibly letting a little of his surprise appear, she remarked quite calmly:

"Oh, well, I expect I've been rather putting it on. I had to be sure what I was going to say, and then I expected it would be you coming, so I had to be ready for you, hadn't I?"

"Why?" Bobby asked. "Why for me in particular?"

"I never thought you so very clever," she told him, speaking slowly, with the air of one considering a problem not very well understood. "Father didn't either. He told me he would think twice before giving you a job anywhere unless it was being a chucker-out at a night club."

"Well, anyhow, I shall know where to apply," Bobby remarked, trying to look pleased.

"I wonder if there's more to it than being clever," Mrs Findlay went on in the same meditative way. "Clever people do like to go roundabout ways sometimes, don't they? I'm clever, and I did. I think you always go straight forward."

"Well," Bobby said, a good deal puzzled by these remarks, "suppose you leave me out of it. I'm only a part of the machinery of the law, and we all depend on law for safety in our homes and our beds. I'm just a grubber-up of facts for really clever people like lawyers and judges to get to work on. What we would like is for you to tell us who it was pushed you down that well. We think we know, but we would like you to say."

She looked at him steadily and was silent. Then she said:

"No one."

"Eh? what?" exclaimed Bobby, quite taken aback, for this was the very last answer he had expected.

"I said 'no one'," she repeated.

"Well, then," Bobby said.

"I fell in by accident," she told him.

"Nonsense," said Bobby.

"That's my story," she said, and now she was smiling to herself in what seemed a kind of mischievous enjoyment of his very evident surprise. It struck him that she was looking much younger, in a way more human, than previously. "You won't get me to alter it, either," she added.

"Do you want to tell me that all those stones, they would certainly have killed you but for the lucky accident of that hole you found, did they fall by accident, too?" he asked.

"Oh, those," she said, still smiling at him with only half-hidden amusement, "No, no, of course not. You see I made a grab, trying to save myself, and I pulled one down and that dislodged the others, so that they all came tumbling after, just like Jack and Jill in the nursery rhyme."

Bobby found himself wondering if ever before in all her life she would have quoted a nursery rhyme. It seemed significant somehow, though he did not quite know what of. He said:

"Why are you saying this?"

But to that she made no reply, only still watched him with that amused, mischievous air of hers, a little like that of a naughty child who feels that parent or teacher has been manoeuvred into an awkward position and does not know what to do next. Bobby got up and moved restlessly about the room. He came back to the bedside and said:

"It was Acton, wasn't it?"

"I've told you it was an accident," she retorted, and he would hardly have been surprised to hear her add: "Put that in your pipe and smoke it."

He sat down again and was silent for a time while she continued to watch him, clearly asking herself what he would do or say next.

"If you mean to stick to that story," he remarked presently, "I don't see there's much we can do about it."

"No," she agreed, and added: "That's what I thought."

"Just between ourselves," he asked, "it was Acton, wasn't it?"

"You haven't got any dictaphones or things fitted up, have you?" she asked cautiously.

"Oh, no," he answered. "I don't think the hospital would approve. And I don't think the courts would be very pleased, most likely they would say it was un-English and not fair."

"Of course it was Charley Acton, the silly man."

"He tried to murder you, then?"

"He didn't succeed," she pointed out.

"What it comes to is that you don't want Acton punished in any way?"

"If you had been really clever, you would have found that out long ago."

"You know he murdered your husband?"

"Yes. Well?"

"You don't want anything done about that, either?"

"If it were, would it bring Ivor back to life?"

"It might save some one else's life. Murderers who succeed once sometimes think themselves so clever they try again—as Acton tried with you."

"Not Charley," she declared. "He's not like that. It was only that he felt he had to save his invention that was his life and more, and Ivor's life was such a small thing in comparison. And I was trying to make him marry me, and he very much didn't want. I expect the well seemed an easy way out."

"The murderer's defence," Bobby commented. Then he asked: "What made you want to marry Acton? I don't think there was any question of being in love with him?"

"Good gracious, no. Just to be as bad as I knew how, to make people shudder and tremble when they thought of me. To marry the man you knew murdered your husband and at the same time make him leave his own wife. I told him he had got rid of my husband, so now he could get rid of his wife.

Poetic justice I told him. You know you can't blame him if he tried to get rid of me instead."

"Speaking as a policeman," Bobby answered, "I find that quite irrelevant. A policeman's duty is to establish facts, not to judge them. Speaking as a man, I must say I think it seems quite understandable."

"So do I," she agreed and seemed to mean it.

He was looking at her thoughtfully, and he was silent so long, that at last she said:

"Well, is that all?"

"I was wondering," he said, "what has changed you so?"

"If you had spent three days dying in a hole in the ground, in your grave, you might understand," she told him. "It doesn't leave you quite the same. A grave is so very real. Sometimes I think I did die. I don't know. I know I slept, and in that sleep had many dreams—if they were dreams. You began it."

"I did? How?"

"You made me look so silly. Marrying Ivor so as to be like Manfred on his mountain peak. I told you. I wanted every one to shrink away from me in horror and fear, and you—you made it all so silly, marrying like any one else. That was one dream."

"Marrying like any one else?"

No, no," she said impatiently. "A sort of universal chuckle, as if all the heavens were being so frightfully amused. I don't suppose in the other place any one ever is amused. But up there it must be hard for them to take being bad very seriously. It's so silly."

"Is that what you found out in what you call your grave?" he asked.

"You think a lot when you are three days dying—dying very slowly," she repeated. "Sometimes I thought you might come. I knew you would be looking. But I didn't much expect it. So I went on thinking—dreaming. If they were dreams. Were they dreams? Well, you know, I wanted to experience everything. I remember father told me once that experience was a universal human need—the need to know everything. Well, I've had it—experience."

"You have," Bobby agreed. "Does Lord Newdagonby know what you've decided?"

"Oh, yes, I told him."

"What did he say?"

"He said I was a fool, and he went on saying it so long that I told him he was getting to be a dreadful old bore. That shut him up. It's the one thing he dreads—becoming a bore in his old age. Afterwards he said it would save a lot of talk."

"Does he know that you, and you alone, can give the evidence to prove who was the murderer?"

"Oh, you know that, do you?" she cried, surprised.

"Of course I do," Bobby answered impatiently. "How else could you have got such a hold on him as to make you think you could force him to divorce his wife and marry you? No wonder he thought that well rather a good idea."

"I saw him on the stairs, coming away from Ivor's room," she explained. "I had been there earlier on to ask Ivor about a cocktail party we were going to give. You found my fingerprints, didn't you? I didn't want to say. You would have gone on asking those beastly questions of yours, wouldn't you?"

"I expect so," Bobby agreed.

"I had forgotten something I meant to ask about, so I had to go back," she continued, "and there was Charley hurrying away, almost running down stairs. He looked funny, and he was trying to stuff a dead guinea pig into his pocket. I couldn't think what he had been doing. Ivor's door was locked, and there wasn't any answer when I knocked. It was like that sometimes. He would lock his door and muffle the 'phone, and you just had to wait till he came out. I expect really he was unconscious. At any rate I didn't get any answer or hear anything, and I came away. It was only afterwards I began to think. I don't mind telling you all this, and it was rather fun watching you blundering along. But if you tell any one, or try to get me to tell any one, I shall say Charley was out with me all morning. He was most of it. I've only to stretch the times a little."

"Well, in that case," Bobby said once more, "I don't see that there's much we can do."

"No, there isn't, is there?" she agreed.

"You think it right your husband's murderer should escape all punishment?"

"I don't think I know any more what's right and what isn't," she answered. "Except not trying any more to hurt any one. But I'll have no share in sending any one to prison—prison must be a little like where I was. Or getting any one hanged. Death's so serious. You'll get no help from me."

Bobby got to his feet.

"Well, that's that," he said. "I suppose it's no good saying anything more. I won't bother you any longer, though I can't promise other people won't. You can be brought into court on a subpoena," he added.

"Did you ever hear of the horse they brought to the water and couldn't make drink?" she retorted.

"I can only say again," he repeated, "you've changed. Shall you change again?"

"I don't think so," she told him. "No. You see, well, after three days in your grave, you aren't quite the same when you come back to life. Was Lazarus, I wonder?"

"It wasn't your grave," he pointed out.

"I thought it was," she answered slowly, and added: "In a sense I think it was."

Later on, when Bobby was called to the Public Prosecutor's office for a conference, he could do no more than repeat that the case was complete, but depended on the evidence of a witness who showed no sign of weakening in her determination to refuse to testify—or alternatively of providing the accused with an alibi.

"Means," said the Public Prosecutor's office disapprovingly, "that a known murderer, guilty also of an attempted murder, is going to get away with it because the wife of the murdered man, and herself the victim of the attempt, wants it that way for reasons best known to herself."

"I don't much think myself," Bobby remarked meditatively, "that it's altogether a case of entirely getting away with it. He'll get his punishment all right."

"If you mean remorse and all that sort of thing . . ." said the Public Prosecutor's office, for that is a department where a certain atmosphere of cynicism is apt to prevail.

"Oh, dear me, no," Bobby answered. "I think Mr Charley Acton is the last person in the world to feel remorse. I expect he considers himself badly ill-used in having such regrettable necessities forced upon him. No, what I mean is that wide publicity has been given to our wanting to get in touch with him because we think he could give us valuable information. Well, he knows—or rather he thinks he knows, having a guilty conscience—what that means. So he has gone into hiding, and in hiding he'll remain, never sure when he won't feel the hand of a policeman on his shoulder. It means the end of his career as an inventor. It means he'll never dare return to this country. It means he'll never know again what it is to feel safe. No, I don't think he'll escape all punishment. I think there'll be a good many days when he'll ask himself if it wouldn't have been better to be hanged and done with it."

"You mean," asked one of the least cynical of those present, "that the wicked flee when no man pursueth?"

THE END

E.R. PUNSHON
CRIME FICTION REVIEWER

E.R. Punshon was for many years a reviewer of crime fiction for the Guardian *newspaper in the U.K. The following five reviews by Punshon were published together in* The Guardian *on 25 June, 1936.*

Busman's Honeymoon, Dorothy L. Sayers
Double Cross Purposes, Ronald A. Knox
Death on the Board, John Rhode
They Found Him Dead, Georgette Heyer
Cry Aloud for Murder, Paul McGuire.

NOT SINCE those spacious days when Sherlock Holmes bestrode the world like a colossus has any writer of detective stories made such an impression on the reading public as has Miss Dorothy L. Sayers. It is interesting, then, to consider the cause of so startling a success. It can hardly lie altogether in the attractiveness of her chief character, Lord Peter Wimsey, for he indeed may be found by some just a little too great and good for a circulating library's daily food. In the three essentials of the art of fiction Miss Sayers emphatically excels, for her characterisation and her skill in narrative are both of the first order and her style is not only admirable in itself but touched with an agreeable flavour of scholarship. But all that can be said of others who have not so impressed the general public, and it seems as if the secret of her achievement must lie in the strange gift of personality—most imponderable of the imponderables. It is the gift by which, for example, Dickens has won a greater fame than has his rival, Thackeray; by which in the last century Henry Irving triumphed over natural defects and made himself the master of the theatrical scene as to-day Miss Sayers is mistress of the detective novel. To adopt the slang of the theatre, Miss Sayers "gets it across."

The plot of her new book, "Busman's Honeymoon," is already familiar, since a stage version has been running for months past in a London theatre, so that many will know that the story deals with the discovery of the body of a murdered man in the cottage Lord Peter and his newly wedded wife have taken for their honeymoon. But knowledge of how the tale goes only enhances admiration for the skill with which Miss Sayers pushes forward the significant clue, plucks it away, dangles it once more before the reader, once more as he attempts to grasp it whisks it away up her sleeve, till he would be ready to swear it was never there at all, but that presently it dawns upon him that all the time it was only Miss Sayers making the quickness of her mind deceive his thought. Nor is this detective interest all there is in the book, for Miss Sayers has included also a careful study of the efforts of two sophisticated, highly intelligent people, already experienced in life, to adjust themselves to the married relationship, with all that it so surprisingly demands and gives so amazingly. Perhaps, for most readers, the greatest interest in the book will lie in watching how she combines the subtle and delicate treatment such a theme demands—a Henry James theme, indeed—with the more robust requirements of the detective interest. There can be nothing but praise for the skill and courage with which Miss Sayers attacks a problem demanding the highest qualities a novelist can display.

* * *

"Double Cross Purposes," by Father Knox, proves again that he possesses a style to which any young writer might do well to play the sedulous ape as well as an abundant wit. But only writers of the highest order have all talents in equal measure, and Father Knox falls a little short in his power of creating character, as also in that direct and clear sense of narrative which many lesser writers possess, that gift which explains how it is that some apparently commonplace authors achieve a success that many learned critics find incomprehensible. The complications in this tale of a treasure found and lost by the banks of a remote Scottish river, of a dead man in a locked garage, of the somewhat tortuous manoeuvres of Miles Bredon grow indeed so tangled as at times almost to bring the narrative to a standstill. In the end Miles Bredon explains everything quite clearly. It may be urged he could have followed a simpler line of country and been more candid both to his companions and to his employers, but then Father Knox would have had smaller opportunity first to tie and then to untie as elaborate a series of knots as any for which even he has been responsible.

* * *

As Miss Sayers dominates the field of detective fiction by sheer force of personality, as Father Knox reigns by brilliance of wit and style, so Mr. John Rhode may well claim the title of Public Brain Tester No. 1. As befits one who is a "big noise" in detective fiction, he starts his new book, "Death at the Board," with a resounding bang—that of an explosion which destroys together a business magnate and his house. Careful details the author gives seem to prove the explosion can have been neither purposed nor accidental. The police are baffled, so is the reader. Both are plunged still deeper in bewilderment when there follows another death, equally contradictory in proven detail. Third, fourth, and fifth murders follow, all of colleagues of the first two victims, all equally puzzling. Fortunately Dr. Priestley is there, and he finally explains both the baffling How and the Who, though the Who the reader may have been as quick as the doctor and a good deal quicker than the police in identifying.

* * *

The reader, too, will probably be quicker than was Superintendent Hannyside in solving the problem set by Miss Georgette Heyer in "They Found Him Dead." Culprit and motive are indeed soon obvious in this tale of how in sequence two senior partners of a business firm are murdered and how on the life of the third in the succession other murderous attempts are made. All that, however, goes for little compared with the excellence of the narrative, the grace and humour of the style, the growing tension of the story. Miss Heyer hardly shows that chessboard ingenuity some writers can display, nor is her work remarkable for originality of plot or characterisation, but within its limits it is of a high order and certain to afford pleasure and entertainment.

* * *

The chief constable who tells the story in the first person in Mr. Paul McGuire's "Cry Aloud for Murder" is an engaging figure, with his modest confession of lack of experience in police work and his ability, when necessary, to call St. Thomas Aquinas in evidence. He is also probably the quickest worker on record, who can combine meeting a girl for the first time, getting engaged to her, getting knocked out by a suspect, and solving a murder mystery in a seaside town all in a day or two. The interest of the book lies, however, less in the solving of the mystery than in the author's clever and interesting study of the psychology of a mind dwelling morbidly upon foolish nightmare terrors of the past that lead in the end to tragedy.